T0324127

NAVIGATING ISLANDS

NAVIGATING ISLANDS

Plays from the Pacific

Victoria Nalani Kneubuhl

University of Hawai'i Press
HONOLULU

© 2024 Victoria Nalani Kneubuhl
All rights reserved
Printed in the United States of America

First printed, 2024

Library of Congress Cataloging-in-Publication Data

Names: Kneubuhl, Victoria N. (Victoria Nalani), author.
Title: Navigating islands : plays from the Pacific / Victoria Nalani
    Kneubuhl.
Description: Honolulu : University of Hawaiʻi Press, [2024] | Includes
    bibliographical references.
Identifiers: LCCN 2023056413 (print) | LCCN 2023056414 (ebook) |
    ISBN 9780824896157 (trade paperback) | ISBN 9780824898298 (epub) |
    ISBN 9780824898304 (kindle edition) | ISBN 9780824898281 (pdf)
Subjects: LCSH: Women—Samoa—Drama. | Samoan Islands—Drama.
Classification: LCC PS3561.N418 N38 2024 (print) | LCC PS3561.N418
    (ebook) | DDC 812/.54—dc23/eng/20231229
LC record available at https://lccn.loc.gov/2023056413
LC ebook record available at https://lccn.loc.gov/2023056414

Cover design by Melissa Olaivar Wong

University of Hawaiʻi Press books are printed on acid-free
paper and meet the guidelines for permanence and
durability of the Council on Library Resources.

CONTENTS

A NOTE FROM THE PLAYWRIGHT

My father was born in Tutuila, American Sāmoa. His mother was Sāmoan and his father a second-generation American from Iowa. My mother was from Hawai'i and part Hawaiian. My parents met, married, and lived in Hawai'i until the early 1960s, when my father thought he might want to move back to American Sāmoa and work in the business my grandfather had established. He made arrangements to visit and check out the situation before making a decision. I was nearly thirteen, and I'm still not sure why he decided that I should go with him. He had not been home for twenty-two years.

I remember vividly the night we arrived at the airport in American Sāmoa. A line of relatives was there to meet us, and as we walked along the line, my father, to my complete shock, began to speak to everyone in Sāmoan. I had never heard him speak Sāmoan and had no idea he was bilingual.

My father stayed for two weeks, but I stayed on with my aunt until the end of the summer. In those days, Tutuila was very different. In most villages, people still lived in traditional fale. The paved road only extended around the harbor and to the airport. Electricity and indoor plumbing were limited to a small part of the island. That summer was my first introduction to what it meant to be a member of an 'afakasi (half-caste) family in Sāmoa. While we were not raised in the fa'a Sāmoa or village life, we did have an extensive family, not only in Tutuila, but on Upolu and Savai'i as well. We were still connected to our family titles and still had genealogical roots that stretched across time. In those days, the 'afakasi community was small and tight-knit, unlike today.

My parents did move to American Sāmoa, and I began spending summers there. One summer, when I was fourteen, my aunt took me and my cousin on a trip to what is now independent Sāmoa. We stayed in Apia at the old Aggie Grey's Hotel. Aggie was still alive and treated us like family. My aunt had a daily schedule of activities organized for us, and one day was devoted to visiting Vailima, the former residence of Robert Louis Stevenson. My cousin and I were given a tour of the house and then taken on a hike to the top of Mt. Vaea, to the gravesite of RLS and Fanny. At that time, the only thing I knew about RLS was that he had written a book I loved called *A Child's Garden of Verses*.

For those of you who have never been there, Vailima is extremely beautiful. Hiking through the vibrant Sāmoan forest to the gravesite on Mt. Vaea, reading the words "Under the wide and starry sky," and seeing the view of Apia and the harbor below would take anyone's breath away. I don't quite know how to say this, but something else happened to me at Vailima. A few places I have been have made a deep and lasting imprint on my psyche. They are places that my mind drifts back to, that I frequently dream about, that seem to have moved inside of me and taken up some kind of permanent residence. The 'āina of Vailima is one of those places. This experience was a cornerstone in forming my personal definition of the phrase "a sense of place." When writing two of the plays in this book, I was returning to that place, a familiar home both inside and outside of myself.

Navigating Islands brings together in a single volume three of my plays set in Sāmoa. Besides all being set there, they share several thematic threads. They all scrutinize how non-Polynesians interact with Polynesians when attempting to navigate an unfamiliar culture. The plays also ask viewers and readers to think about how the outside world's impressions of Polynesians were shaped by the perceptions and stories of non-Polynesians. But perhaps the plays' strongest connections involve nineteenth- and early twentieth-century women, Polynesian and non-Polynesian, as they struggle to achieve individuality and a true self in the face of unfair expectations, negative societal projections, and historical misrepresentations of female characters in literature.

In 1968, I moved to American Sāmoa for seven years and then returned to Hawai'i. *Aitu Fafine* was inspired by the stories I heard there. Not only are there many ghost stories, but, without embarrassment, many Sāmoans still respect and fear aitu. As a young substitute teacher in Sāmoa, I also had to deal with a student who had ma'i aitu, ghost sickness. She apparently went into the bush, made loud, inappropriate, disrespectful noises, and became possessed. I have never forgotten her or her story. *Aitu Fafine* draws on the traditional stories of female ghosts, in Sāmoa and in other cultures, using these stories to examine the demonization of women. The play also asks us to question the role of story creators/writers and their responsibility in shaping ideas about various groups of people. I hope, too, that it suggests stories can sometimes heal, change our lives, and help us to move into new realms.

As a writer, I am sometimes unexpectedly but powerfully attracted to certain subjects. I have to admit that, even decades later, I am still fascinated by Fanny Stevenson and her daughter Isobel (Belle) Strong. In *Fanny and Belle*, I explore their lives and their mother-daughter relationship. Both women were unconventional, adventurous, bohemian, and full of spunk. A review of their lives also challenges our preconceived ideas about nineteenth-century women. They lived and traveled all over the globe, from the parlors of Europe to out-of-the-way Pacific villages. Through their striving to shape their own lives, we can see a foreshadowing of the issues women struggle with in our own time—although it is their time in Sāmoa that most interests me, and the indelible mark it left on their lives.

The seeds for *The Holiday of Rain* must have been germinating in my mind since my very early teens. My parents' first home after returning to American Sāmoa was in Malaloa, very near the old building reputed to have been the boarding house where Somerset Maugham and Gerald Haxton stayed. Staying there at the same time was a Honolulu prostitute who supposedly inspired the character Sadie Thompson in Maugham's short story "Rain." Although he wrote several stories set in the Pacific, "Rain" is probably the piece of Western literature most associated with American Sāmoa. At the time, Maugham was a famous and technically accomplished writer, but he was not kind to Polynesian women, and particularly to "half-caste" women—like me.

Of course, he created images of islanders through the lens of his own time, culture, and prejudices, but because of his fame, what is especially unfortunate about his images is that they joined with others fashioned by Western writers to shape how the outside world viewed Pacific Islanders. When researching Maugham's personal

life, I found myself disliking him as a person, yet feeling sympa-
thetic about the external and internal trials he faced as a gay man in
the early twentieth century. This play looks at "Rain" and Maugham
through my own lens as a woman of Polynesian ancestry—I hope
without rancor, and with some meaning and humor.

I would like to welcome and thank any readers who pick up
these plays and spend time in the fictional worlds I have fashioned.
Reading plays is an exercise for our interior and imaginative fac-
ulties, and I hope you are able to find, as I have, some enjoyment
and some truth in these illusions. As I have always thought of the
stage as a place in our lives where mystery and magic might still
be present, these stories have taken form as plays. They mix fact
with fiction, and reality with the imaginary. I hope the end result
is pleasure.

ACKNOWLEDGMENTS

My sincere thanks to the University of Hawai'i Press for publishing a second volume of my plays, and to the anonymous reviewers of my manuscripts for their enthusiastic support. To Emma Ching, my editor, thank you for your kind and steady support and guidance. My heartfelt thanks also to Adriana Cloud, Malia Collins, and Wendy Lawrence from the UH Press production team for their careful attention and help. To Craig Howes and the Center for Biographical Research, mahalo for decades of support for my work, and for the years of genuine friendship and collaboration. Fa'afetai lava to Dr. Evile Feleti of the Samoan Studies Institute at the American Samoa Community College for helping me with the Sāmoan language, and also to my brother James Kneubuhl of the American Samoa Community College for facilitating. To my husband, Philip D. Haisley, goes my great appreciation for the cover illustration. I would also like to acknowledge the State Foundation on Culture and the Arts for awarding me the Individual Artist Fellowship in 1996, which allowed me to travel to do research for *Fanny and Belle*. Mahalo to Kumu Kahua Theatre, for years of support and for commissioning the play *The Holiday of Rain*. And to our Hilo-based play-reading hui, Keakalehua, affectionate thanks for reading *Aitu Fafine* and for your feedback and aloha. And to all the actors, directors, and theater technical and office personnel who have worked to bring my plays to life, I offer my heartfelt gratitude.

In closing, I would like to acknowledge three people, no longer with us, who helped and encouraged me to find a creative voice and who gave me the confidence and inspiration to write: my analyst, Rita Knipe; my teacher and mentor Dennis Carroll; and my uncle John Alexander Kneubuhl. Ke aloha nui iā 'oukou.

INTRODUCTION

Craig Howes

In the "Note from the Playwright" in this collection, Victoria Nalani Kneubuhl vividly describes Sāmoa's influence, second only to Hawai'i's, on her life and art. This introduction provides a more detailed account of how she went about writing these plays, and of what she hoped to convey through the historical and fictional characters, including Sāmoa itself. Following the precedent set in *Hawai'i Nei: Island Plays*, the many quotations in this introduction are from a February 2023 interview, in which Kneubuhl talked at length about her artistic process, her history with each of these plays, and her thoughts about what the theater has offered her as a Hawaiian Sāmoan playwright.

In the twenty years since the publication of that first collection, Kneubuhl has been prolific in several genres. All the plays in this collection were produced by Kumu Kahua Theatre: *Fanny and Belle* in 2004, *The Holiday of Rain* in 2011, and *Aitu Fafine* in 2024. Her earlier plays have enjoyed productions as well. *Ka'iulani* (1987) was remounted by Kumu Kahua in 2015; the version of *Emmalehua* (1996) in *Hawai'i Nei* was produced elsewhere in 2003; *The Story of Susanna* (1998) has been staged seven times at universities and theaters across the United States; *Ola Nā Iwi* (1994) has also been presented through readings and productions, including in 2007 at Kumu Kahua Theatre; and *The Conversion of Ka'ahumanu* (1988) has been remounted twice by Kumu Kahua Theatre and produced at five other locations.

As a script writer and co-producer, she has been responsible for five documentaries in the *Biography Hawai'i* series—*Maiki Aiu Lake* (2002), *Harriet Bouslog* (2003), *Ruth Ke'elikōlani* (2004), *Koji Ariyoshi* (2005), and *Joseph Nāwahī* (2009), broadcast on PBS Hawai'i—and for *Ka Hana Kapa* (2014), aired extensively on public television in Hawai'i and throughout the United States. She also wrote the scripts for *Heartbeats of a Dance Maker* (2003), on the life of dance pioneer Donald McKayle; *Jack Hall: His Life and Times* (2007), on the Hawai'i union leader; and many shorter documentaries and training films for the Center for Labor Education and Research, University of Hawai'i—West O'ahu, and for the Hawai'i Department of Education. Subjects ranged from picket captain training to women poets, historic sites, Hawai'i ranching life, and the island of Lāna'i. Kneubuhl has written many living-history programs as well. The Kona Historical Society commissioned works on coffee production (2003), the residents of Kalukalu (2004), and the adventures of visiting writer Isabella Bird (2005). For the Mānoa Heritage Center, Kneubuhl created programs on the history of Mānoa Valley (2006) and on Hawaiian painters (2007). Running for seven consecutive years (2013–2019), *The Beginning of a Garden* features three important figures in the history of Foster Botanical Garden. Her most sustained living-history collaboration has been with the Hawai'i Pono'ī Coalition, an organization dedicated to foregrounding Hawaiian history in the islands. In addition to *Ke Kauā o Ka Lāhui: The Life of Prince Jonah Kūhiō Kalaniana'ole Pi'ikoi*, a commissioned production performed on the grounds of 'Iolani Palace in 2022, three commemorative productions that Kneubuhl wrote in the 1990s have been regularly performed as part of the coalition's *Mai Poina* (Never Forget) series. *The Overthrow* walking tours dealing with the events of January 1893 ran annually from 2009 to 2019 at 'Iolani Palace; *The Trial of a Queen: 1895 Military Tribunal* was produced in 2015; and *The Annexation Debate* in 2013 and 2018.

Kneubuhl has also written an impressive amount of fiction. Published by the University of Hawai'i Press, *Murder Casts a Shadow* (2008), *Murder Leaves Its Mark* (2011), and *Murder Frames the Scene* (2016), a trilogy of mystery novels set in 1930s Hawai'i, feature Mina and Fatu, romantic partner detectives who first appeared as characters in *Ola Nā Iwi*. *Murder Frames the Scene* received the Ka Palapala Po'okela Award for Excellence in Literature in 2017. Kneubuhl's short story "Ho'oulu Lāhui" (2000), a work of Hawaiian speculative fiction, has been republished twice.

In 2007, Kneubuhl served as distinguished writer in residence at the Department of English at the University of Hawaiʻi at Mānoa. She was also instrumental in establishing the Mānoa Heritage Center, serving as its director of education programs from 2003 to 2007. Her community service has been notable—as a trustee for the Hawaiian Historical Society from 2007 to 2013, and as a member of the State Historic Preservation Review Board from 2004 to 2006. She has taught playwriting at various times over the past twenty years, and in 2006 her achievements as a writer were recognized with the Elliot Cades Award for Literature. She had already received the Hawaiʻi Award for Literature in 1994, the state's highest recognition for literary and dramatic achievement.

Victoria Kneubuhl has always occupied a space where the otherworldly, the realm of dreams, and the mundane matters of life are all in play. Her childhood reading was partly responsible. "I had a big imagination," she recalls, and she nourished it with the Grimms' fairy tales, L. Frank Baum's Oz books, and the animal stories in *Old Mother West Wind*, by the American conservationist author Thornton Burgess. When buried in a book, Kneubuhl "felt like I was in another world." Her family environment also fed her imagination. Stories from Hawaiian and Sāmoan elders profoundly influenced her sense of the islands that are her ancestral and present homes. Her inner worlds were therefore rich, interesting, and rewarding, and she spent much of her childhood living there.

But she also came to understand that the external world did not entirely approve of such a person, and as an adolescent and young adult, she increasingly felt "hammered into a kind of way of life that didn't have a creative outlet." Only in her late twenties did she find a way to bridge the supposed chasm between the imaginative and material worlds, when she took a course from Dennis Carroll, a director, playwright, and professor in the Department of Theatre and Dance at the University of Hawaiʻi at Mānoa. Carroll introduced her to the work of Richard Schechner, professor of performance studies at NYU. Kneubuhl was especially taken with his idea of the theater as a liminal space—not a specific location or shape, but a threshold, or a sill, offering a passage between realms. The bridge therefore becomes the scene, creating "all kinds of possibilities." For Kneubuhl, such notions had two important effects. First, her inner life "got way less stressful"—either/or could now be both/ and. Second, the theater became a practical space for realizing the products of her imaginative nature, which, because it now had an outlet, "didn't really make me crazy anymore."

Reading "The Samoan Identity," an essay by her uncle and noted Pacific playwright and screenwriter John Kneubuhl, created an additional passageway between her theater training and Hawaiian and Sāmoan culture and history. He calls attention to the Sāmoan saying "Teu le va," which stresses the importance of "tending the space." If, for instance, disagreements or tensions disrupt personal relationships, attention must be directed toward healing the breach. Always a synthetic thinker, John Kneubuhl blends together his extensive knowledge of Western theater history and his equally rich familiarity with Sāmoa and the Pacific by extending the notion of "tending the space" to suggest how individuals should navigate the spaces between their internal lives and the world. In his hands, Aristotle's famous emphasis on pity and fear as the appropriate responses to tragedy becomes a method for such navigation personally and artistically. Pity is transformed into a sense of personal compassion for the impulses and revelations felt within the internal life—forces often attributable to ancestral spirits. Fear fuels the equally important need to back away from such powerful forces when they threaten too greatly the ability to live an individual life in the world. Thanks to her uncle, Victoria Kneubuhl no longer needed Richard Schechner to be her principal teacher regarding liminal space. Her Polynesian ancestors already occupied and enriched it. Recalibrating her focus on that portal space as "a part of normal reality" from a Pacific perspective, she concluded that embracing this liminal realm, rather than constantly fighting its influence, would make people feel and act more confidently.

In all of her plays, and especially those in this collection, the realms of dream, reminiscence, and imagined interactions between natural and supernatural characters from different times and places fill the theatrical space. What is also striking, however, is how frequently the represented interactions become redemptive—for the characters, and, ultimately, for the audience. As a child of the fifties greatly puzzled by the civil rights clashes and violence reported on the news, Kneubuhl was constantly unsettled by social expectations that made little or no sense, offered paltry rewards, and even at times seemed to demand cruelty and hate. Over time, and thanks to a number of teachers, she came to believe that her deeply felt spiritual, ancestral, and imaginative life was the means for accepting and celebrating herself as something more than what those external pressures dictated. "Tending the space" rather than maintaining it offered a method for integrating all her possibilities.

Kneubuhl strongly believes that access to what the imaginative self offers, even if it cannot always be fully realized in the outer world, is essential, because, ultimately, "nothing is created physically unless we open ourselves up to that world. All of these people who are considered great have said that about themselves. It's their imagination, and it's their listening to their inner world that has helped them create some of the most amazing things in life. So why is the imagination so denigrated? I don't understand that." Individuals and the world therefore have an inherent capacity to change, and the theater is a place where we can imagine this process—how it comes about, and how difficult it can be. Almost an artistic watermark, this conviction informs all of Kneubuhl's plays. Wending their way through great challenges, her plots move characters toward a sense of redemption or peace, often shared, that marks the journey's end.

A range of theatrical conventions became tools for realizing this effect. She recalls that her fascination with the affinities between theater as a liminal space and her felt understanding of Hawaiian and Sāmoan culture meant that "I structurally gave up the well-made play mostly." She was also influenced by British feminist playwrights' commitment to a shared equality of parts for actors. "I never really liked the idea of one big star anyway," Kneubuhl recalls, so "once I was introduced to that idea of not one protagonist and not a focus on one single person, I just couldn't really ever go back." Though *Emmalehua*, her first full-length play, has a principal character, she is one profoundly unsettled by intimations of a liminal landscape. In that realm, her ancestors urge her to accept her kuleana, or responsibility, to her history and culture, as Hawai'i careens out of territorial status into statehood and an even tighter embrace by American culture. The Native American character

Hank undergoes a similar process. The co-written *Ka'iulani* offers many versions of the main character, and in *The Conversion of Ka'ahumanu*, five characters follow different arcs, all leading toward some kind of reconciliation, or at least greater personal knowledge. And for Kawehi and Liliha, *Ola Nā Iwi*'s emotionally beleaguered main figures, their journey ends with one of the most lyrical yet powerful imaginings of peace and reconciliation found in any play.

For more detailed discussions of how this impulse informs *The Conversion of Ka'ahumanu*, *Emmalehua*, and *Ola Nā Iwi*, consult the introduction to *Hawai'i Nei: Island Plays*. If anything, the plays in this new collection are even more detailed explorations, within theater's liminal space, of how multiple characters can be redeemed. "It's taken me a while, but I realize that what I've wanted to say is that we all have the possibility to change ourselves," Kneubuhl explains, and *Fanny and Belle, The Holiday of Rain*, and *Aitu Fafine* employ a host of dramatic techniques, often in surprising ways, to dramatize this belief.

FANNY AND BELLE

Fanny: We'll have a great adventure, you and I.
[. . .]
Belle: I couldn't let it all slip away.

The earliest-composed of this collection's plays, *Fanny and Belle* focuses on the lives of Frances Matilda Van de Grift Osbourne Stevenson (1840–1914), eventual wife of the immensely popular Scottish writer Robert Louis Stevenson (1850–1894), and her daughter, Isobel Osbourne Strong Field (1858–1953). A staged reading of the play took place in 1999; after a long period of revision, it was produced by Kumu Kahua in 2004. Looking back almost twenty years later, Kneubuhl is struck by how much she had to leave out—partly the reason for writing *Aitu Fafine*, although she still regrets not having space in either play for Oscar Wilde's visit to Belle in San Francisco, or Fanny's introduction of vanilla vines and cocoa to Sāmoa, or Belle's involvement in Hawai'i with Walter Murray Gibson. But Kneubuhl is still happy with what *Fanny and*

Belle manages to accomplish in "that short two hours of theater about the lives of these two women."

What little regret lingers results from how much research she managed to do. Kneubuhl's plays almost always have a detailed historical component. *Ka'iulani* is set in the 1880s and '90s, *The Conversion of Ka'ahumanu* in the 1820s and '30s, and *Emmalehua* in the 1940s and '50s. *Ola Nā Iwi* ranges from the 1820s to the 1990s, with brief stops at landmarks of racist history along the way. Even *The Story of Susanna* juxtaposes an apocryphal biblical narrative with its largely contemporary plot. But for *Fanny and Belle*, a Hawai'i State Foundation on Culture and the Arts Individual Artist Fellowship in 1996 allowed Kneubuhl to conduct research "in a way that I usually don't get a chance to do." At the University of California, Berkeley, she read some of Fanny's early writing, and at what is now the Robert Louis Stevenson Museum in St. Helena, California, she examined some of Fanny's canvases painted in Grez, Belle's own sketchbooks, and other memorabilia.

But Kneubuhl's principal motivation was to explore the relationship between mother and daughter, with a special emphasis on the amazing parallels in their lives. Some were uncanny. Both lost young sons with the same name, and Belle eventually married Edward Salisbury "Ned" Field, her mother's late-in-life and thirty-eight-years-younger secretary and companion—who was also twenty years younger than Belle. Other aspects of their lives still intrigue Kneubuhl. "After all these years," and even after revisiting Fanny and Belle in *Aitu Fafine*, she remains "fascinated" by "these two women—the places they traveled and the things that they did."

Racing through three-quarters of a century, *Fanny and Belle*'s episodic plot is punctuated by Belle's lyric reminiscences at Vailima, the family's Sāmoan home. Kneubuhl chose this structure partly because, unlike with her previous plays, she "really knew what the ending was"—the laying of Fanny to rest next to her husband Robert Louis Stevenson, with the added reveal of Belle's marriage to Ned short months after Fanny's death. In retrospect, Belle's monologues are therefore musings not just about her relationship with her remarkable mother, but also about the rightness of her very recent marriage to a man barely three years older than her son. But like *Ola Nā Iwi*—another play with two striking female figures—*Fanny and Belle* explores many other characters along the way: Robert Louis Stevenson, most notably, but fathers, mothers, lovers, husbands, brothers, sisters, and children as well.

The play begins in what Kneubuhl calls "the Vailima space": "A memory place used by Belle and Fanny" where "time is suspended, overlapping with what came before and what comes after." This liminal space, which can be "a particular place on the set, or special lighting, or simply an acting mode," will be frequently returned to, sometimes only for moments, to capture intimate interactions between mother and daughter—pauses in a plot that propels them, together and separately, from Indiana to Panama; Reese River, Nevada; the Bay Area of California; Paris and Grez-sur-Loing, France; then back to San Francisco and Monterey, California; and on to Honolulu; various sites in Europe; Sydney, Australia; and finally Sāmoa, where Belle's arrival in the historical narrative, and her return into the Vailima space, coincide to end the first act. Over half of the second act takes place at Vailima— the longest interval within a single setting. Then, with the death of Stevenson, mother and daughter return to San Francisco, where they remain until Fanny dies. The play concludes with Belle and Ned's return to Sāmoa to reunite Fanny with Robert, and with Fanny and Belle's reunion within the Vailima liminal space.

Kneubuhl's handling of characters mirrors this frenetic shifting of locations. Only the actors performing Fanny and Belle have a single role. The other actors—four women and four men—take on between them over fifty additional roles—some as substantial as Stevenson, others only present for a moment. These endless permutations require the audience to register instantly each character, then to abandon that identification, often just as quickly, when the actor slips into another role. The liminal space of Vailima is therefore surrounded by the liminal space of theater itself. This whirlwind of episodes, actors, and movement does not, however, undermine the main characters' steady progress toward self-knowledge, harmony, and change that Kneubuhl sees as central to all of her dramatic work. Despite the first act's breakneck pace, and the personal conflicts bordering on madness and despair in Vailima for much of the second, for all their sharp disappointments and suffering, Fanny and Belle both achieve a state of reconciliation and peace—made possible through important interventions by a small handful of others, but primarily through their mutual and undeniable love and support.

THE HOLIDAY OF RAIN

Maugham: This is Pago Pago, for God's sake! What kind of an inn do you think they'll have? And we'll be stuck with those dreadful people.
[. . .]
Tina: And if it's the last thing I do for you, when you wake, your world will be new.

The Holiday of Rain (2011) was a substitute. After receiving a commission from Kumu Kahua Theatre, Kneubuhl began working on an early version of *Aitu Fafine*—a return, though with a very different approach, to the subject material of *Fanny and Belle*. But the writing proved "so hard to begin with" that shifting to *The Holiday of Rain* offered a welcome release. Though not composed as quickly as *The Conversion of Ka'ahumanu*, the drafting time was relatively short, and while the play has some serious elements—racist and sexist depictions of Sāmoa and Pacific Islanders, for instance, and the need for many characters, with varying degrees of success, to change, heal, or redeem themselves—the plot and tone owe a great deal to the theatrical conventions of comedy. When she was a kid and "television was new," Kneubuhl especially liked to watch screwball comedies. Lighthearted rather than aiming for explosive laughter, they were verbally clever yet dramatically frenetic—"people screaming in the closets and stuff," or "crossing and doing things at the same time." *Ola Nā Iwi* (1994) had been an earlier attempt to blend playful physical and verbal comedy with "a super serious subject," and "some people understood it." When Kneubuhl returned to this model sixteen years later, even though she felt that audiences might be a "little more sophisticated," and therefore better at processing "two things together," she nevertheless chose subjects for *The Holiday of Rain* that were not as dire or demanding as the abuses of Indigenous human remains central to *Ola Nā Iwi*.

But troubling nevertheless. As a playwright, Kneubuhl keeps "coming back to how Western writers looked at Polynesians, and how male writers looked at females," and Somerset Maugham was an especially egregious case on both counts. It was also personal for her. Because the place where he and Gerald Haxton had stayed in Pago Pago "was right down the street from my parents' house," she had known about Maugham since her teenage years. (Her grandfather would say, "Oh, yeah, I remember when that man came.") Maugham's famous, now notorious, short story "Rain" was the result of that stay, and the hotel was later renamed and is still advertised as the Sadie Thompson Inn—a major inspiration for *The Holiday of Rain*. (At one point in the play, Blake, the 'afakasi handyman, even carries in the "Sadie Thompson" portion of the sign, removed temporarily for the purposes of the twenty-first-century role-playing scenario.)

Kneubuhl's fascination with the story's combination of the horrific and the unintentionally ridiculous had been prodded in 2002, when a Honolulu theater produced the stage version of "Rain." "I couldn't even understand why they wanted to do the play," she recalls, and she had "some trouble not laughing when I was watching it. Some of the lines!" But it also reminded her that "the terrible thing is that short story is the one piece of literature about Sāmoa that everybody knows." When she set *Aitu Fafine* aside, and decided to write a comedy instead, she therefore began looking into Somerset Maugham, seeking to learn more about what motivated him to write the story that had provoked so much amusement and outrage on the same evening of theater. She began with the story itself. First published as "Miss Thompson" (1921), and only later acquiring the title "Rain," it was immensely popular. A dramatic adaptation appearing the following year ran for 608 performances in New York, and two movies soon followed—a silent version starring Gloria Swanson (1924) and a sound version featuring Joan Crawford (1932).

Kneubuhl then read some of Maugham's other work, soon recognizing a pattern of white men asserting their superiority in the Pacific, in Africa, and over women generally. Biographies did not soften the picture—his treatment of Syrie Barnardo Wellcome, his wife and the mother of his child, was "pretty awful." Given this information, Kneubuhl did not intend to use him in a play—until she learned about his connection to the outrageous Aleister Crowley. She was already familiar with his mesmerizing personality, magical and occult predilections, prolific artistic endeavors, and pansexuality, and she soon learned that he had even visited Hawai'i, staying in Waikīkī. Most intriguing, however, were his vicious confrontations with Maugham over the latter's use of Crowley as a model for a satiric portrait in his novel *The Magician* (1908). "I had never put those two people together in my mind before," recalls Kneubuhl. But once they were there, the thought emerged of having them face off in Sāmoa in a contemporary bed-and-breakfast cashing in on the fame of Maugham's famous and notoriously misogynist and racist short story. Made theatrically plausible by Crowley's mystical and occult proclivities, it also sounded like fun.

As is often the case for Kneubuhl, drawing figures from the past into her plays stimulates rather than restricts her imagination. Instead of inventing "a character that's totally fictitious . . . you have a set of givens that you can play with." And play she does. In *The Holiday of Rain*, the three historical figures coexist with the characters from Maugham's short story, the contemporary 'afakasi playing those roles, and a supernatural figure and former spiritual companion of Aleister Crowley pretending to be a contemporary Sāmoan and the native housekeeper from "Rain." Orchestrating all of these players led to further ingenious experiments, all in the interest of having fun. Take, for example, the conversations between Effie, the American expatriate who will play Sadie Thompson, and Charmian, the 'afakasi Pacific Island literature professor on sabbatical. Composed entirely of questions, these moments of clever repartee would be at home in screwball comedies, right down to the stage directions indicating that the women are filing their nails. But these scenes have a hidden function as well. Communicating necessary information about previous events and relationships to an audience is always a challenge. Because the characters usually know this information, why would they be telling each other? Kneubuhl felt she had found a "fun and different" solution to the exposition problem through these Effie and Charmian scenes. Because the subjects of conversation are new and famous arrivals, details about them could quite plausibly be known by one woman but only vaguely familiar to the other. Their bantering questions also lighten the characters' potential heaviness. Effie is a depressed individual who must impersonate the despairing Sadie Thompson. Charmian is an earnest but humorless academic. But in these scenes, they display a playful sprightliness that offers hope for both of them.

Broad humor is a constant in *The Holiday of Rain*. Blake's muttered replies to Maugham's racist condescension are an in-joke for audience members familiar with Sāmoan. Offstage knees to the groins of predatory males are important plot devices. Kneubuhl herself is especially fond of Charmian's belief that Maugham's very real racism and sexism are actually evidence of a masterful performance designed to deconstruct such categories by exposing them to view. Her wish to have Maugham visit her theory classes offers an entire comic scenario for audiences to imagine. But above all, the play's entire premise, laid bare in its first few minutes, turns the bathetic excesses of Maugham's short story into farce. "I had great fun making fun of 'Rain' in the play within a play after I saw that production," Kneubuhl recalls, taking special satisfaction from the double hypocrisy of Aleister Crowley's over-the-top performance as the Reverend Davidson, from Maugham's obsessive attraction to "Davidson," and from Maugham's racist and sexist revisions when drafting his story to make what he actually witnesses agree with the stereotypical beliefs of his white readers and himself regarding native savagery.

The slapstick, the unexpected entrances thanks to broken bells, and the hilarious misunderstandings inevitably resulting from time travel and clashes between realms of being make *The Holiday of Rain* the most comic of Kneubuhl's plays. Yet even here, her interest in people's capacity for difficult but positive change despite personal, cultural, and historical trauma drives the plot. The posturing villain Aleister Crowley is of course hopeless, and, quite properly, Tina, an actual angel in disguise, and the protector of her Sāmoan friends, propels him into the netherworld with a knee to the groin. But even Somerset Maugham receives some small measure of sympathy. Though his prejudices, cruelties, and ignorance are condemned through ridicule, Kneubuhl observes that "when people aren't allowed to be themselves," they often make "a mess of their own lives, and a mess of other people's lives too." As necessarily closeted gay men, the historical Maugham and Gerald Haxton found negotiating the early twentieth century a challenge. Because she "kind of [feels] sorry for them," and in keeping with the actual events, she grants Maugham the blessing of ultimately realizing that he truly loves Gerald.

And for all of the play's absurdities, the backstories and challenges of several of the fictional characters are as extreme as those found in Kneubuhl's *The Story of Susanna* (1998), and in some cases mirror them closely. Effie and Theo, the 'afakasi woman who will play Reverend Davidson's wife in the "Rain" reenactment, are struggling with a profound sense of failure and unworthiness only made worse by their assumed roles, and Theo's former lover Reed, Charmian, and even Blake are all dealing with past mistakes. As a playwright and novelist, Kneubuhl has long been fascinated by how "stories and literature shape our view of ourselves and other people," and "especially in *The Holiday of Rain*, I was thinking about all of the ways we internalize racism in ourselves as people of color." Gender-related trauma is also a strong presence—in Effie certainly, but especially in Theo, whose turbulent, guilt-ridden, and violent past "makes her extremely vulnerable," and, thanks to Crowley, the one in greatest danger. But to some degree, all the women characters are traumatized and spinning their wheels when the play begins, and their movement toward self-acceptance becomes the driving narrative impulse.

The embodiment of this force is Tinamoni, the literal guardian angel for all those under her influence and care. The Sadie Thompson Inn is a home for individuals recovering from historical and personal trauma, and Tina draws on all her supernatural and empathetic powers to help them regain traction in their lives. Though she offers her support widely and frequently, her most significant intervention is with Theo. Tina's powerful words cut through the fog of self-loathing that Crowley has exploited and through the gender stereotypes that have been pursuing Theo for much of her life. "Now listen very carefully, darling, because I don't have much time," Tina commands.

Tina: You are *not* some sexy slut like Sadie or some buttoned-up missionary like Mrs. Davidson. Don't you dare fall for those images. They're very convenient for men like Reverend Davidson—like Peter Crow, or like Somerset Maugham, but they are *not* you. Do you understand? They are made up, false, phony, fun-house images. Have you heard everything I've said?
Theo: Yes, Tina.

To save Theo, Tina sacrifices herself to Crowley's will—what he has been hoping for all along while manipulating the other characters for his own amusement. But the angel and her well-placed knee ultimately prove too strong for him, and Tina returns to a new world at the Sadie Thompson Inn. The historical figures are expelled, her charges have all been freed from their passivity and despair, and the play ends with tea, cake, and jokes. In *The Holiday of Rain*, Kneubuhl therefore fulfills her intention "to combine things that might be serious with comedy," because "some part of me feels like people are more likely to think about things and accept the messages that you might want to get across if there's some fun in it."

AITU FAFINE

Louis: Will it be difficult?
Manu: Oh, no, Tusitala, it's very easy.
Vai: As easy as crossing a stream.

Several characteristics distinguish *Aitu Fafine* from the other Sāmoan plays in this collection. The handling of the location is one of them. *The Holiday of Rain* unfolds almost entirely within the walls of a kitschy tourist fun house, and though much of *Fanny and Belle* takes place at Vailima, its main characters roam the world. While *Ola Nā Iwi* and *The Holiday of Rain* demonstrate that Victoria Kneubuhl has "always loved that collision between the past and present," encounters between "the other world and an everyday world" also fascinate her. In *Aitu Fafine*, she sets all of these worlds into conversation within a liminal space that is Sāmoa. Her principal figure also represents a departure. "I have to admit that *Aitu Fafine* is the first play where there was so much focus on the male character," Kneubuhl remarks. "I'm usually focused on women." As the husband and stepfather of its title characters, Robert Louis Stevenson had of course played an important role in *Fanny and Belle*. But his prominence in *Aitu Fafine* as a male character who comes to recognize his weaknesses, and to redeem himself in his own eyes and those of the women around him, is something new in Kneubuhl's work. Male figures such as Adrian Clearwater in *Emmalehua*, Gustav or Erik in *Ola Nā Iwi*, and the Sāmoan men in *The Holiday of Rain* show some signs of self-awareness and progress as men. As a famous historical figure, however, both Stevenson's personality and his literary reputation have to be accounted for. Kneubuhl's hope for him results from "the kind of woman he picked for a partner." Because Fanny did not fit "into the mold of the nineteenth-century woman," she "was pretty extraordinary for her time." Stevenson therefore "must have been attracted to that kind of independent, strong-willed, strong-minded person." His biography's overlap with Kneubuhl's other long-held interests also explains his return as a subject. Her own experience has convinced her that writers often write "because they need to understand something about themselves and the process of living." When researching *Fanny and Belle*, she noticed that "Stevenson, right at the end of his life, and in one of the last things he was working on," began "to write a female character that was actually not so wooden" as most of his woman figures—"more like a whole person." Wondering whether "that's the direction" he would have moved had he lived, she soon found herself imagining "what it would be like for a man to just all of a sudden start thinking 'Wow! What have I been writing all these years? How have I been looking at something, and how could I have missed it?'" Because her long familiarity with Stevenson had convinced her that "he was a pretty compassionate person," she concluded that "he's one of the male writers of that time that might have been open to something like that." Kneubuhl does not therefore return to Vailima in *Aitu Fafine* to tell us more about Robert Louis Stevenson. Along with Fanny and Belle, he offers her an already-familiar starting point for exploring very different concerns.

The play had one of the longest gestation periods in Kneubuhl's career. She began writing it when Kumu Kahua Theatre commissioned a play for its 2010–2011 season, but "it seemed too hard," and the subject was even "a little intimidating": "I wasn't quite sure where it was going, or how it was going to work out." Putting it aside, she wrote *The Holiday of Rain* instead. Only in 2020, when "COVID started and I had to stay home," did she return to it. She recalls little or nothing about the process: "I just remember that I sat down, and somehow the story started happening. . . . It's kind of a big fog in my mind, but it all came together—for me, anyway. I hope it comes together for an audience." As for the structure, "it's a bardo," inspired in part by the story of Dasa in Hermann Hesse's novel *Magister Ludi* (*The Glass Bead Game*). After encountering a yogi in the forest, Dasa undergoes a complex and detailed series of encounters and actions making up a sizable portion of a life, only for it to be revealed at the story's end that this entire narrative has taken place in a few seconds. He still stands in the forest. In *Aitu Fafine*, Stevenson goes through a complex process of self-discovery, personal redemption, and reconciliation with those closest to him— all in the few seconds between the onset of his brain hemorrhage and his death. Kneubuhl "borrowed" other details from Hesse for Stevenson's imaginative adventure—the crossing of the steam, and even the cup of water.

This narrative strategy is in keeping with what Kneubuhl feels is most compelling about theater. Because "we can't compete with film anymore, because films just do realism perfectly," playwrights "have to look for every way that we can to open up that space" by making it more distinctively dramatic and experimental. Paradoxically, theater "has survived for a pretty long time" because it can withstand innovation, granting her the license to "push the boundaries"—first, because "it's super fun" and "super free to do that," but second, because "every play is a different experience of the theater." Kneubuhl takes great satisfaction from using "that space in the freest, most adventurous way," since "it's the one playground where nobody's going to tell me I'm doing something wrong."

What is especially striking about this bardo is that almost all the other characters go through redemptive arcs during the tiny interval as well. (Self-satisfied in his sense of masculine superiority when he is not rendered submissive or unconscious by the aitu inhabiting the young woman Vai, Lloyd Osbourne, Fanny's son, is the exception.) Stevenson provides the through line. In the imaginative world he occupies only for a moment, Fanny, Belle, and Vai above all are agents for transforming his understanding of women, and his representations of them in his writing. Micro therefore enables macro in the theater's liminal space. Between Stevenson's stroke and his death, Kneubuhl grants him an entire play, complete with conflict, personal realization, and redemption. Although Fanny and Belle also travel difficult trajectories in this imagined liminal space—Fanny in relation to her embedded racism and thwarted ambitions, and Belle in response to being discounted or dismissed because of her tumultuous past as a wife and mother—their narratives are not foregrounded, because they have already been the subjects of their own play. "I knew an awful lot about Fanny and Belle" when writing *Aitu Fafine*, Kneubuhl notes, "so it was a little easier for me to point in the direction of what was going to happen after this episode." Here, they serve primarily as secondary agents within Stevenson's journey.

What is truly remarkable about *Aitu Fafine*, however, is Kneubuhl's handling of the aitu figures Manu and Vai, and especially of Nanny, Stevenson's early nurse, who not only shapes his early attitudes about women but also participates in his eventual redemption, and even makes Vai's salvation possible. The bond between Vai and Manu is one of the most culturally grounded aspects of the play. "In Sāmoa, the brother-sister relationship is really tight," Kneubuhl explains, with brothers often upholding "the wishes of their sisters over their wives" because of loyalty to their family, and especially to "their older sister." For this reason, although she toyed with the idea of having Manu as an aitu who would seduce and take total control over both Fanny and Belle, and therefore would be "doing the same thing" that Vai was "doing to Lloyd," Kneubuhl ultimately decided to emphasize "the brother role of protecting his sister." Manu's heightening of the tensions between mother and daughter, tensions meticulously explored in the earlier play, is therefore largely unintentional. Nevertheless, he does provoke a number of Fanny's "do as I say, not as I do" moments that Belle responds to with actions leading to similar results, anticipating events such as Fanny's and Belle's eventual relationships with the much younger Ned Field. In this sense, *Aitu Fafine* is a prequel to *Fanny and Belle*.

The most important fictional figure in the Vailima liminal realm existing between Stevenson's stroke and death is Vai, the aitu fafine of the play's title. She performs two distinct yet carefully integrated functions. First, she is the major agent for making Stevenson rethink the attitudes about women present in his writing. Through bold statements and pointed conversations, Vai annoys, exasperates, but ultimately prods Stevenson into considering how and why he relates to and represents women in the ways that he does. The result is a more mature and appreciative understanding, if only for a few seconds, of the women in his life and art. This young woman is intelligent, articulate, self-confident, reasonable, and compassionate—the Vai who captivates the hearts of Vailima.

But in a more familiar and terrifying sense, Vai is also an aitu, a demonic spirit who seduces then possesses men. Although an aitu can be male, Kneubuhl "was interested in why a female spirit would be doing that same activity over and over and over and over again, for however many centuries people have been talking about it." This figure is very well-known. "Anybody who's from Sāmoa who sees the play and hears this story is going to know what I'm talking about," Kneubuhl remarks. But she also suggests that frightening female spirits may be the product of violence against women. "The women always got blamed for everything—any kind of adultery, or having an affair," she observes, and "they always got punished for it, sometimes in physically brutal ways. But not men—that never happened to men." In Kneubuhl's play, the aitu is therefore a supernatural being who inflicts vengeance on males who perform, but are never held responsible for, actions that lead to women paying a terrible price.

Vai undeniably embodies this figure, and Lloyd, an all-too-typical male chauvinist, is an easy target. But only part of her carries out this agenda, and Kneubuhl is especially interested in exploring how Vai's personal history feeds her aitu nature. "I wanted to say something about stress and trauma in people's lives, and what happens when people are super-traumatized," Kneubuhl recalls. The result is a series of hints culminating in Nanny's circus tale, which reveals how Vai's innocent attractiveness as a girl led to an infatuated young man's obsession and suicide. Blaming her for his death, his family exacts revenge by killing her parents, blackening her reputation by declaring her "an evil temptress," and persecuting her relentlessly. Ultimately, their "rage and violence," and her own desire for "protection and revenge," lodge the aitu in her. Vai's personal journey in the play's liminal realm is therefore toward the eventual expulsion of the aitu, allowing her to live only as the kind, intelligent, and beautiful loving sister who serves as the primary agent for Stevenson's own redemption.

How women replace externally imposed feelings of futility and worthlessness with a sense of self-worth is one of Victoria Kneubuhl's themes—a battle fought by Pali and Hannah Grimes in *The Conversion of Ka'ahumanu*, by the title character in *Emmalehua*, by Kawehi in *Ola Nā Iwi*, by all the women in *The Story of Susanna*, by both title characters in *Fanny and Belle*, and by Effie and especially Theo in *The Holiday of Rain*. In almost all instances, redemption follows embracing a narrative other than the one assigned to them as women. "There's a certain power in storytelling," Kneubuhl believes. "Sometimes when there are things about ourselves that we can't see, we can see it in a story that is not pointing the finger at us, but is telling the same kind of story that we find ourselves living in." In *Aitu Fafine*, "I wanted to write about how, in literature and storytelling and all kinds of art, [women] can see ourselves in something that we're a little bit detached from in our everyday lives." Such a recognition "helps us change." Because the transformative power of story is so important in *Aitu Fafine*, although four of the characters are historical figures, Kneubuhl calls it "probably the play where I had to do the least amount of real research," because "the things that happen in the play are mostly fictitious."

The most audacious example of how stories can direct and redirect lives is Nanny, Stevenson's childhood nurse and governess. For much of the play, she appears in his dreams as the source of his unconsciously misogynist attitudes toward women, due to her harsh, self-righteous religious instruction, reinforced by "her bogey tales" of she-devils and female demons, who act as "the most willing servants of Satan." But in Stevenson's momentary dream world, Vai challenges Nanny by pointing out that these tormenting female "bogeys" are almost always her tales' victims. The truly terrifying actors are the men and women who have cruelly abused them.

Kneubuhl grimly notes that such stories, and historical events, are apparently universal: "Women have taken the blame for a lot of stuff." Referring to Vai's horrible early experience, she insists that "things like that didn't just happen in Sāmoa," but "all over Europe, because that's the entire roster of Nanny's stories."

Kneubuhl could have locked Nanny into flashbacks as the tainted source of Stevenson's buried attitudes toward women. Instead, precisely because of her formidable storytelling abilities, Nanny becomes a crucially important agent for change. This transformation begins early in act 2, when Louis begs her to tell him the story of Medea. When Vai shows up once more to disrupt the scene, Nanny somewhat surprisingly accepts her challenge to let Medea tell her own story. Medea does so, ending with a denunciation of Euripides's influential narrative, which "for centuries" has condemned her to star "as an archetypal evil present in *all* women." This is of course the formula Nanny follows in all her stories, but at least within the liminal realm of Stevenson's last moments, she comes to recognize her own guilt in demonizing women through narrative. But not before a scene with Vai beside the āoa tree in scene 10. Vai accuses her of creating "an appetite" in Louis for "stories about those kinds of women." Nanny responds that "life is stories. We are made from stories. Every moment is part of a story. We live in a forest of stories." At this moment, these two characters' agendas start to converge. Vai tells Nanny that she is "younger than I imagined," suggesting a possibility for change. This moment comes as a surprise for the reader, and Kneubuhl admits she took "a big liberty with Nanny," because even though she initially comes across as an older, proper, and judgmental figure, she "actually outlived Stevenson." In this dream scene, though, Nanny not only intuits that Vai's story is "a very sad one," but that the two of them are "kindred spirits," who through stories affect people's lives.

This realization soon leads Nanny to reconsider her role in raising Stevenson. Telling him that "lately, I'm feeling very bad, very bad indeed," she confesses that "the stories I've always told you . . . about the women" might not have been "good for you—or them." Having revealed this to her charge, she suddenly realizes that she must go to Vai, now fully possessed by the aitu spirit, "to tell her a story, one story" that might offer "a way to tell her, by not telling her, another way of seeing"—perhaps "the story I was meant to tell all along." The ensuing scene is the actual climax of *Aitu Fafine*. A story was always going to be the tool for freeing Vai from the aitu cycle of vengeance, and initially, Kneubuhl thought that Stevenson, the famous author, would be the one to tell it. But she soon realized that "no, that's a really bad idea." Although it might seem idealistic, "it was important to me that Nanny did it," because "I just wanted it to be a woman who did that for another woman." At the moment of telling, the redemptive power of stories literally becomes a matter of life or death. About to convince Lloyd to kill himself, as the aitu, Vai rejects Nanny's offer to tell her a story. Nanny responds with a proposition: "You listen to the story, and afterwards, if you still want the lad, he's yours." Then, drawing on a circus motif that the aitu contemptuously suggests, Nanny tells the story of Vai, the woman suppressed but present within the aitu, which leads Vai to expel the evil injected into her by others. She then offers Nanny thanks for her salvation through story, but Nanny replies that "the telling of it was a blessing," for it has led her to face her own culpability in shaping Stevenson's mind, and to seek to atone for it.

At this moment, the play acknowledges its setting—within Stevenson's mind, in the brief seconds left between life and death. Standing together, Nanny and Vai witness his passing, confident that their stories have redeemed him at the last moment. And like so many of Kneubuhl's plays, *Aitu Fafine* ends with what amounts to a benediction. Vai and Manu reenact the story of "Vailima, water in the hand"—this time to bestow the water of life upon Stevenson, who rises from the dead, walks to the āoa tree, and crosses the stream with his spectral companions to the other side. In the theater, "the lights fade to black."

When Vai remarks in *Aitu Fafine* that "not only do readers believe what they read, but then the people being written about start to believe it about themselves," she is issuing Robert Louis Stevenson a warning that sets him, however unwillingly, on a path toward change. But if we also think of this warning as a description of a playwright's artistic practice, the connotations are much more positive. In these Sāmoan plays, Victoria Nalani Kneubuhl offers audiences a chance not only to exercise that "willing suspension of disbelief, which constitutes poetic faith," but also to think about themselves differently when they leave the theater. For Hawaiian and Sāmoan readers, so familiar with the impact of stories told about them by others, she offers a guide for navigating the Pacific's racist, sexist, and psychologically treacherous history. For women readers, she tells stories free from the all-too-familiar assumptions of misogyny. And for all readers, she creates liminal spaces in which almost anyone, if motivated, passionate, and humble enough, can imagine themselves free from guilt and shame—and perhaps even have some fun along the way.

AITU FAFINE

FOREWORD

Aitu Fafine was first produced by Kumu Kahua Theatre in January 2024 and directed by Lurana Donnels O'Malley with the following cast:

Fanny Stevenson (Aolele)	Amy K. Sullivan
Robert Louis Stevenson (Tusitala, Trout)	Scott Robertson
Belle Strong (Teuila)	Sorcha McCarrey
Lloyd (Loia)	John D'Aversa
Nanny	Eleanor Svaton
Vaimanu (Vai)	Thoren Laga'ali Black
Manutagi (Manu)	Kekoa Shope

THE CAST OF CHARACTERS

Fanny Stevenson (Aolele)
Robert Louis Stevenson (Tusitala, Trout)
Belle Strong (Teuila)
Lloyd (Loia)
Nanny
Vaimanu (Vai)
Manutagi (Manu)

NOTE

Actors take all roles in ghost stories as suggested. When Vai appears in her aitu (*ghost*) persona, there is particular music and lighting.

THE SET

There are three set areas: 1) A *Study Area* for Louis that includes a desk, a chair, and a daybed. 2) The *Āoa Tree* and symbolic stream. The *Āoa Tree* has a laufala (pandanus) mat under it. The stream flows by, and on the other side is a bench or some other sitting place. 3) The *Playing Area* for all other scenes, with perhaps a table and chairs.

THE TIME

Late nineteenth century and other space-times.

THE PLACE

Vailima, Sāmoa.

Act I

(*Lights up on LOUIS as he sits at his desk in the Study. FANNY watches him from the edges of the light.*)

FANNY: Are you sure you're alright, Louis?

LOUIS: I'm fine, love.

FANNY: Do you need me? Can I get you something?

LOUIS: No, I'm perfectly fine.

FANNY: What are you working on?

LOUIS: *The Weir of Hermiston.* I'm going over yesterday's work.

FANNY: Oh.

(*There is a silence.*)

LOUIS: Well, I must work, Fanny, if we want our bread and butter.

(*LOUIS starts reading the manuscript.*)

FANNY: Don't exhaust yourself now. I want you here.

LOUIS: (*Not looking up*) I'm right as the rain, love.

(*FANNY exits. As soon as he's sure she's gone, he pulls out a blank piece of paper and a pen and excitedly starts writing.*

He begins to write while speaking, but soon abandons the pen, speaking directly to the audience, as if addressing his friend.)

LOUIS: My dear Colvin, the most remarkable thing happened to me yesterday. There is something deliriously fine about keeping a secret, but also about confessing one. And I know you have heard me go on and on about our supposed aitu fafine (*woman ghost*) here at Vailima—our beautiful, irresistible, resident lady ghost, who kills by attracting and then putting her victims into a slow fatal sleep. So, you will all the more appreciate my narrative. The adventure began well after lunch. Fanny had been in a bit of a funk, but when I saw her in the late afternoon, she was all smiles.

(FANNY, whistling, at a table with kitchen utensils in the Playing Area. LOUIS enters.)

LOUIS: Ah, the clouds have parted for the sun. What are you doing, my love?

FANNY: I'm making something special, our Vailima mayonnaise.

LOUIS: And how could I be part of this enterprise?

FANNY: You could cut and squeeze this lemon.

(LOUIS takes a knife and a lemon and cuts it once. He suddenly drops the knife. His hands go to his head.)

LOUIS: Oh my God! The pain.

FANNY: Louis?

LOUIS: Do I look strange?

FANNY: Are you alright?

(LOUIS sits and puts his head between his knees. The lights go out and slowly rise on FANNY's line. She is kneeling beside him.)

FANNY: Louis, talk to me. Are you alright?

(*LOUIS, after a beat, raises his head. He's a little dazed.*)

LOUIS: I, I think so. It came so suddenly.

FANNY: Are you sure you're alright?

LOUIS: Yes, I think so. It seems to be gone.

FANNY: Let me help you to your room. I'll finish this.

(*LOUIS and FANNY move to his room, where he settles into the easy chair.*)

LOUIS: Strange, I do feel a bit sleepy.

FANNY: (*Kisses his forehead*) Of course, you're just tired, that's all.

(*FANNY exits. LOUIS goes back to his letter.*)

LOUIS: Well, Colvin, I must have been very tired because I slept right through until the next morning. And I woke up feeling better than I had in years—fit and eager and bright as the dawn. No one was awake, and as the day looked so fine, I decided to take a walk in the bush.

(*LOUIS strolls into the Playing Area.*)

LOUIS: Soft beams of morning light filtered through the canopy, and the birds were wheeling through vines and branches. A scent, a faint perfume of leaves and flowers, hung in the air. I was so bewitched by it all that, before I knew it, I found myself in a part of the forest I didn't recognize. And there, just across a small stream, stood a magnificent āoa tree. (*Lights rise on the scene*) And under the tree sat a beautiful young woman, reading. There was a quiet serenity all around her. I cannot say how long I watched, when suddenly she stood up, and looked straight into my eyes. Startled, I took a step back and—

(*LOUIS takes a step back but slips and falls. The lights go out and slowly rise. LOUIS is holding his head. VAIMANU, the young woman, is kneeling beside him.*)

LOUIS:	Oh my God! The pain.
VAI:	Are you alright?
LOUIS:	Fanny, do I look strange?
VAI:	It's not Fanny.
LOUIS:	Oh, what a wallop. I must have hit my head.
VAI:	You've had a shock.
LOUIS:	Where am I? I don't recall this place.
VAI:	Do you remember anything?
LOUIS:	I . . . I think I was going for a walk.

(*LOUIS sits up.*)

LOUIS:	I'm a little dizzy. Where are we?
VAI:	The vā (*space/distance*) has many dimensions.
LOUIS:	(*Confused*) What?
VAI:	You should rest in the shade.
LOUIS:	I've never walked this way before.
VAI:	Come, see, just across this little stream on the other side.

(*VAI helps him over the stream, and he sits on the mat, leaning against the tree.*)

LOUIS:	(*Closing his eyes and leaning back*) So, of course, my dear Colvin, the first thing I thought was that I'd seen the aitu fafine.
VAI:	Did you say aitu fafine?
LOUIS:	Did I?
VAI:	(*With a laugh*) I don't think she's your type at all.
LOUIS:	(*Amused*) And why is that?

VAI: Because Tusitala likes women that are . . . women that are more original.

LOUIS: You know me?

VAI: Everyone in Apia knows Robert Louis Stevenson.

LOUIS: Well, go on, lass, about the women.

(*Pause. VAIMANU looks at him hesitantly.*)

LOUIS: Please, you have my full attention.

VAI: Well, you seem to like women who have inner strength, who defy convention, brave women, like Fanny.

LOUIS: Like Fanny?

VAI: Not like the women in your stories. They're a little wooden.

LOUIS: How is it I've never met you?

VAI: I'm Vaimanu.

LOUIS: We know all the 'afakasi (*half-caste*) families in Apia, but I'm sure I've never seen you before.

VAI: I'm just visiting . . . my mother's 'āiga (*family*).

LOUIS: Where do you live?

VAI: My parents died, and I live with my aunt and uncle north of San Francisco Bay, my father's 'āiga.

LOUIS: I've lived there myself, in Silverado.

VAI: I know.

LOUIS: Your aunt and uncle must support female education.

VAI: They used to teach at Mills. I can't believe you would think I was that aitu fafine.

LOUIS: A beautiful young woman, alone in the woods—

VAI: I guess those kinds of stories appeal to *some* men.

LOUIS: That's how the stories go, they—

VAI: And the women always get blamed for what men want!

LOUIS: Whatever does that mean?

VAI: How do you feel?

LOUIS: I think I feel . . . odd.

VAI: Let me get you some water.

(*VAIMANU rises with a coconut cup, but LOUIS stands shakily.*)

LOUIS: (*Taking the cup away from her*) No, lass, I can get it myself.

(*LOUIS crosses the stream and bends to fill the cup.*)

VAI: No, Tusitala, don't go back—

(*Lights on VAIMANU dim, and lights on FANNY rise as she enters.*)

FANNY: Louis!

(*LOUIS puts down the cup and steps back across the stream.*)

FANNY: What are you doing here?

LOUIS: I went for a walk, and I slipped and fell and she . . .

(*LOUIS looks back and no one is there.*)

FANNY: She?

LOUIS: Well, I fell and—

FANNY: I've been searching all over for you. They're all waiting with breakfast for you. We have to go back.

LOUIS: (*Looking toward the tree*) But look, Fanny, isn't it beautiful here? Why don't we stay for a bit?

FANNY: Come on now, Louis, we have to get back.

(*She takes his arm and leads him back. LOUIS goes to his Study and resumes his letter.*)

LOUIS: Well, what do you think, my friend? I can hardly keep myself at my work. Such a remarkable girl, and the tree and all of it, like something from one of my stories, something I dreamed up. I plan to return to the spot as soon as possible and make sure I'm not going mad. But I'll have to evade Fanny. She seems to think that if I wander off, I might never come back.

(*Lights dim on LOUIS as he watches LLOYD and FANNY in the Playing Area.*)

SCENE 2

(*Playing Area.*)

FANNY: Lloyd, I tell him these things over and over again, but he never listens!

LLOYD: He's not a child, Mother.

FANNY: Sometimes he behaves like one.

LLOYD: I thought you loved the boyish charm.

FANNY: Maybe you could talk to him.

LLOYD: About what?

FANNY: About keeping to the house a little more. About not wandering off.

LLOYD: But he loves walking in the bush.

FANNY: He could have had an accident. He could fall. Who would be there?

LLOYD: It's one of his only pleasures.

FANNY: He's been sick. He could have a relapse.

LLOYD: You can't chain him to his room.

FANNY: It would be better for him.

LLOYD: What?

FANNY: If he waited, until he was well, I mean.

LLOYD: Mother, he's been waiting all his life to be well.

SCENE 3

(*Lights to LOUIS back at his letter.*)

LOUIS: I tell you, Colvin, I am feeling a little thrill of terror, much the same as I did when I was a young lad and burglarized an empty house on my own dare. Oh, adventure and fear! Life still has its little joys.

(*Lights rise on NANNY in the Playing Area. She wears a black shawl as a scarf and has a distinct Scottish accent.*)

NANNY: As his nanny, I could tell you, Louis was much like other bairns, whilst very naughty indeed. But I taught him the shorter catechism, and made sure he knew his Psalms. These are most important against the grasping ways of the devil. (*Calls out*) Trout!

(*LOUIS's voice comes from his space.*)

LOUIS AND NANNY:

My soul he doth restore again
and me to walk doth make
within the paths of righteousness
ev'n for his own name's sake.
Yea, though I walk in death's dark vale
yet will I fear none ill,
for thou art with me and thy rod
and staff me comfort still.

NANNY: That's a good lad. Now if you'll behave yourself, later we'll go on a nice walk to Warriston Cemetery. Oh, but we must be careful as ever that we don't catch any of those resurrection men lifting the dead out of their graves and then carting them away and wickedly disassembling the poor corpses. Lord, what would become of us if they was to see us discovering them at their foul deeds—such easy prey, a poor nanny and her charge. Say your prayers now, Trout, and ask God for acceptance while you've still the breath to do it.

(*LOUIS lies back in the easy chair.*)

LOUIS: If I should die before I wake, I pray the Lord my soul to take.

NANNY: That's a good lad, Lou. And be on your guard against those she-devils, the most willing servants of Satan.

LOUIS: Yes.

NANNY: Especially those female demons, those, those—

SCENE 4

(*Lights start to fade on NANNY and come up on LOUIS, who is still asleep and dreaming. LLOYD enters.*)

LOUIS: Aitu fafine.

NANNY: (*Fading out*) What do you say?

LOUIS: Aitu fafine!

LLOYD: Louis, wake up!

LOUIS: Oh, Lloyd, I was having a dream.

LLOYD: You were shouting in your sleep.

LOUIS:	More like a nightmare.
LLOYD:	I have to tell you something!
LOUIS:	First pour me a whiskey.
LLOYD:	(*Pours him a shot*) It's awfully early.
LOUIS:	Now what's the news?
LLOYD:	I've met the most beautiful girl.
LOUIS:	What?
LLOYD:	Why are you shocked? You know I like girls.
LOUIS:	And which girl is it now?
LLOYD:	She's 'afakasi, visiting, from somewhere near San Francisco. It was like love at first sight.
LOUIS:	That's unbelievable.
LLOYD:	Why should it be unbelievable? You're always writing about it.
LOUIS:	Where did you meet her?
LLOYD:	I was riding, and she was just sitting by the side of the road, reading. You know, the rest fale (*house*) just before Vailima. She looked up and . . . that was it.
LOUIS:	Does she seem to return your feelings?
LLOYD:	Well, I don't really—I mean, I'm not 100 percent sure, but it doesn't matter. *I'm* sure I love *her*.
LOUIS:	I wouldn't tell your—
LLOYD:	I can't tell Mother—not just yet anyway.
LOUIS:	Lloyd, I—
LLOYD:	I know, she's a native girl, but I'm telling you she's extraordinary. She's educated, well read, sweet, and lovely. If Mother just met her, she'd come around. I just know it.
LOUIS:	You're treading on dangerous ground, lad.
LLOYD:	I need your help, Louis. I need you to invite her for lunch or something.
LOUIS:	(*Loud*) What?

LLOYD: You know, with her family or whomever.

LOUIS: (*Still loud*) I can't just go—

(*Enter BELLE.*)

BELLE: What's all the shouting?

LOUIS: Your brother's gone mad, Belle.

BELLE: Fanny said to warn you.

LOUIS: About what?

BELLE: About the girl.

(*A beat as LOUIS and LLOYD stare at each other and then at BELLE.*)

BELLE: What's the matter with you two? You look like you've seen a ghost.

LOUIS: What ghost?   LLOYD: What girl?

BELLE: The girl who's coming to stay here. Fanua's 'āiga.

LOUIS: Coming to stay here?

BELLE: Fanua is going to Pago Pago with her husband, and she asked Mother if this girl could stay here— something about not leaving her without any other women around.

LOUIS: Where is she from?

BELLE: She's just visiting. She lives with her pālagi aunt somewhere near San Francisco.

SCENE 5

(*FANNY and VAIMANU sit in the Playing Area drinking tea. LLOYD, BELLE, and LOUIS wander in.*)

FANNY: We lived for years in Oakland. Belle and I went to the California School of Design in the city.

VAI: My aunt is a great friend of Dora Williams.

FANNY: (*Excited*) Why, I must write straight to Dora and
            tell her I've met you.

VAI: Dora helped me learn to draw. Do you and Belle
            like sketching?

BELLE: We love it! Maybe we could plan a sketching picnic.

LLOYD: That would be splendid.

FANNY: You said your aunt and uncle teach at Mills?

VAI: They've retired to a kind of colony with some
            others. They tutor us, the students.

BELLE: That sounds ideal. I didn't like school very much.

VAI: They're devoted to our education.

FANNY: It sounds wonderfully progressive.

VAI: We read lots of novels with my aunt—we've read
            your work, Tusitala—and we have long discussions
            with her.

LOUIS: And what do you discuss?

VAI: We always discuss the women.

LLOYD: The women?

VAI: She says we should pay attention to what people
            write about us in novels.

FANNY: What a marvelous idea!

BELLE: A fascinating idea!

LLOYD: (*Amused*) Why would you want to pay attention to
            the women?

VAI: Because people believe things they read in novels,
            about groups of people.

LOUIS: What are you saying?

VAI: What does *Othello* say about the Moors or *The
            Merchant of Venice* about the Jew? Don't people
            believe that?

LLOYD: Perhaps it's true, in a general way, I mean.

VAI:	(*To LOUIS*) See? People write things about groups of people over and over again, and readers believe them.
LOUIS:	And your aunt supposes that women are one of these groups?
VAI:	Yes.
LOUIS:	And what does she say about my women?
VAI:	Well . . .
LOUIS:	Go on, lass, don't be shy.
VAI:	Well, she says they're mostly nonpersons, not whole characters like the men, but in the story set in Falesā, you were starting to see the light.
LLOYD:	The theory sounds preposterous. She couldn't possibly find any support for it.
VAI:	Why not?
BELLE:	And what do you think?
VAI:	I think not only do readers believe what they read, but then the people being written about start to believe it about themselves.
FANNY:	I think that's an astounding idea.
LLOYD:	I think you've been misguided by a crank!
BELLE:	I think it's something we should all look into.
VAI:	And what does Tusitala think?
LOUIS:	(*Exiting*) I think I need a whiskey and a smoke.

(*LOUIS goes to his Study, and pours another drink.*)

SCENE 6

LOUIS:	She's a minx, Colvin. Her damn idea has been haunting me ever since it came out of her mouth.

I'm trying to work, but my mind always wanders back to the subject, and I feel more than a little disturbed about it. Have I unwittingly caused injury? Damn it, man! Do you see what's happening? One day I'm perfectly happy, and the next a slip of a girl has nearly unhinged me.

(*Enter LLOYD.*)

LLOYD:	Louis, we have to help her.
LOUIS:	Ah, enter the white knight.
LLOYD:	I'm serious.
LOUIS:	She hardly seems to need our help.
LLOYD:	She's been under the influence of a female Svengali.
LOUIS:	(*Slightly sarcastic*) The inspiring aunt?
LLOYD:	She's probably one of those suffragists who is always going on about women voting.
LOUIS:	Don't talk that way in front of your sister. I don't want another three-day ruckus.
LLOYD:	I wonder what happened to her parents?
LOUIS:	Ask her.
LLOYD:	But she is beautiful, don't you think?
LOUIS:	Lovely.
LLOYD:	You're together with me on this, aren't you?
LOUIS:	On what?
LLOYD:	On this female stuff.
LOUIS:	Listen, my boy, I've never completely understood what goes on with women, but I know enough to be careful. So, I'll give you this good advice: be careful.
LLOYD:	I knew Mother would like her. Didn't I tell you?
LOUIS:	Still, I wouldn't—
LLOYD:	No, no, of course not. She'll have to get used to the idea gradually.

LOUIS:	Your mother or the object of your affection?
LLOYD:	I'm sure she doesn't believe even half of the things she says. She's just repeating what she's been taught.
LOUIS:	It's what most people do, laddie.
LLOYD:	Yes, but most people have been taught by responsible people. Not some, not some crazy woman.

SCENE 7

(*VAIMANU and FANNY are drawing pictures of each other.*)

FANNY:	I was separated from my first husband, living in Paris. Then my youngest child, Hervey, died after a long illness, and the doctor sent me to rest in the country.
VAI:	You must have been very sad.
FANNY:	I felt like I was out of this world—everything became so distant.
VAI:	I felt like that once.
FANNY:	When?
VAI:	After my parents died.
FANNY:	How did they . . .
VAI:	There was a fire. It was so long ago, but sometimes it seems like yesterday.
FANNY:	That's exactly how I feel about Hervey. Anyway, I went with Belle and Lloyd to this place in the countryside, on the river. At first, we were alone at the inn, but then, all of these artists showed up.
VAI:	And Louis came with them?
FANNY:	When I first met him, I couldn't stop staring. He held my gaze. His face, his whole body was so thin,

and his bones! It looked like at any moment they could break through that delicate skin. I thought, he needs someone to look after him or he could evaporate into thin air.

VAI: I understand you've been quite a nurse to him.

FANNY: I know what it's like to battle with death.

VAI: People say—

FANNY: Oh, I know what people say about me: that I'm a witch, a shrew, a demon who keeps him under my thumb and separates him from his friends.

VAI: You brought him back.

FANNY: In every serious illness with Louis, there has been a moment.

VAI: A moment?

FANNY: A moment when he's almost left me, and then there's a turning, a looking back, toward life. And that's when I've held on.

VAI: And how did you do that?

FANNY: I became an anchor.

VAI: An anchor?

FANNY: For his spirit.

VAI: Sometimes anchors are useful, Aolele.

FANNY: (*Smiles*) I see you've discovered my native name.

VAI: But sometimes they're just dead weight.

SCENE 8

(*LLOYD and BELLE in the Playing Area.*)

LLOYD: You don't have to encourage her.

BELLE:	Encourage her?
LLOYD:	I mean with all this stuff about women in stories and Othello and everything.
BELLE:	*She* brought it up.
LLOYD:	Yes, but you and Mother egged her on. It's not good for her.
BELLE:	Why, Lloyd, you fancy her!
LLOYD:	How can you tell? Is it that obvious?
BELLE:	I'm your sister, remember?
LLOYD:	Well, let's not get off the point.
BELLE:	What *is* the point?
LLOYD:	It may be all right for someone like you to have these ideas about women and suffrage and all that rot, but it's no good for someone like her.
BELLE:	Someone like her?
LLOYD:	Yes, someone who's innocent and vulnerable.
BELLE:	But they're all right for someone like me?
LLOYD:	You're divorced. You've had a child and everything.
BELLE:	What?
LLOYD:	You've already slept with men. I mean *a* man.

(*Pause. BELLE is stifling her rage and hurt.*)

BELLE:	Does Mother know how you feel?
LLOYD:	You won't tell her, will you?
BELLE:	Yes! Your soiled, used-up witch of a sister just might!
LLOYD:	Alright, I'm sorry. I'm sorry.
BELLE:	(*Still mad*) Have you seen Louis? I'm supposed to be looking for him.
LLOYD:	No. Now, promise you won't tell.

BELLE: You have no idea where he is?

LLOYD: He's probably just gone for a walk. Will you . . .

(*BELLE walks away from LLOYD.*)

LLOYD: Belle!

SCENE 9

(*BELLE moves toward the Āoa Tree, looking for LOUIS and obviously stung by LLOYD's remarks.*)

BELLE: (*To herself*) You're divorced. You've had a child and everything. You've already slept with a man!

(*Lights up on a young Sāmoan man, MANUTAGI, sitting on a mat by the Āoa Tree. He is polishing a Sāmoan hair comb. BELLE looks up and sees him. Fascinated, she watches. He sees her, stands, and looks straight at her, smiling. She begins to back away and then slips and stumbles. He rushes over to help her.*)

MANU: Are you hurt?

BELLE: My ankle.

MANU: (*Feeling her ankle*) I think you've twisted it.

(*BELLE likes it, but is embarrassed at the way he has touched her.*)

BELLE: Yes, I—

MANU: (*Takes her to sit*) Come and rest, Teuila, then I'll help you home.

BELLE: How do you know my name?

MANU: Everyone in Apia talks about the beautiful daughter living at Vailima.

BELLE: Whose husband preferred another woman?

MANU: People say he's a fool, and now I know why.

BELLE: That's very kind of you.

MANU: (*He engages her eyes*) I'm not saying it to be kind.

BELLE: (*Engaged*) I've never seen you in Apia before.

MANU: I'm just a visitor.

LLOYD: (*Offstage*) Belle? Belle, where are you?

BELLE: (*A little frightened, standing*) I think I should go home now.

MANU: Let me help you.

LLOYD: (*Offstage*) Belle!

BELLE: No, I hear my brother.

MANU: Teuila, let me . . .

BELLE: (*Turns and moves away from him*) No, please, I'm fine. Lloyd! I'm here!

(*MANUTAGI slips away as LLOYD enters.*)

LLOYD: Belle! There you are. Louis was in his room all the time.

BELLE: Lloyd, I've met the most—

(*BELLE turns to where MANUTAGI was and is dazed to see that there is no trace of him.*)

LLOYD: I'm sorry, Belle, about what I said. Things just slip out.

BELLE: He was just—

LLOYD: I don't know why.

BELLE: What?

LLOYD: I said things slip out, and—

BELLE: (*Still dazed*) That's lovely, dear, can you help me home? I think I've hurt my ankle.

SCENE 10

(*LOUIS sleeps in his easy chair, and NANNY enters in a dream.*)

NANNY: Oh, my darling boy, are you feeling poorly?

LOUIS: Nanny?

NANNY: Would you like a nice bogey tale?

LOUIS: Nothing would be better.

NANNY: Oh, but I don't know. I wouldn't want to frighten you out of your wits, now, would I?

LOUIS: Tell me about Pearlin' Jeanne.

NANNY: Very well then. The young Robert Stuart, pride of his family and handsome as the devil himself, was sent from his home for schooling in Paris.

(*Enter LLOYD with a swagger as ROBERT.*)

ROBERT: (*With a Scot's accent*) He was young, and cocksure, with a swagger in his walk and an eye for the ladies.

NANNY: There, he fell in love with Jeanne, a young lass of fifteen.

(*Enter BELLE as JEANNE. She is wearing a habit, and crosses herself as if saying a prayer.*)

ROBERT: She was about to become a papist nun, when he spied her in the cloister courtyard.

(*She sees ROBERT. She tosses her habit and runs to him.*)

JEANNE: (*With a French accent*) But she soon lost herself, forsook her vows, and did all for him.

(*They meet and begin to dance. He twirls her around and they embrace.*)

NANNY: She was bonny and bright—

JEANNE: And she thought the sun rose and set in his eyes.

NANNY: And as his schooling drew to a close—

JEANNE: She yearned for the day when they would go to Scotland, and she would become his bride.

(*ROBERT and JEANNE move to separate sides of the stage.*)

NANNY: But the scoundrel had no such plans. He knew very well that his family would never allow their marriage.

ROBERT: So, he decided it would be best to sneak away, and leave Paris without her knowing. And early one morning, he called for his coach.

(*ROBERT sneaks away as if boarding a coach, and holding the reins.*)

NANNY: But no sooner had the carriage begun to roll when Jeanne herself, in her pearlin' white dress, came crying out to him, and ran on the side of the coach to his window.

JEANNE: My love, where are you going?

NANNY: She cried out.

ROBERT: Home to my family in Scotland.

NANNY: He shouted back.

JEANNE: Oh, Robert, you cannot leave me, you cannot leave me. Take me with you and make me your wife.

ROBERT: Never! Never in my life will I marry you!

NANNY: Then, the young lass flew into a passion, as the French are wont to do, and she screamed—

JEANNE: Fie on you, Robert Stuart! Never may you have a moment's peace! May your life be ever cursed, and if you dare to marry, I will bathe your house in blood.

NANNY: No sooner had she uttered these words than he turned the coach toward her.

ROBERT: Begone, you bitch!

NANNY: And the carriage wheels rolled over her neck. She was dead.

(*JEANNE falls over as if dead, then quickly exits.*)

ROBERT: Robert flew swiftly away, thinking to leave all his misdeeds behind him. And a few weeks later, he rode up to his ancestral seat, relieved at the sight of home.

NANNY: But, as he approached the gatehouse, his horses shied and turned, and he had to keep urging them on.

ROBERT: Then a cold chill filled the air, and a dark mist rolled down around him.

(*JEANNE reenters with a bloody face, in a bloody white cape, her neck tilted, and only one good eye.*)

NANNY: And there was Jeanne, floating before him in her pearlin' white dress—

ROBERT: With blood dripping over her twisted face, staring at him with her one good eye.

NANNY: Jeanne kept her word, for the house was never the same but for her screamin' and throwin' the furniture about, and walking the halls with her bloody face.

ROBERT: No, please. I'm sorry.

JEANNE: HAH!

(*JEANNE chases ROBERT around and off the stage, snarling and screeching.*)

NANNY: And she haunted Robert Stuart to an early grave, where he was punished by God for his sins.

(*VAIMANU has wandered into the dream.*)

VAI: That's not a nice thing to tell a little boy.

LOUIS: This is my dream. What are you doing here?

NANNY: Who is this vixen?

VAI: Poor Jeanne.

LOUIS: Poor Jeanne? She haunted him until he died.

VAI: And the bloody face bit, that's just too much.

NANNY: This is a fine bogey tale, young lady!

VAI: He probably conjured her up.

NANNY: (*A little curious*) Why would you say that?

LOUIS: Why?

VAI: Calling her back there, and smearing her poor spirit with his bloody guilt.

NANNY: Her poor spirit?!

VAI: *She* was the one who never got to rest!

LOUIS: Can't you just leave me alone in my own dream?

(*LLOYD enters, as NANNY and VAIMANU fade out.*)

LOUIS: Just leave me alone!

LLOYD: Louis, wake up!

LOUIS: Oh, Lordy, I was having a frightful nightmare.

LLOYD: Speaking of nightmares, they're planning a literary meeting to discuss female characters.

LOUIS: Good God.

LLOYD: We need to stick together.

LOUIS: You can stick together with her brother.

LLOYD: Whose brother?

LOUIS: (*Picking up a letter*) Her brother. I got this message from Fanua that she's sending Vaimanu's brother to stay with us too. I haven't told Fanny. (*Looking at note*) Says he's handsome, charming, and very smart.

SCENE 11

(*FANNY alone.*)

FANNY: I don't know what's happening to me—why, in a moment, I'm suddenly craving things I thought didn't matter to me. Do you know what it's like to be married to a man who lives in his mind? To feel so shut out? To watch as all love and desire spills out onto the page until there's nothing left? I feel as if I've just woken up to see I'm in a trap. I've been trapped for so long, and now I'm starving. I've been famished for years and years, with this overwhelming longing—this longing to feel that warm touch, the affection of encircling arms, the low breath of love . . . just below my ear, in the soft, slow curve of my neck.

(*Lights rise on BELLE rubbing her ankle. FANNY turns to look at BELLE, walks in and picks up a strip of cloth, and starts bandaging BELLE's ankle.*)

FANNY: This is just what I'm talking about. Louis could walk alone in the bush and hurt himself too.

BELLE: Louis isn't as clumsy as I am.

FANNY: Belle, I have a little secret.

BELLE: Really?

FANNY: Early this morning, I walked down to the village below Vailima, and on the way back, I met an extraordinary young man.

BELLE: What did he look like?

FANNY: Oh, he was very handsome. He was in the little rest fale (*house*), just near the village, and I stopped and talked for a moment. He was an 'afakasi, and he spoke perfect English. We just exchanged a few words, but when I left, I felt so . . .

BELLE: Yes?

FANNY: I've never wished I was young again. I've never wished I could go back but . . . Well, I'm blushing just to think about it, darling.

(*Enter LLOYD.*)

LLOYD: Louis wants to know about the young man.

FANNY AND BELLE:

            What?

LLOYD: If it's all right with you, Mother, Fanua's sending her nephew to stay with us too. Vaimanu's brother.

FANNY: (*To herself*) Why yes, he certainly could have been . . .

BELLE: (*To herself*) He did remind me of someone . . .

LLOYD: What are you talking about?

FANNY AND BELLE:

            What?

LLOYD: I said what are you talking about?

FANNY AND BELLE:

            Nothing!

FANNY: I mean, I was just going to say that . . .

BELLE: I just wanted to . . .

FANNY: You can tell Louis the boy's very welcome.

BELLE: Yes, very welcome.

SCENE 12

(*VAIMANU and MANUTAGI at the Āoa Tree.*)

VAI: Manu, you got here.

MANU: If you need me, I'm always here for you.

VAI:	Things aren't as easy as I thought they would be.
MANU:	Some people just have to learn the hard way.
VAI:	And some people never learn.
MANU:	Do they like you?
VAI:	Yes, they like me, and I'm sure we have some time.
MANU:	Let me guess. My job will be to distract the ladies.
VAI:	Be careful. They're both a little complicated.
MANU:	You know you can trust me.
VAI:	And they're sensitive too.
MANU:	And pretty.
VAI:	Manu!
MANU:	I knew you were going to need me, so I just decided to meet them on my own.
VAI:	Don't tell me. They're already half in love with you.
MANU:	You should talk.
VAI:	I don't do it on purpose.
MANU:	I don't either.

(*BELLE limps in with her sketchbook, anxious and looking lost. She pauses at the edge of the stream.*)

VAI:	(*To MANUTAGI*) Go away now, I want to talk to Belle.
MANU:	Why can't I talk to her too?
VAI:	Because I said so. Alu (*Go*)!

(*MANUTAGI exits. VAI crosses over the stream to talk.*)

VAI:	Belle?
BELLE:	Oh, Vaimanu, you scared me. What are you doing here?
VAI:	What are *you* doing here? You should be resting your ankle.

BELLE:	I just came out to do a little sketching, and I guess I wandered farther than I thought.
VAI:	Sit down for a minute. You look flushed.
BELLE:	No, I'm fine.
VAI:	Would you like some water?
BELLE:	I said I'm fine!
VAI:	You don't seem fine.
BELLE:	I'm sorry. I don't mean to—it's just that some-times—between Louis and my mother and my brother, I think I might just go crazy!
VAI:	I thought you all got along so well.
BELLE:	I just don't know why Louis and Fanny insisted I come here. The three of them are their own team. Now that I'm divorced, they treat me like an embarrassing appendage.
VAI:	You have to be careful about other people.
BELLE:	What other people?
VAI:	My aunt says, if the people around you think of you as an embarrassment, then you might believe it—even if you're not.
BELLE:	Being married to Joe Strong, now that was embarrassing.
VAI:	You have to protect yourself from the way people want to see you.
BELLE:	Like my brother thinking of me as a used-up old hag?
VAI:	Why is it that sex "spoils" women and makes men more powerful?
BELLE:	(*Laughs*) Maybe you should ask Lloyd. It might shock him into doing some real thinking. You know he's gone sweet on you.

VAI: Your brother is still a child.

BELLE: I hope my mother doesn't find out.

VAI: Why?

BELLE: Because she doesn't want him involved with island women. Because she might send you away.

VAI: Is that so?

BELLE: There was a beautiful Sāmoan girl in Apia. Poor thing, I think he was really in love. Fanny put a stop to it.

VAI: But isn't her sister married to a Mexican man in California?

BELLE: Oh yes, and Fanny adores Adolfo, but when it comes to her dear Lloyd, she's a bit of a hypocrite.

SCENE 13

(*LOUIS is alone in his Study.*)

LOUIS: Do you think there is any possibility to this so-called theory, Colvin? I would very much like your opinion. I'm ashamed to even be asking you about what my mind tells me may be cobbled-up nonsense, and yet I have to admit it brings up these sprouts of doubt and insecurity. They surface several times a day and sometimes at night. I have this sudden fear that there is some kind of web, some secret stream of connections that I may have been blind to all my life. And then I become sick with worry about my writing. I think there may be consequences, things I may have unwittingly caused—actual people I may have harmed. I know, these sound like the ravings of a lunatic, and even as I listen to myself, I know what you must be thinking: Louis has finally gone mad. He steered himself away from civilization, out to the ends of the earth, and now he's fallen over the edge.

SCENE 14

(*LLOYD and MANUTAGI in the Playing Area.*)

LLOYD: So, do you live in this colony with your sister?

MANU: Yes, but it's more like a family, like an 'āiga here in Sāmoa.

LLOYD: I thought it was some kind of school.

MANU: It's an 'āiga, and a school.

LLOYD: Are any of the teachers men?

MANU: Of course.

LLOYD: And do they teach all of this female nonsense too?

MANU: What nonsense are you talking about?

LLOYD: These things I've heard your sister talk about— looking at how women appear in literature, and this notion that people believe what's written about them.

MANU: Do the ideas bother you?

LLOYD: I find it all preposterous.

MANU: You don't agree that women are always judged in literature from a male point of view?

LLOYD: Well, I agree that it's mostly men who are writing the books, but it doesn't mean they're wrong.

MANU: And if it were the opposite?

LLOYD: I imagine we would all be romantic heroes or despicable villains.

MANU: And we might end up believing that's all we could be.

LLOYD: I hardly think so.

MANU: If you keep telling someone they're weak and incapable, don't you think eventually they might believe it?

LLOYD: But we're talking about books! Novels! They're harmless entertainment.

MANU: (*Shakes his head*) Tālofa e (*Oh, my goodness*)!

(*Lights rise on the Āoa Tree. LLOYD looks at it, entranced.*)

LLOYD: Why, look at this! Why have I never noticed this part of the bush before?

MANU: Let's go back now.

LLOYD: And look, there's a mat under the tree. Someone has been here.

MANU: Don't cross the stream, Loia.

LLOYD: (*Crosses the stream and goes to the tree*) Why not? Let's rest here. It's so inviting.

MANU: Come back. There could be an aitu in that tree.

LLOYD: (*Laughing*) You've heard about our resident lady ghost?

MANU: I wouldn't laugh about it like that out here in the bush.

LLOYD: (*Yawns*) Your sister is certainly beautiful.

MANU: (*Goes to LLOYD*) And you mustn't fall asleep here.

LLOYD: And the air here—there's a perfume.

MANU: Get up!

LLOYD: I am *so* tired.

MANU: (*Shaking him*) Stay awake!

LLOYD: (*Half asleep*) I dream about her, you know.

(*Dreamlike lights and strange music. MANU fades away. VAIMANU appears from behind the tree. She moves in a slow, seductive way. LLOYD sits straight up with wide eyes. He speaks as if he is possessed.*)

LLOYD: You've come for me.

VAI: You've called me.

LLOYD: I want you.

VAI: (*Echoes*) I want you.

LLOYD: I don't care what they say.

VAI: I don't care . . .

LLOYD: Mine, you're mine.

VAI: Mine.

LLOYD: I am lost in you.

VAI: Lost.

LLOYD: Day and night.

VAI: Night.

LLOYD: Every night.

VAI: (*She moves to him, they kiss*) Endless night.

SCENE 15

(*FANNY is sitting and drawing a picture. She is humming the same strange music from the previous scene. MANU appears at the edge of the light, watching.*)

FANNY: It's you.

MANU: Yes, it's me.

FANNY: Before you appeared, I sensed you.

MANU:	Sensed me?
FANNY:	I knew you were coming.
MANU:	You knew?
FANNY:	I thought so.
MANU:	How did you know?
FANNY:	I saw your image emerging.
MANU:	You can see things, Aolele.
FANNY:	Forming from the darkness.
MANU:	An anchor.
FANNY:	A spirit.
MANU:	A spirit anchor.
FANNY:	Moving toward me.
MANU:	(*Moves close to her, looks at the picture*) You have brought me to life.
FANNY:	(*Puts down her pencil, takes his hands in hers, looks into him*) No, *you* have brought *me* to life.

SCENE 16

(*LOUIS and BELLE. BELLE sits with a notepad, ready to take his dictation.*)

BELLE:	Do you want me to leave?
LOUIS:	No, I just don't know what's wrong.
BELLE:	Every writer must have a bad day or two.
LOUIS:	I feel as if I have nothing more to say.
BELLE:	That couldn't be true.
LOUIS:	As if I've run out of words.
BELLE:	Now that sounds very dramatic.

LOUIS:	Perhaps I need Lloyd's opinion.
BELLE:	(*Slight sarcasm*) Of course.
LOUIS:	Are you angry with your brother?
BELLE:	I just don't know why I came here.
LOUIS:	Where else would you go? You're divorced and on your own.
BELLE:	I could go back to Sydney. I was happy there.
LOUIS:	In that boarding house? With those theater types?
BELLE:	I had work. I had friends.
LOUIS:	It was asking for trouble.
BELLE:	What does that mean?
LOUIS:	Nothing. (*Pause*) These things Vaimanu says about the influence of literature, about how people see themselves.
BELLE:	Is that what's troubling you?
LOUIS:	What do you think?
BELLE:	Maybe there is some truth to them.
LOUIS:	Go on.
BELLE:	Well, maybe we do believe what we read about ourselves. Maybe sometimes you *do* have to protect yourself from the way other people want to see you.
LOUIS:	You think, as a writer, I may have done some harm?
BELLE:	No, no, I wasn't thinking about you at all.
LOUIS:	I go over and over all my characters, wondering.
BELLE:	Really, I wasn't.
LOUIS:	And I have such an uncertain feeling.
BELLE:	(*To herself*) Welcome to the club.
LOUIS:	As if something isn't quite right.
BELLE:	Does it have to do with our visitors?

LOUIS:	They both seem so lovely.
BELLE:	Don't they?
LOUIS:	So lively and bright.
BELLE:	So kind and understanding.
LOUIS:	And Fanny seems quite taken with Manutagi.
BELLE:	It doesn't bother you?
LOUIS:	Why should it?

(*Pause. She looks at him.*)

BELLE:	And are you quite taken with Vaimanu?
LOUIS:	(*Laughs*) Not the way your brother is.
BELLE:	My brother needs to grow up.
LOUIS:	He's a fine young man.
BELLE:	He's a baby who's never had to be on his own. He wouldn't know what to do without you and Fanny.
LOUIS:	He went off to school by himself.
BELLE:	And then he came right home to be coddled by Mother and fussed over by you.
LOUIS:	Belle!
BELLE:	Isn't this just what you wanted?
LOUIS:	I wanted a family around me.
BELLE:	But just look at him! What has he ever done on his own?
LOUIS:	Why are you so angry?
BELLE:	I don't know. I don't know. It's just—sometimes I feel so trapped!

(*BELLE stomps off. She walks toward the Āoa Tree and finds VAIMANU, who has been crying.*)

BELLE:	Vai, what's wrong?
VAI:	Nothing. I don't know. Sometimes, something happens.

BELLE:	What happened?
VAI:	Something. It was something!
BELLE:	Did someone hurt you?
VAI:	I don't know—
BELLE:	I don't understand.
VAI:	I don't either.
BELLE:	Vai, I—
VAI:	There's nothing you can do. Just please, leave me alone.

SCENE 17

(*BELLE leaves her and moves toward the house. She encounters MANUTAGI.*)

MANU:	Teuila, have you seen my sister?
BELLE:	She said she wanted to be alone.
MANU:	(*Disheartened*) Oh.
BELLE:	I think she was crying.
MANU:	It's hard for her.
BELLE:	What is?
MANU:	Having to—having to be so attractive.
BELLE:	That's nothing to cry about.
MANU:	She always cries.
BELLE:	What is it, really?
MANU:	I shouldn't tell you.
BELLE:	You can trust me.
MANU:	You won't tell the others?
BELLE:	I promise.

MANU: (*Pause, remembering*) It was long, so long ago when we were children, living in a village with our family.

BELLE: What happened?

MANU: Some people set fire to our home and our parents died. It was terrible. My mother's family took me in, but they wouldn't have Vai. She wandered around, sleeping in the bush. She was all alone. She wanted to die. I kept trying to help, but I was just a boy. She was almost at the end, but then . . . they came.

BELLE: Who came?

MANU: Our 'āiga. They heard, and they came looking for us.

BELLE: Your aunt and uncle? Your father's family?

MANU: They took us away with them.

BELLE: I can't believe you came back here. I can't believe they would let you.

MANU: They said it would be good for us.

BELLE: Even after what happened?

MANU: I'm her brother. I should have been able to protect her.

(*Pause.*)

BELLE: Are you falling in love with my mother?

MANU: (*Laughs*) No.

BELLE: I've seen how she looks at you. You don't seem to be discouraging her.

MANU: (*Shrugs*) Maybe.

BELLE: Oh, so that's how it is with you.

MANU: I don't really want to.

BELLE: Right.

MANU:	I just can't help it.
BELLE:	That's a very bad line.
MANU:	I didn't write the script.
BELLE:	Who else did?
MANU:	I can't tell you.
BELLE:	That makes no sense.
MANU:	I wish things were different between us.
BELLE:	What does that mean?
MANU:	We have to move past each other because we're always watching out for others.

(*MANU takes her hand and looks at her.*)

| MANU: | You must promise not to tell, about Vai. |

(*BELLE returns his gaze.*)

| BELLE: | I would never hurt her. |
| MANU: | Fa'afetai (*Thank you*), Teuila. |

(*He kisses her on the forehead. BELLE smiles at him and leaves. He watches her go.*)

SCENE 18

(*VAIMANU is asleep under the Āoa Tree. She is crying out in her sleep. LOUIS enters.*)

VAI:	No! Come back.
LOUIS:	(*Calls out*) Vai, wake up.
VAI:	Come back.
LOUIS:	Vaimanu!
VAI:	(*Sitting up*) Tusitala.

LOUIS: Were you having a nightmare?

VAI: (*Crosses the stream*) It was so real.

(*They sit on the bench.*)

LOUIS: I've been having dreams too.

VAI: There was a girl. I was on a path, walking behind her. She turned around and scowled at me. Then we walked a little further, and she picked up some stones and threw them at me. One of them hit me right in the forehead. I tried to talk to her, ask her what was wrong, but she was so angry.

LOUIS: Teu le vā (*Tend to the space/distance*).

VAI: What?

LOUIS: I'm sure you know what that means.

VAI: I'm surprised you do. Most pālagi think that between us, in the vā, between things and places, there is only empty space.

LOUIS: Teu le vā, this idea of tending to that space between ourselves and others, has always intrigued me.

VAI: It is for balance.

LOUIS: And perhaps safety?

VAI: Safety?

LOUIS: To draw away from fear or danger, to move close with compassion or understanding. It is hard to know.

VAI: The vā has many dimensions.

LOUIS: And sometimes I think it's also about recognizing our own darker side—these spaces inside ourselves. We draw close and look when it is safe, and move away if it's not.

VAI: And you think this has to do with my dream?

LOUIS: There could be a Jekyll and Hyde in all of us.

VAI:	You sound like one of my teachers.
LOUIS:	So many of my stories, my most vivid characters, have come to me in dreams.
VAI:	But most times dreams aren't logical. They make no sense.
LOUIS:	Logic doesn't tell us everything, much less what we might desperately need to know.

SCENE 19

(*LLOYD is sitting and staring into space. FANNY enters.*)

FANNY:	Where have you been? I've been calling and calling.
LLOYD:	What?
FANNY:	Why, Lloyd, how well you look.
LLOYD:	I feel wonderful!
FANNY:	What are you doing here?
LLOYD:	Just daydreaming.
FANNY:	I need you to cut some ginger flowers for the table.
LLOYD:	Ginger flowers, they're like a lovely woman.
FANNY:	I suppose.
LLOYD:	So delicate, but such a potent perfume.
FANNY:	What were you daydreaming about? Or should I ask whom?
LLOYD:	How many do you want?
FANNY:	About five or six stalks.
LLOYD:	(*Exiting*) I'll get right to her. I mean, it.
FANNY:	(*Calling after him*) Get ones with lots and lots of flowers.

(*FANNY watches him leave. She moves into the Study. LOUIS is working.*)

FANNY: What's wrong with Lloyd?

LOUIS: What's that, dear?

FANNY: Something is wrong with Lloyd.

LOUIS: I haven't noticed.

FANNY: I find that hard to believe. You notice everything.

LOUIS: What's wrong with him?

FANNY: He's acting like he did before.

LOUIS: When?

FANNY: When he was besotted with that native girl.

LOUIS: The one you made him give up?

FANNY: I made him do the sensible thing.

LOUIS: You may have created forbidden fruit.

FANNY: Just what does that mean?

LOUIS: What do you think?

FANNY: Is he infatuated with Vaimanu?

LOUIS: I didn't say—

FANNY: How could I have missed that?

LOUIS: Maybe your mind's been elsewhere.

FANNY: That little sneak.

LOUIS: I don't think the lass returns his affection.

FANNY: She's probably just playing hard to get.

LOUIS: I don't think she's playing at anything.

FANNY: Of course, she is! He's a catch for a girl like her.

LOUIS: I really don't think—

FANNY: She'll have to leave.

LOUIS: No, she won't.

FANNY: I won't have him falling for another native girl!

LOUIS: I said, I don't think the lass wants him!

FANNY: And I don't care. She has to leave!

LOUIS: If she leaves, her brother leaves with her.

FANNY: What?

LOUIS: You heard me, if she leaves, then he leaves too!

(*FANNY glares at LOUIS and marches off.*)

LOUIS: (*Begins writing and then speaks to audience*) My dear Colvin, how rapidly things can change in our lives. And how interesting to see, at my age, that things I took for granted may not be so. I can't believe how I'm feeling, how I'm behaving. Fanny is attracted to a young man, and I don't even care. Not only do I not care, I feel a little relieved. Yes, relieved to have all that passion, all that intensity, all that scrutiny, all that need turned away from me. Yes, I feel relieved, as if I can breathe, as if another door is just about to open to a new space, as if there is still a little wonder in the world.

SCENE 20

(*Evening. Everyone is gathered together. The atmosphere is tense. BELLE is sketching VAIMANU, who is reading. FANNY is mending a shirt. LLOYD and MANUTAGI are looking over some maps. LOUIS walks in, stands, and paces.*)

LOUIS: Now, Manu and Vai, won't you tell us a little more about your literary studies. I'm quite curious.

VAI: I don't want to make people feel uncomfortable.

LOUIS: You won't make anyone uncomfortable. We're all very broad-minded here. Lloyd, are we not?

LLOYD: (*Repeats*) Very broad-minded.

FANNY:	Louis, don't be a bother.
LOUIS:	(*To VAI*) You don't feel I'm bothering, do you?
VAI:	What would you like to know?
LOUIS:	Who were some of the women characters your teacher approved of?
VAI:	(*Remembering*) Mostly ones written by women. She liked Jo March in *Little Women*.
FANNY:	Sentimental trash.
MANU:	Alcott presented many possibilities for women.
FANNY:	Well, I'm all for women and possibilities.
VAI:	She liked Jane Eyre. She said Jane had a real voice.
FANNY:	She was a blind slave to her love for Rochester.
MANU:	(*Looks at BELLE*) I thought they were more like soulmates.
VAI:	And I especially liked Uma in your story *The Beach at Falesā*.
FANNY:	Of course, the native girl heroine.
VAI:	Also, the story was a good critique of colonialism and imperialism.
FANNY:	And what would you know about those things?
LOUIS:	Fanny, be civil.
FANNY:	She just likes using big words.
VAI:	I'm sorry, Aolele.
LOUIS:	You have nothing to be sorry for.
FANNY:	What do you say, Lloyd?
LLOYD:	I'm not saying anything.
FANNY:	Say something like you said before.
LLOYD:	I have nothing to say.
FANNY:	Well, I do. I want an end to all this nonsense about women characters and imperialism and colonialism!
LOUIS:	Yesterday you were all for it.

FANNY:	Well today I'm sick of it, and I want it to stop!
MANU:	Aolele, perhaps you would like to go for a walk?
FANNY:	(*A pleading look*) Yes, please, take me out of here. I feel as if I'm suffocating.

(*MANU and FANNY exit. LOUIS and BELLE watch them.*)

VAI:	Does she want us to leave?
LOUIS:	No, no.
VAI:	I think she doesn't want me here.
LOUIS:	Don't mind her.
VAI:	If she asks me to leave, I have to—
LOUIS:	Nonsense! *I* want you here.
VAI:	Really?
LOUIS:	Yes. Why, we all do. Right, Belle?
BELLE:	(*Looking at LOUIS*) Of course we do.
LOUIS:	Lloyd.
LLOYD:	(*Enraptured with VAI*) Of course.
LOUIS:	Now about these women characters—

(*LLOYD, who has been staring at VAI, begins to drift off.*)

BELLE:	Lloyd, are you alright?
LLOYD:	I feel so tired.
BELLE:	Wake up, we have to get ready for tonight.
LLOYD:	Tonight?
BELLE:	Yes. Remember our plan for tonight?
LLOYD:	Oh, right.
BELLE:	Come on, get up and help me.

(*BELLE grabs her brother and they exit. VAI watches.*)

VAI:	Tusitala, did you mean what you said?
LOUIS:	About what?
VAI:	About not wanting me to leave.

LOUIS:	Yes, I did.
VAI:	Vailima is so beautiful.
LOUIS:	Sometimes it feels like a beautiful birdcage.
VAI:	You feel caged?
LOUIS:	And haunted by things that are just out of reach.
VAI:	What things are those?
LOUIS:	(*Faraway*) I'm not sure, but I've always sensed, maybe even longed for the unknown.
VAI:	You've faced the unknown since you were a child.
LOUIS:	I've stepped up to those passages, but I've always turned back.
VAI:	Called back. Sometimes we are called back.

SCENE 21

(*LOUIS moves slowly into a soft light in the Study Area.*)

LOUIS:	And I must say, I can't believe how tired it all makes me feel.
NANNY:	Come to bed now, Trout.

(*LOUIS lies down on his chair with his feet up on the ottoman and drifts off, as NANNY creeps out of the dark and VAI fades away.*)

LOUIS:	As if I could sleep for a hundred years.
NANNY:	Growin' lads do need their rest.
LOUIS:	And a bogey tale, Nanny.
NANNY:	But first, tell me—what do you think of the young lass and her idea?
LOUIS:	Vai?

NANNY:	About the guilt and all?
LOUIS:	Nanny, please, just tell me a story.
NANNY:	Oh, very well. And what fine bogey tale would you like to hear, my love?
LOUIS:	Tell me about Kittie Rankie.
NANNY:	(*Giggling*) Ah, but it might be scaring the pants off you!
LOUIS:	Tell me now.
NANNY:	Well, laddie, as ye well know, on the south bank of the River Dee lies the tower house of a castle. Its old and ancient walls be three-foot thick to keep out the enemies of the Gordons, but there be no defense against the evil that comes from within. Kittie Rankie was a woman who came to work there, a woman who was said to practice the black arts. And the mistress of the house, who thought herself ever so fine, was always callin' on Kittie to use her powers.

(*Enter FANNY as the MISTRESS OF THE CASTLE. She is wearing a tiara and a velvet cloak.*)

MISTRESS:	Kittie Rankie! Where be thee, woman?

(*Enter BELLE as KITTIE RANKIE. She wears an apron and has a peasant shawl over her head.*)

KITTIE:	Pardon, Madame. I did not hear thee call.
MISTRESS:	Now, Kittie, I want you to be asking your spirits— what's become of my fine pearl necklace?
KITTIE:	Oh, Madame, they are looking. They say you shall find the necklace on the floor of the wardrobe, underneath your soft silk shawl.
MISTRESS:	And, Kittie, I want you to be asking them—what's become of the fine new pony brought home for our bairns?

KITTIE: Oh, Madame, this little pony, they say, has run to the hill in the eastern vale and there he be eating in the fine tall grasses.

NANNY: Oh, but one day the mistress asked a terrible question.

MISTRESS: And now, Kittie Rankie, ask your spirits, where is my husband and why is he so many days late in returning to our home?

KITTIE: Oh, forgive me, Madame, they cannot see.

MISTRESS: (*Angry*) I say, tell me, Kittie Rankie, or you shall go without food and water.

KITTIE: Oh, no, Mistress, do not ask me, for they say no good will come of it.

MISTRESS: (*Grabs her by the hair*) Tell me what they see, Kittie, or you shall suffer.

KITTIE: I'm sorry to say, sweet Mistress, he lies with another. She is young and fair and her hair is gold and her eyes are green, and she is telling him she carries his child.

MISTRESS: Lies! Lies! You foul sorceress!

NANNY: The mistress shrieked—

MISTRESS: Lock her in the cellar!

(*LLOYD enters with a black hood over his head. He grabs KITTIE and throws her down.*)

KITTIE: No, Madame, no. It's not me! It's him who betrays you! It's him who should be punished! It's him!

NANNY: At these words, the mistress only flew into a greater rage and in a fit and a fury she screamed—

MISTRESS: Take the slut, the foul witch, to the hill Craig-na-Ban. Tie her tight to the stake and burn her for her wicked crimes.

(*LLOYD marches KITTIE to the center of the Playing Area and leaves her as if tied to a stake in a spot of light. The light gradually gets redder and redder. KITTIE collapses and lights black out suddenly.*)

NANNY: But little did the Mistress know that now the Gordons would never be rid of Kittie Rankie. For up rose her ghost—

(*Soft light on KITTIE rising up in a slow, ghostly way.*)

NANNY: And ever after, she walked the castle.

(*KITTIE walks very slowly, pointing, with a creepy smile on her face.*)

NANNY: Now in the cellar, now in the tower.

(*KITTIE slowly raises the palm of her hand. A bell tolls three times.*)

NANNY: And she appears before them and makes the old bell toll when death and misfortune are coming, and everyone is greatly afeared to see her and to hear the ringing as it echoes through the castle. For who knows, they all think, but the bells could be tolling for me.

SCENE 22

(*At the Āoa Tree.*)

VAI: Fanny has turned against me.

MANU: It's not your fault.

VAI: Maybe it is.

MANU: Stop punishing yourself.

VAI: What?

MANU:	Nothing. Why has she turned on you?
VAI:	You know why.
MANU:	Has she—
VAI:	No, she hasn't told me to leave.
MANU:	Do you think she might?
VAI:	I think he's stopping her, for now.
MANU:	Then just ignore her.
VAI:	You know our teachers' rules. If Fanny or Louis tells us to leave, it's over.
MANU:	So, we might not have much time.
VAI:	Exactly.
MANU:	You have to pull yourself together.
VAI:	What if I can't?
MANU:	You're halfway there.

(*They watch BELLE and LLOYD set six laufala mats in the Playing Area.*)

VAI:	What are they doing?
MANU:	It looks like some kind of game.
VAI:	A game?
MANU:	They love to do odd things.
VAI:	(*A beat*) Were you talking to her about me?
MANU:	How can you tell?
VAI:	Why did you do that?
MANU:	I felt like I had to.
VAI:	Why?
MANU:	I don't know why! Look, it's not that easy for me either!

(*LOUIS and FANNY join BELLE and LLOYD in the Playing Area. They stand behind their mats, leaving space between the two men for VAI, and between the two women for MANU.*)

VAI: They are a little odd, aren't they?

MANU: We have to go along with them.

VAI: More than a little odd . . .

MANU: Come on, they're waiting.

(*VAI and MANU join the others as a bell tolls three times.*)

LLOYD: But who knows, they say—

BELLE: But the bell could toll for me.

(*They all lie down on their backs on the mats and close their eyes.*)

LOUIS: This is what happens when you die.

LLOYD: You lie still in a dark cocoon.

BELLE: Still as a standing stone.

FANNY: Still as a lonely crow.

LOUIS: There is only a dark quiet.

LLOYD: Sometimes a faint murmur.

BELLE: Far away, a distant rustle.

FANNY: The sense of something just beyond.

LOUIS: But you lie still.

LLOYD: Swaddled in shadow.

BELL: Still as a frozen lake.

FANNY: Still as a barren tree.

BELLE: Still as the silent moon.

LOUIS: The bell tolls and you lie.

LLOYD: Waiting.

BELLE: Forever wanting.

FANNY: Wanting forever.

(*VAI and MANU stand and move to their own light.*)

VAI: On some nights, we would lie on the grass, out on our malae (*village green*). We would close our eyes and count, and then all together we would open our eyes to the night sky, the star-laden meadow with the glittering path of the Milky Way.

MANU: How can our hopes fail us, when every night we are invited to this miracle? How can we not embrace our genuine longing? How can we not feel the resonant brilliance of our being, illuminated and clear?

BELLE: (*Sits up and looks at MANU*) The Spirit is neither born, nor does it die at any time. It does not come into being, or cease to exist.

LOUIS: (*Sits up and looks at VAI*) I am the resurrection, and the life: he that believeth in me, though he were dead, yet shall he live.

End ACT I

Act II

(*LOUIS is sleeping in his Study. NANNY enters.*)

LOUIS: Nanny, I want a bogey tale.

NANNY: Which one would that be, Trout?

LOUIS: I want to hear about *her.*

NANNY: Not her!

LOUIS: Yes, her, Nanny, I want *her.*

NANNY: She's a demon if there was one. Are you sure?

LOUIS: Yes, please, yes!

NANNY: Well, here she is, lad.

(*A light to MEDEA, played by FANNY. She knits as NANNY talks. VAIMANU creeps in and watches in the shadows.*)

NANNY: There she is. The murderess, the witch, the sorceress, the Medea. She had a grand passion for Jason
and helped him get the Golden Fleece. And she
killed her brother as they were running away, cutting up his body and scattering it about. She could
drive men mad, and she got the daughters of old
King Pelias to kill their father by slashing him up
and throwing the pieces in a boiling pot. Then,
when Jason meant to abandon her for the younger
princess, Glauce, out of jealousy she killed Glauce

with a golden dress laced with deadly poison. And then, she did the worst, most horrid of all crimes— to wreak revenge on Jason, she killed her own bairns, two boys, more lovely than the sunshine—

VAI: I don't believe this!

NANNY: You again.

VAI: Yes, me.

NANNY: Why do you keep popping up?

VAI: (*To LOUIS*) Do you ever question these stories?

LOUIS: Why? It's just a story in a dream.

VAI: You should ask questions.

LOUIS: And what would I be asking?

VAI: (*Points to MEDEA*) You might ask *her* about her life since she's sitting right there.

LOUIS: Nanny?

NANNY: (*After thinking*) Maybe we should give the lady a chance.

LOUIS: Really?

NANNY: We don't want to close our minds, Trout.

LOUIS: (*To MEDEA*) Madame, would you?

MEDEA: Would I?

LOUIS: Would you care to talk?

MEDEA: Well, kind sir, I have been waiting forever to talk. No one ever asks *me* to talk. (*Short pause*) In the first place, people forget I'm descended from the sun god, Helios. I am the niece of Circe. I have magical abilities. I am a mythological being, and mythological beings are always up to one thing or another, aren't they? And I did *not* develop a passion for Jason—Hera and Aphrodite forced those feelings on me with one of their spells. I would never have fallen for that dim-witted toy boy on my own—although he was very handsome and handy in certain departments. But honestly, he was always just a few oars short of a crew. He couldn't have gotten that fleece without me. I practically had to throw it in his lap. And as for those other crimes: I did *not* kill my brother—that stupid Jason did. And it's not *my* fault Pelias died. His brainless daughters spied on me when I was practicing rejuvenation magic on an old ram, and decided to try it on their father. It's not my fault those nitwits filleted him and boiled him with herbs. I'm telling you, ancient Greece was full of idiots! And as for Glauce—please, oh, please! If I had been unfaithful to Jason, they would have called me a whore, and no one would have blinked twice if he killed me or my father, in or out of a jealous rage. And once and for all, I did *not* kill my beautiful boys. The citizens of Corinth performed that cruelty. I have been falsely accused by that writer, that poet, that maker of dramas. Euripides is the bastard's name. He sentenced me to centuries of condemnation for the sake of making a sensational impression. And I am not the only one who has inherited his stamp of depravity. For centuries I have starred as an archetypal evil present in *all* women. And I ask you, how many women have been judged and suffered because of his pack of lies? How many have suffered because of his arrogant egotistical pen—just so he could make his audience gasp in horror!

LOUIS: Enough!

MEDEA: How many?

LOUIS: Enough! Get out! All of you!

(*Everyone exits. LOUIS turns, calling out in his sleep. MANU enters.*)

LOUIS:	It's not my fault.
MANU:	Tusitala?
LOUIS:	I'm sorry.
MANU:	Tusitala. Wake up.
LOUIS:	(*Half awake*) I'm so sorry.
MANU:	Sorry for what?
LOUIS:	For everything.

SCENE 2

(*In the Playing Area, LLOYD is sleeping on a mat. He is wearing a lavalava and has a flower behind one ear. VAIMANU is draw-ing him. FANNY enters. VAI doesn't look at FANNY.*)

FANNY:	I know what you want.
VAI:	Do you?
FANNY:	You can't have him.
VAI:	Can't have whom?
FANNY:	Don't pretend you don't know what I'm talking about.
VAI:	He looks so peaceful in his sleep.
FANNY:	You may have Louis fooled, but you don't fool me.
VAI:	Who do you think haunts his dreams?
FANNY:	How much do you want?
VAI:	What?
FANNY:	How much? How much money do you want?
VAI:	Money?
FANNY:	To leave him alone.
VAI:	(*Laughs*) I don't want money.

FANNY:	Everybody wants money.
VAI:	This is beneath you, Aolele.
FANNY:	So, what do you want? What will it take to make you leave him alone?
VAI:	It all depends—
FANNY:	Depends on what?
VAI:	It depends on what *he* really wants.
FANNY:	(*Looking at her drawing*) Just what do you think you're drawing?
VAI:	You don't like it?
FANNY:	He doesn't look like he's sleeping. He looks like he's dead.

(*Exit FANNY and VAIMANU.*)

SCENE 3

(*LOUIS and BELLE enter.*)

BELLE:	I guess you know. She's having a fit.
LOUIS:	About Vai?
BELLE:	And Lloyd.
LOUIS:	She does like to organize our lives.
BELLE:	(*Angry*) You mean control?
LOUIS:	I was trying to be kind.
BELLE:	Are you suggesting I'm unkind?
LOUIS:	No!
BELLE:	She's so desperate . . .
LOUIS:	For what, I wonder?
BELLE:	Isn't that obvious?

(*They come upon LLOYD.*)

LOUIS: The lad's asleep again.

BELLE: (*Feeling his forehead*) He doesn't feel quite right. He feels cold and clammy.

LOUIS: Is he ill?

BELLE: (*Checks his pulse*) And his pulse is so faint. (*Alarmed*) Something is very wrong!

LOUIS: We should get him up to the house.

BELLE: I'll get some help.

SCENE 4

(*LOUIS alone in his Study.*)

LOUIS: My dear Colvin, how I miss your steady friendship. How I miss my friends so far away. These past days I have sorely wished I'd been born strong enough to live out my days in my own homeland among the hills and lochs and heather. You find us in a fine state here! Lloyd has some mysterious tropical malaise and has been in a coma-like state for days. We fear for his life. And between Fanny's bad behavior and Belle's simmering resentment, I wish I could run away. What I wouldn't give to meet you under a street lamp and amble into a pub for a pint or four. And now I see that this is becoming a treatise in self-indulgent pity. Even worse, a sorry confessional. I'll just stop this whining. I'll just rip this apart . . .

(*LOUIS rips up the letter.*)

LOUIS: And go for a walk.

SCENE 5

(*LOUIS begins to walk out. FANNY intercepts him.*)

FANNY: Where are you going?

LOUIS: I'm going for a walk.

FANNY: I don't think you should go walking in the bush by yourself.

LOUIS: Oh, the lady cares.

FANNY: I've always looked after you.

LOUIS: And tell me, Fanny, has it been a pleasure or a duty?

FANNY: I'm your wife.

LOUIS: That's not what I'm asking you.

FANNY: What are you asking me?

LOUIS: Maybe I've never been your pleasure.

FANNY: Are you accusing me?

LOUIS: And all along I've been the livelihood.

FANNY: What?

LOUIS: You know, the stepping stone—so you could have all of this, be the wife of a celebrated author, elevate yourself into a higher social class.

FANNY: Don't be ridiculous. When I married you, you were sick, penniless, and no one had ever heard of you!

LOUIS: Perhaps you saw me as a worthwhile investment.

FANNY: And you, of all people, should know I've never given a fig for social class. Or are you going to tell me again that I have the soul of a peasant?

LOUIS: What is really happening with you, Fanny?

FANNY: I don't know.

LOUIS: You don't know.

FANNY: Everything has become so . . . everything that's familiar to me has become so strange—you, Belle, even Lloyd—as if our little world is now a strange wilderness. I know you feel it too.

LOUIS: Maybe I—no, I just don't see what you mean.

FANNY: No, maybe you can't see. Not yet.

(*LOUIS exits and FANNY watches him.*)

SCENE 6

(*LOUIS walks up to the Āoa Tree. VAI sits under the tree. LLOYD kneels behind her, brushing her hair and kissing her neck and shoulders adoringly. LOUIS is awestruck.*)

LOUIS: What is this? Lloyd, I thought you were sleeping in the house. You're awake!

(*Enter MANU.*)

MANU: He can't hear you.

LOUIS: How did he get here?

VAI: (*To LLOYD*) Desire brought you here.

LOUIS: I don't understand.

(*VAI holds her arm out. LLOYD puts down the comb and massages her hand and fingers.*)

VAI: (*To LLOYD*) Your desire enters me like a stray song from the air. It enters me and tries to possess me. I will not be overcome.

(*LOUIS tries to cross the stream, but he is thrown back by an invisible force.*)

VAI: (*To LLOYD*) You are lost.

(*VAI extends her other arm. LLOYD rushes to massage her other hand.*)

LOUIS: What am I seeing?

(*VAI picks up a coconut cup.*)

VAI: Water!

(*LLOYD takes the cup and scoops up water for her.*)

LOUIS: Lloyd!

(*LOUIS tries again to cross the stream, and again he is thrown back. VAI drinks the water, and LLOYD continues to fawn over her.*)

MANU: It's no use, Tusitala.

LOUIS: Can we stop this?

MANU: She's too powerful.

LOUIS: She's what?

MANU: And she's had way more practice.

LOUIS: This can't be happening. Vai, lass, listen to me.

MANU: (*He pulls TUSITALA away*) Come away.

LOUIS: Lloyd, son!

MANU: He's lost.

LOUIS: But he's—

MANU: My sister is lost.

LOUIS: Why is she—

MANU: She doesn't know she does this. It's the aitu.

LOUIS: What?!

MANU: The aitu possesses her. And she doesn't know!

LOUIS: Can't we reason with her? Can't we talk to her when she's not—

MANU: NO! You can't talk to her.

LOUIS: Why not?!

MANU:	I planned to once, a long time ago but . . .
LOUIS:	But?
MANU:	But the aitu came to me in a dream. It was so real. She threatened to . . .
LOUIS:	Kill her?
MANU:	There are things—things much worse than death.
LOUIS:	There must be something—
MANU:	I have to protect her!
LOUIS:	We have to do something.
MANU:	I told you. I've tried.
LOUIS:	You've seen this before?
MANU:	Too many times.
LOUIS:	How does it end?

(*Pause.*)

MANU:	The man fades away.
LOUIS:	Dies?
MANU:	'Ioe (*Yes*).
LOUIS:	He's going to die?
MANU:	'Ioe.
LOUIS:	We can't let this happen.
MANU:	Where they are—we can't touch them. She keeps us outside.
LOUIS:	But where are they?
MANU:	I'm not sure. We can only watch. We can't get in there.
LOUIS:	There must be something.
MANU:	'O le 'i'o i mata o le tama o le teine.
LOUIS:	What?
MANU:	The sister is the pupil of the brother's eye. She's the first thing to protect.

LOUIS:	I don't think it's your fault.
MANU:	(*Defeated*) If I had been older, I could have kept her safe.
LOUIS:	Perhaps we can find a way.
MANU:	What way is that?
LOUIS:	Isn't that what she keeps trying to tell us? That there's always another side, another way to look at something?

SCENE 7

(*FANNY and BELLE are drawing each other.*)

BELLE:	Did you know the Greeks thought women were not quite human? That only men were fully human?
FANNY:	No, I didn't know that.
BELLE:	So, I guess it didn't start with the Bible.
FANNY:	What's that?
BELLE:	You know, being just a rib.
FANNY:	I have no idea what you're talking about.
BELLE:	You're not even listening to me.
FANNY:	I have a lot on my mind.
BELLE:	I'm sure you do.
FANNY:	And what is that supposed to mean?
BELLE:	Nothing.
FANNY:	Have you been saying things to Louis about me?
BELLE:	No. What kind of things?
FANNY:	And where is that girl? Have you seen her?
BELLE:	She has a name.
FANNY:	She needs to be watched.

BELLE:	I don't know why you're so beastly to her.
FANNY:	She wants to take him away.
BELLE:	I don't think—
FANNY:	But I won't let her.
BELLE:	Mother—
FANNY:	He belongs here with me, with us.
BELLE:	Everything is about Lloyd.
FANNY:	You've always been so jealous of your brother.
BELLE:	You've never understood me.
FANNY:	And have you ever understood me? Maybe you're jealous of me too.
BELLE:	What?
FANNY:	Manu *is* very handsome.
BELLE:	And very young.
FANNY:	He seems to have a preference.
BELLE:	And you're very married.
FANNY:	(*Laughs*) That never stopped you. Don't think I don't know all the things you were up to in Honolulu, *and* Sydney.
BELLE:	You know nothing about me!
FANNY:	(*Goes to look at BELLE's drawing*) You're drawing me again in that ugly way you always do.

(*BELLE snatches up her drawing and exits.*)

FANNY:	It's not fair for her to judge me, for any of them to judge me. All these years, I've done everything for them, and they don't even think about it. I'm the one who's held everything together. I'm the one who's waited on everyone, protected everyone, nursed everyone, dealt with every big or petty problem. None of them see how they've used me up and drained all the life out of me—cornered me into the dull and mechanical half-life of a drudge. So, can

you blame me for responding to this candle? Can
you blame me for responding to this young man
who has brought some light back into my meaning-
less life? This boy who makes me remember what
it's like to be alive, to want to live, to want to turn
and shed my skin, to want to feel my wings slowly
spread apart and begin their steady beat as I rise,
floating above and away from this dismal prison.

SCENE 8

(*BELLE is pacing. MANU enters.*)

MANU: What's wrong, Teuila?

BELLE: My mother is so insulting.

MANU: She's frightened.

BELLE: I wish she'd just fly away on her broomstick.

MANU: She's scared of losing something.

BELLE: I don't see why she has to take it out on me.

MANU: Because you always forgive her.

BELLE: One day, I might not.

MANU: The space between you is tangled.

BELLE: I'll say.

MANU: You often want the same thing.

BELLE: Or the same person?

MANU: (*Smiling*) Or the same person.

(*Pause.*)

BELLE: Can you believe how beautiful it is here? I wonder
how we talk ourselves into being unhappy when
the world is so lovely.

MANU:	This world is beautiful. But when we leave, I'll be wishing you could have come with us.
BELLE:	And what about my mother?
MANU:	What about her?
BELLE:	Are you the something my mother thinks she might be losing?
MANU:	I couldn't tell you.
BELLE:	And how will it all end?
MANU:	How do you think?
BELLE:	You're not really visiting from California, are you?

(*FANNY calls MANU from offstage.*)

BELLE:	Right on cue. Tōfā soifua (*Goodbye*).

(*BELLE exits. FANNY enters.*)

FANNY:	There you are.
MANU:	Yes, here I am.
FANNY:	That Belle is so awful to me.
MANU:	I'm sure she doesn't mean to be.
FANNY:	And Louis, he practically accused me of marrying him for his money.
MANU:	Maybe he thinks you pay too much attention to me.
FANNY:	He's not jealous, if that's what you mean.
MANU:	No?
FANNY:	No, he's irritated. I'm merely an irritant.
MANU:	Do you care how he feels?
FANNY:	I scarcely know how *I* feel anymore.
MANU:	We're all a little lost.
FANNY:	It's like we're all under a spell.
MANU:	Part of you sees what others don't.
FANNY:	(*Laughs*) And part of me is blind. You're the only one here who understands.

MANU:	Yes, I do, but remember, I will have to go away.
FANNY:	Maybe I could go with you. Maybe we could go away together.
MANU:	You know that's not possible.
FANNY:	I know. I just don't want your beautiful light taken away from me.
MANU:	There will be another light, Aolele, much brighter.
FANNY:	Are you seeing the future?
MANU:	It's a feeling I have.
FANNY:	Listen, Manu, I have a feeling too.
MANU:	What is it?
FANNY:	I have a feeling something terrible is about to happen.
MANU:	What?
FANNY:	I'm not sure. I just feel like the whole world could fall apart.

SCENE 9

(*BELLE is watching LLOYD sleep. VAI wanders in, looking before she enters.*)

VAI:	I like the way he looks when he's asleep.
BELLE:	I don't understand what's happening to him.
VAI:	He looks so innocent.
BELLE:	The doctor doesn't know either.
VAI:	But maybe he's not.
BELLE:	What do you mean?
VAI:	What do any of us mean?
BELLE:	You and your brother talk in riddles.

VAI:	You can trust my brother.
BELLE:	I'm not so sure about that.
VAI:	Do you trust *your* brother?
BELLE:	Why shouldn't I?
VAI:	Because he's never seen you as a person. He only sees you as a sister.
BELLE:	But I am his sister.
VAI:	It's dangerous when they don't see you as a person.
BELLE:	Dangerous?
VAI:	You aren't quite real.
BELLE:	I admit, he is a little self-involved, but—
VAI:	If you're not quite real, you become an object. Objects don't have real lives.
BELLE:	You mean, like the Greeks?
VAI:	I've been trying to tell you—these things we've talked about are not just in books.
BELLE:	But he's my only brother.
VAI:	What did he do when your husband betrayed you?
BELLE:	We never discussed it.
VAI:	He saw you as a used-up hag, remember?
BELLE:	I don't think he really meant to say that. It just slipped out.
VAI:	Just slipped out? Where do you think it slipped out from?
BELLE:	I don't know.
VAI:	Yes, you do.
BELLE:	He's my brother.
VAI:	Brother, father, cousin. Why do you keep defending them?
BELLE:	I'm not.

VAI:	You are. You have to see it going on around you, otherwise it's just talk.
BELLE:	See what?
VAI:	See that you already half believe what he thinks about you, what they think about you.
BELLE:	(*Getting angry*) You mean that I'm a lost cause, a desperate spinster of loose morals that nobody will ever really want, that they have to take care of forever?
VAI:	If you refuse to see, another part of you sees.
BELLE:	Another part of me?
VAI:	It can become mean. That's why you have to stop it.
BELLE:	(*Frustrated*) Another riddle.
VAI:	I'm trying to tell you, trying to warn you. If you believe what they say, you'll lose yourself!
BELLE:	Why are you harping on me like this?
VAI:	Because you're lost!
BELLE:	(*Angry*) Why can't you stop badgering me?!

(*Short pause.*)

VAI:	(*Covering her eyes, exiting*) I don't know. I don't know. I'm sorry. I'm sorry. Sometimes things just take over.

SCENE 10

(*Distraught, VAI walks to the Āoa Tree to find NANNY sitting there.*)

VAI:	What are you doing here?

NANNY:	I can't say. What a fine tree! What sort is it?
VAI:	It's an āoa tree. Don't change the subject. How did you get here?
NANNY:	I found myself here.
VAI:	I thought you were only in his dreams.
NANNY:	This isn't his dream?
VAI:	Why do you say that?
NANNY:	Perhaps I'm getting mixed up.
VAI:	What do you want here?
NANNY:	Where is here?
VAI:	You really don't know?
NANNY:	As you said, I'm used to being in his dreams.
VAI:	You're younger than I imagined.
NANNY:	Because I was young when I first came to him.
VAI:	And full of those stories.
NANNY:	*Life* is stories. We are made from stories. Every moment is part of a story. We live in a forest of stories.
VAI:	But the ones you tell . . .
NANNY:	I tell him what he loves to hear.
VAI:	You've created an appetite.
NANNY:	And what's the harm in it? The lad nearly died a dozen times. His hunger kept him coming back.
VAI:	For the stories about those kinds of women.
NANNY:	Aye, lass, but those are the stories that gave him life. (*Pause*) And what of you?
VAI:	Me?
NANNY:	What business do you have here?
VAI:	I'm just visiting.
NANNY:	A clever answer from a clever girl.

VAI:	You're a clever girl too.
NANNY:	Yes, and I recognize a kindred spirit.
VAI:	You think I'm a kindred spirit?
NANNY:	Oh, yes. And maybe *you* have a story.
VAI:	Not important.
NANNY:	And from the look of you, lass, it's a very sad one.
VAI:	I don't know what you're talking about.
NANNY:	Sometimes stories come together. Maybe that's why I'm here?
VAI:	Maybe you don't belong here.
NANNY:	We'll see about that, lassie. Now if you'll excuse me, I think I hear him calling.

SCENE 11

(*NANNY walks back to the Study. LOUIS sits, waiting for her.*)

LOUIS:	Nanny, where have you been?
NANNY:	Are you asleep, now?
LOUIS:	I think so.
NANNY:	Have you said your prayers like a good lad?
LOUIS:	Yes, Nanny.
NANNY:	And are you ready?
LOUIS:	Yes, Nanny. Yes!
NANNY:	Many years ago, in ancient Japan—

(*NANNY spreads out a tatami mat for a stage. VAI has followed her and is watching from the shadows.*)

LOUIS:	Japan?
NANNY:	Yes, in faraway Japan, there lived a maid.

(FANNY enters, dressed in a kimono and carrying a tray.)

NANNY: Her name was Hime, and she was the good wife of Nobunaga, a great warrior.

(MANU enters with a swagger, dressed like a samurai with a dagger and a sword in his sash. He kneels down on the mat.)

NANNY: Hime revered her husband and served his every wish.

(HIME puts the tray down in front of him and bows. There are two cups and a sake bottle. She pours him a drink, bows, and leaves.)

NANNY: They had been together for many years, and year in and year out, she obediently tended to his desires.

(HIME returns with sushi on a tray, bowing and serving him, and then leaves.)

NANNY: But Nobunaga grew tired and restless and one day turned his eyes another way.

(Enter BELLE dressed in a kimono with a fan. She walks by flirtatiously.)

NANNY: And a great desire arose in him for a young and pretty wife.

(HIME enters with another small tray of food. She bows and stands.)

HIME: Is there anything else you wish for, my husband?

NANNY: And he made a wicked plan to get rid of Hime by poisoning her.

NOBUNAGA: Fetch me some fish, cooked the way I like it, and some rice with a sprinkling of sea salt. Then I wish that you, dearest wife, should sit and eat with me.

(*HIME bows and leaves. NOBUNAGA turns over a second cup. He pours himself some sake, and then pours a second cup. He reaches inside his robe for a vial of powder that he sprinkles in the second cup. HIME returns with the fish and rice and kneels, sitting across from him.*)

NOBUNAGA: And now, my beloved, you must share a drink of sake with me.

(*NOBUNAGA hands her the poisoned cup. They stare at each other and then sip from their cups. HIME begins to cough. She stands. Choking and gagging, she runs offstage.*)

NANNY: Nobunaga hid the circumstances of Hime's death, and after a time, he took a new and younger bride.

(*BELLE enters again with her fan, walking and flirting, but soon comes around to NOBUNAGA. They face each other, bow, and freeze.*)

NANNY: But so great was Hime's anger that she became a wrathful spirit, ready to seek revenge on her murdering husband and his young bride.

(*HIME enters in a black kimono with a white ghost mask, and her hair sticking out in disarray. She creeps around, looking at NOBU and his BRIDE. NOBU and his BRIDE separate, looking in opposite directions. HIME creeps back and forth, frightening them. HIME, NOBUNAGA, and the BRIDE enact NANNY's narrative and freeze in an ending tableau.*)

NANNY: First she tormented them with her frightening appearances. Then one day, she attacked the young bride and strangled her, throwing her corpse down in front of Nobunaga.

HIME: Whore!

NANNY: Nobunaga flew into a mad frenzy. He yanked out his dagger, knelt down, and committed hara-kiri.

LOUIS:	What is that, Nanny?
NANNY:	He slit open his stomach, lad, and his guts poured out of him.
LOUIS:	She was a very bad ghost.
NANNY:	Revenge is a powerful force, my boy. It infects both the living and the dead.

(*NANNY turns to VAI, who has been staring at the tableau.*)

NANNY:	And what say you, lassie? Do you think she was a very bad ghost?
VAI:	He betrayed her! He murdered her! Maybe she had a right . . .
NANNY:	To revenge?
VAI:	(*Stressed, exiting*) Yes, she has a right!
NANNY:	(*To LOUIS*) Do you see, Lou? Somewhere inside, the poor thing knows.

SCENE 12

(*LOUIS is in his Study. BELLE enters.*)

BELLE:	They're all waiting like you wanted.
LOUIS:	How is Lloyd?
BELLE:	He's in the same deep sleep.
LOUIS:	(*Shakes his head*) I'm worried, Belle.
BELLE:	Are you sure this is a good idea?
LOUIS:	I'm sure we can all be civil.
BELLE:	I'm glad *you're* sure.

(*LOUIS and BELLE enter the Playing Area. MANU is reading. VAI is drawing. FANNY is knitting.*)

LOUIS:	Well, here we are.
FANNY:	Just as you ordered.
LOUIS:	Now, I wanted to have one of our little discussions.
FANNY:	About?
LOUIS:	I'm thinking of writing a story, with a demon in it, a female demon. I wanted to get your impressions on things you've read or heard. It's quite a fascinating subject.
FANNY:	Wasn't your Nanny quite an expert on nasty females?
LOUIS:	Yes, but she's not here now.
MANU:	What sort of demon is in your story, Tusitala?
LOUIS:	She isn't quite wholly formed yet, but I think we could call her a vengeful spirit.
BELLE:	Who are her victims?
LOUIS:	Men, mostly, but women too, if they get in her way.
FANNY:	I suppose she was married once.
LOUIS:	I haven't decided.
MANU:	Is she a seductress?
LOUIS:	She does have a seductive nature.
BELLE:	I assume she's a shape-shifter? Vai, you're so quiet.
VAI:	I'm thinking.
LOUIS:	Would you care to share your thoughts?
FANNY:	Oh, here we go.
VAI:	I'm thinking about things these female ghosts and demons have in common in stories and literature.
LOUIS:	And?
VAI:	Most of them were once human. Many became demons because of bad things men did to them. And as you say, many of them are seductive.

LOUIS:	And why do you suppose that is?
FANNY:	Because they're stories! They're meant to frighten people! What is more frightening than an evil, seductive woman?
LOUIS:	Vai?
VAI:	Um, I think men create these images of wanton, seductive, dangerous women, because that's what they want. They're fascinated with being overwhelmed and aroused. It both frightens and excites.
LOUIS:	You think men are responsible?
VAI:	Aren't you fascinated by aitu fafine?
BELLE:	And let's face it. Men do most of the writing.
FANNY:	You don't have to join in, Belle.
BELLE:	Why not?
FANNY:	All this men doing this and men doing that, and these sex factors. Can't you see she just loves attention?
LOUIS:	Everyone may say what they want here.
FANNY:	Then I will say what I want. Louis, you are so gullible. You don't actually think a girl like her has any real ideas, do you? All you see is her lovely young skin, her long flowing hair, and those big innocent brown eyes. Well, she's not innocent. She's just out for what she can get.
LOUIS:	(*Raised voice*) Fanny, for God's sake!
VAI:	It's alright. I know she doesn't like me.
FANNY:	(*Standing*) That's right! I don't like you.
VAI:	I'm very sorry, Aolele, if I've said something that offends you.
LOUIS:	You have nothing to be sorry for.
FANNY:	Don't play the innocent with me. You conniving native girls are all the same. You just want to worm your way into our family. Well, I won't let you!

(*VAI stands up to leave.*)

BELLE: I knew this was a bad idea.

LOUIS: No, Vai. Don't leave.

VAI: But she doesn't want me here—

FANNY: Yes! I *don't* want you here. Why don't you just get out!

(*VAI runs out.*)

LOUIS: I can't believe you, Fanny. In all our years of marriage, I have never been so ashamed or disgusted by your behavior.

(*LOUIS exits.*)

BELLE: Bad form, Fanny. I can't bring myself to call you Mother.

(*BELLE exits.*)

FANNY: (*To MANU*) Are you leaving too?

MANU: (*Standing*) She's my sister.

FANNY: And you prefer her company to mine?

MANU: You can see, Aolele, but you were right. Part of you is very blind.

FANNY: I know. I can't help it. When it comes to my family, I'm . . . possessed.

(*MANU exits, leaving FANNY. Distraught, she hides her face with her hands.*)

SCENE 13

(*LOUIS returns to his Study, reclines, and closes his eyes.*)

LOUIS: Where are you, Nanny?

(*NANNY enters.*)

NANNY: You're so tired, Trout.

LOUIS: It's a long story.

NANNY: Trout, I've been thinking. And lately, I'm feeling very bad, very bad indeed.

(*Silence.*)

LOUIS: Nanny?

NANNY: It's about the stories I've always told you . . . about the women. Perhaps they weren't good for you—or them.

LOUIS: Them?

NANNY: Them. Women folk. I don't know, laddie. Seeing that young lass, listening to her. I think I may have been at fault.

LOUIS: (*He takes her hand*) Well, Nanny, maybe we've all been at fault. But listen, your love and stories of ghosts and demons poured life into a very sick child, kept the blood pumping through his veins, made the world of his imagination vivid and real, and I owe you so much. You were my own, my good, aitu fafine.

NANNY: I wish there was something we could do for the lass, Trout.

LOUIS: I thought discussing demons would make some connection but it blew up. I'm running out of ideas.

NANNY: I hate to think of her sitting under that tree, nursing on her pain.

LOUIS: You've seen that?

NANNY: Perhaps you could tell her, the good one, I mean.

LOUIS: No, her brother said, if we told her, if we tried to talk to her, the aitu would do something terrible.

NANNY: (*Inspired*) Trout, I think I must leave you now.

LOUIS:	Nanny, no! Please don't leave me.
NANNY:	Yes! I must leave you now and go to her.
LOUIS:	Why?
NANNY:	Why, to tell her a story, one story.
LOUIS:	What story?
NANNY:	(*Strokes his head*) Perhaps it's a way to tell her, by not telling her, another way of seeing. Perhaps it's the story I was meant to tell all along.
LOUIS:	Please, I don't want you to go.
NANNY:	It's the least we can do, lad. You know that, don't you?
LOUIS:	(*Holds her*) Yes, Nanny, I know.

(*LOUIS watches as NANNY exits. He closes his eyes.*)

SCENE 14

(*FANNY enters the Study.*)

FANNY:	Louis, are you alone?
LOUIS:	(*Not friendly*) Yes.
FANNY:	I thought I heard voices.
LOUIS:	As you can see, there's no one here.
FANNY:	I've come to apologize.
LOUIS:	I'm not the one who deserves your apology.
FANNY:	If you think I should—
LOUIS:	I do, Fanny. Oh yes, I do.
FANNY:	If you think that I'm going to—
LOUIS:	Egads, Fanny, what do you want?
FANNY:	Why do you treat me as if I were a monster?

LOUIS:	Why have you become so cruel?
FANNY:	Have I?
LOUIS:	Yes, you have behaved very badly.
FANNY:	Perhaps I feel trapped.
LOUIS:	Trapped.
FANNY:	I think back to when I painted my own pictures, when I wrote my own stories. Of course I never thought I would be famous, but I felt so . . .
LOUIS:	I saw what you gave up.
FANNY:	It was a small voice.
LOUIS:	And I said nothing.
FANNY:	But it was mine. (*Pause*) Can you feel us drifting away?
LOUIS:	I feel the distance between us growing.
FANNY:	I've tried so hard to keep you with me.
LOUIS:	(*He holds her*) And I'm still here, Fanny.
FANNY:	(*Faraway*) I know she wants to take something away. (*Short pause, looks at him*) And have you noticed how dark it's become?
LOUIS:	The night has fallen.
FANNY:	But even the days have grown dark.
LOUIS:	Yes, now that you mention it.
FANNY:	And none of us are ourselves.
LOUIS:	What do you mean?
FANNY:	I feel as if I'm being unraveled and used, as if I've fallen into . . .
LOUIS:	Into?
FANNY:	Somewhere. I don't know. (*A beat*) Maybe we've been together too long. When we were younger, we could give each other what we needed.
LOUIS:	Are you saying you need something different now?

FANNY:	Don't pretend you don't too.
LOUIS:	I guess everyone needs change.
FANNY:	If I've been cruel, I'm sorry. I never meant to be cruel to you.
LOUIS:	I think you need some rest.
FANNY:	It doesn't mean I don't love you.
LOUIS:	(*Takes her to the bed*) Come, my darling, why don't you lie down and close your eyes.
FANNY:	Because I'm afraid. I'm afraid of what lies in this darkness.

SCENE 15

(*VAI is at the Āoa Tree in the aitu persona and atmosphere.*)

VAI:	Loia! Sau. Fa'avave. (*Come. Hurry.*)

(*LLOYD appears obediently.*)

VAI:	(*Handing him a comb, kneeling*) Comb my hair.

(*LLOYD begins to comb her hair and to kiss her neck.*)

VAI:	I have to leave sooner than I expected.
LLOYD:	Please don't leave me.
VAI:	You want to be with me forever?
LLOYD:	Forever—
VAI:	I have to rush things a little.
LLOYD:	And ever.
VAI:	The final sleep will come sooner.
LLOYD:	Soon enough.
VAI:	Suddenly. You'll have no time to drift off.
LLOYD:	Suddenly, forever.

VAI: I brought you something to help.

(*VAI hands him a rope with a noose. He stares at it and smiles. She smiles back.*)

VAI: You know what to do.

(*LLOYD takes the noose and moves to the tree. He is about to throw the rope over a branch when NANNY, who has been watching from the side, steps up to the edge of the stream.*)

NANNY: Stop!

(*LLOYD freezes.*)

VAI: What are you doing here, Nanny?

NANNY: The aitu knows who I am?

VAI: I know who you are. I watch the things she does.

NANNY: But she doesn't know you.

VAI: What she doesn't know won't hurt her.

NANNY: That's another matter, lassie.

VAI: She's naïve and foolish. And you need to get out of here.

NANNY: I'm afraid I can't leave. Let the boy go.

VAI: You can't make me.

NANNY: (*Steps across the stream*) Maybe I could.

VAI: How did you do that?

NANNY: Why, we're kindred spirits. Cut from the same cloth. We just have different ways about us.

VAI: (*To LLOYD*) Do it! Loia, I said do it.

(*LLOYD stays frozen.*)

NANNY: Too bad, lassie.

VAI: What do you want?

NANNY: I want to tell you a little story.

VAI: I don't want to hear any of your ridiculous stories.

NANNY: I'll strike a bargain with you, Missy She-Devil. You listen to the story, and afterwards, if you still want the lad, he's yours.

VAI: Hah! Is that all?

NANNY: But she will have to be listening too. Can you make her?

VAI: I can push her where I want, if you promise he's mine.

NANNY: So, you agree?

VAI: I agree, but this better not take all night. What is it? One of your bogey circus tales?

NANNY: What did you say?

VAI: I said, is it one of your stupid bogey circus tales?

NANNY: Aha, a circus! Just the setting for a tale—yes, a night at the circus. Let's see, I think we need a ring, a circus ring! And maybe a barker!

SCENE 16

(*Lights to the Playing Area. Carnival music as BELLE and FANNY set out a ring. MANU enters with a top hat and a cane as the BARKER.*)

MANU: Step right up—

(*NANNY pushes VAI over the stream and into the Playing Area.*)

MANU: Step right up to the circus bogey tale of *YOU!*

(*MANU points at VAI.*)

MANU: Yes, step right up to your own thrills and chills, to your own sorrow, to your very own pain, all destined to become your very own impossibly heavy burden. Your very own perpetual nightmare. Now step right up and let us begin at the beginning. Nanny, please, you have the honor.

NANNY: Once upon a time, there was a girl. She was happy and cheerful, kind and thoughtful, and full of goodness.

(*Enter BELLE, in a school uniform. Her hair is in a ponytail. She is drawing in a sketchbook.*)

MANU: And don't forget, she said her prayers.

NANNY: Oh yes, her prayers.

BELLE: *My soul he doth restore again*
And me to walk doth make
Within the paths of righteousness
E'vn for his own name's sake.

NANNY: She was every girl with everything bright to look forward to. But, as she grew older and more lovely, she began to attract the attention of men.

(*BELLE takes out her ponytail and lets her hair hang down, brushing it. LLOYD with sunglasses watches her, walks by, keeps watching her. She does not notice.*)

NANNY: The son of someone powerful and important, a veritable chief in his own way, fell in love with her. And when he declared himself, she had no idea what to do.

(*LLOYD rushes up to her with flowers and a ring. BELLE jumps up, shocked and surprised. She shakes her head and hides her face. Rejected, LLOYD fades away.*)

NANNY: Confused and startled, she told him to go away. And he did go away. And the foolish lad took his own life.

(*BELLE resumes her sketching.*)

NANNY: But that was not the end of it. Oh, no. His friends, his family, decided she was to blame.

(*LOUIS, LLOYD, and MANU have on sinister clown masks to become CLOWN 1, CLOWN 2, and CLOWN 3. They march in front of BELLE and call her names.*)

CLOWN 1:   Bitch.

CLOWN 2:   Slut.

CLOWN 3:   Whore.

(*FANNY, wearing a mask, steps forward.*)

NANNY: Seeking revenge, his family set fire to her home.

(*FANNY strikes a match.*)

NANNY: And her parents died.

(*FANNY blows the match out.*)

NANNY: Then, they remade her into an evil temptress.

(*CLOWN 1 paints BELLE's lips red. He laughs at what he has done.*)

CLOWN 1:   Bitch.

(*CLOWN 2 places a garish feather boa around her neck and pulls down her blouse on one side to reveal her shoulder. He laughs at what he has done.*)

CLOWN 2:   Slut.

(*CLOWN 3 arranges BELLE in a very seductive pose. He points at her and laughs.*)

CLOWN 3:   Whore.

NANNY: And then, they relentlessly pursued her.

(*The CLOWNS snatch BELLE off her feet. They form a triangle and violently push her to one another, with increasing violence and speed.*)

CLOWN 1:   Bitch.

CLOWN 2:   Slut.

CLOWN 3:   Whore.

CLOWN 1:   Bitch.

CLOWN 2:   Slut.

CLOWN 3:   Whore.

CLOWN 1:   Bitch.

CLOWN 2:   Slut.

CLOWN 3:   Whore.

NANNY: And then they, and then they—

(*The CLOWNS push BELLE down in the ring and onto the floor in the dark. They freeze, standing over her in a dim light.*)

NANNY: Over and over again they injected her with their own anger, with their own hate, with their own violent rage, until the life flew out of her, and they left her for dead.

(*The CLOWNS turn away, and FANNY, as a figure under a red cloth, enters. She kneels down beside BELLE, and they both are covered together.*)

NANNY: Oh, maybe her poor body was dead, but something else was born. Born from the rage and violence. Born for protection and revenge. Born into forever.

(*The red cloth swirls around, and FANNY is revealed with a demon mask. She snarls at each of the CLOWNS in turn, who react as if something is choking them. They stagger away in pain. This action is repeated three times, each more chaotic.*)

VAI: (*Yells*) Stop! Stop all of this.

(*FANNY rushes up to VAI, hissing and circling her like prey.*)

VAI: I said stop, because I see you now.

(*FANNY continues her assault.*)

VAI: You are not me. You can't use me like this.

(*VAI pushes FANNY away.*)

VAI: I don't want you. I don't need you. You can just get out!

(*FANNY whirls away and collapses into a heap.*)

VAI: You can all go away now. This story is ended.

SCENE 17

(*The lights dim as NANNY takes VAI back to the Āoa Tree. LLOYD is no longer there.*)

VAI: Is she gone?

NANNY: All gone.

VAI: (*Distressed*) I've been something horrible, haven't I?

NANNY: Not you, lass. Those who did the harm and caused the deep pain created her. It was never your fault.

VAI: She had so much power.

NANNY: Because you couldn't see.

VAI: How could I not see?!

NANNY: Pain builds the wall to protect, but it also hides the dark things. When the pain is bearable—

VAI: In a story, I could see her in the story.

NANNY: In this story, the wall crumbles, and darkness gives way to light.

VAI: And the aitu flies away.

NANNY:	(*Hugs VAI*) And the power returns to you, as a treasure.
VAI:	You are the treasure, Nanny. How can I ever thank you?
NANNY:	I need no thanks. The telling of it was a blessing.

(*Enter MANU. He rushes to hug VAI.*)

MANU:	Vai!
VAI:	It's over.
MANU:	I wish I could have—
VAI:	Be quiet, Manu. You did everything you could. I couldn't ask for a better brother.

(*Enter LOUIS. NANNY fades away. LOUIS does not cross the stream.*)

LOUIS:	I've just had the most extraordinary dream. And when I woke up, Lloyd was awake and chattering away like his old self.
VAI:	What was your dream about?
LOUIS:	I think you know.
VAI:	I know the world is full of surprises.
LOUIS:	What would your teachers say?
VAI:	Something simple, like revenge makes things worse.
LOUIS:	And what do you think would make it better?
VAI:	A change in how we all see each other.
LOUIS:	Something simple and maybe impossible.
VAI:	If we can imagine it, it may *be* possible.
LOUIS:	Are you really going to leave?
MANU:	Yes, we will be leaving.
LOUIS:	Fanny didn't mean those—
VAI:	Tusitala, it's not because of Fanny.
LOUIS:	No?

MANU:	No. It's just—our time here is coming to an end, and we have to go.
LOUIS:	(*Disappointed*) Oh, I don't suppose I could persuade you—
VAI:	But there is one last thing.
LOUIS:	What is that?
VAI:	You'll see.
LOUIS:	What is it?
VAI:	Just go back now, and we'll see you later.

(*LOUIS exits. NANNY steps into the light.*)

NANNY:	You've been so kind to him.
VAI:	I hope he understands.
NANNY:	I think he will, lass. I think he will.

SCENE 18

(*Lights fade to half. NANNY and VAI watch what follows. LOUIS enters the Playing Area, where FANNY is at a table.*)

LOUIS:	Ah, the clouds have parted for the sun. What are you doing, my love?
FANNY:	I'm making something special, our Vailima mayonnaise.
LOUIS:	And how could I be part of this enterprise?
FANNY:	You could cut and squeeze this lemon.

(*LOUIS takes a knife and a lemon and cuts it once. He suddenly drops the knife. His hands go to his head.*)

LOUIS:	Oh my God! The pain.
FANNY:	Louis?
LOUIS:	Do I look strange?

FANNY: Are you alright?

(*LOUIS sits and puts his head between his knees. The lights go out and slowly rise on FANNY's line. She is kneeling beside him.*)

FANNY: Louis, talk to me. Are you alright?

(*FANNY panics.*)

FANNY: (*Yelling*) Lloyd, Belle, help! Something is wrong with Louis.

(*LLOYD and BELLE rush in.*)

BELLE: What happened? Oh no, Louis!

LLOYD: I'll go for the doctor!

FANNY: First let's get him to his bed.

(*FANNY, BELLE, and LLOYD pull LOUIS up, take him to the bed in his Study, and lay him down. Lights to near dark, and rise on NANNY and VAI.*)

NANNY: It was very quick, wasn't it?

VAI: Yes, very.

NANNY: And my lad didn't suffer, did he?

VAI: (*Touching her*) No, no it was very quick, and there was no suffering.

NANNY: Am I finished here?

VAI: There is only the final story, and it is very short.

NANNY: (*Kissing VAI on the forehead*) I pray he hears you, lass.

(*NANNY fades away. LLOYD, FANNY, and BELLE arrange LOUIS's body. As they speak, they cover him with a dark sheet.*)

LLOYD: He sleeps so still in his dark cocoon.

BELLE: Still as a barren tree.

LLOYD: Still as a frozen lake.

FANNY: Still as a standing stone.

BELLE: Still as a lonely crow.

LLOYD: Still as the silent moon.

FANNY: 'Ia manuia lau malaga (*May your journey be blessed*), my love.

(*FANNY kisses LOUIS's forehead and covers his face. FANNY, BELLE, and LLOYD step back and turn away, as they all freeze in a tableau of grief.*)

SCENE 19

(*VAI and MANU in the Playing Area.*)

VAI: This is the story of Vailima, water in the hand.

MANU: There was once a man and a woman who were trying to cross the island of Upolu. The journey was very difficult.

VAI: They suffered many trials and many storms, and they went without food and water for many days.

MANU: Finally, the man was unable to go on, and he lay dying of hunger and thirst.

VAI: So, the woman, weak as she was, went in search of water. She searched and searched, and found a spring, a spring so clear and cool, a spring whose water rose up from the deepest places.

(*VAIMANU kneels at the stream.*)

VAI: She scooped up the water and carefully held it in her hands.

(*VAIMANU scoops up water in her joined, cupped hands. She is joined by MANU, and they walk in ceremony to TUSITALA. MANU peels back the sheet and raises TUSITALA's head. VAI offers him the water in her hands.*)

VAI:	And he drank of the life-giving water.
MANU:	And they entered the new world.
VAI:	Le aso ma le taeao (*The morning of the day*).

(*LOUIS gets up, and the three of them walk toward the Āoa Tree. MANU and VAI cross over the stream and turn to LOUIS, who stops and looks back.*)

LOUIS:	It's so hard to let go.
MANU:	Yes, we know.
LOUIS:	And all of this, since I . . .
MANU:	The vā has many dimensions.
VAI:	Everyone leaves in a different way. This was your way.
LOUIS:	It seems a shame, that only now I see how much they loved me.
VAI:	Yes, many people love you.
LOUIS:	She brought me back so many times.
VAI:	You wanted to go back.
LOUIS:	And this time . . .

(*LOUIS turns away, and looks at MANU and VAI.*)

MANU:	We are here for you.
VAI:	Our teachers sent us.
MANU:	To be here for you.
VAI:	Are you ready?
LOUIS:	Will it be difficult?
MANU:	Oh, no, Tusitala, it's very easy.
VAI:	As easy as crossing a stream.

(*MANU and VAI each extend a hand to him. LOUIS takes their hands and steps across the stream. The lights fade to black.*)

CURTAIN

FANNY AND BELLE

**The Story of Mrs. Robert Louis Stevenson
and her daughter, Belle Osbourne**

FOREWORD

Fanny and Belle was first presented by Kumu Kahua Theatre on March 11, 2004. The production was directed by John H. Y. Wat with the following cast:

Fanny	Jennifer Robideau
Belle	Laura Bach
Player 1	Laurie Tanoura
Player 2	Victoria Gail-White
Player 3	Michelle Crush
Player 4	Terri Seeborg
Player 5	James Rudy
Player 6	Wil T. Kahele
Player 7	John R. Watson
Player 8	Eric Schonleber

THE CAST OF CHARACTERS

Fanny

Belle

Eight Players: Four Women and Four Men for Multiple Roles

Player 1: Woman 4, Mother, Maud, Flirting Woman 1, Undermining Woman 1, Female Artist 3, Aunt Maggie

Player 2: Woman 1, Jo, Flirting Woman 2, Undermining Woman 2, Female Artist, Market Woman, Via

Player 3: Woman 2, Flirting Woman 3, Undermining Woman 3, Female Model, Lagi

Player 4: Woman 3, Flirting Woman 4, Female Artist, Nellie, Clara

Player 5: Father, Robert Louis Stevenson

Player 6: Man 1, Shadowman, Prospector 2, M. Fleury, Male Artist 1, O'Meara, Adulfo, Henley, Dr. Richards, Dr. Mueller

Player 7: George, Man 2, Stationmaster, Prospector 1, Male Model, Doctor, Male Artist 2, Joe Strong, Ned

Player 8: Sam, Male Artist 3, Lloyd

THE SET

The *Great Hall* at Vailima, a large redwood-paneled room about forty by sixty feet. A grand staircase from the upper floor flanked by two bronze Buddhas is the *Hall*'s most prominent fixture. The *Hall* can be used in any imaginative way, with moveable, flexible props to create the different scenes. The *Vailima Space* is a memory place used by Belle and Fanny. Here, time is suspended, overlapping with what came before and what comes after. It could be a particular place on the set, or special lighting, or simply an acting mode.

THE TIME

1860 to 1915.

THE PLACE

Vailima, Sāmoa, and, by way of memory, Indiana, Panama, Reese River, Oakland, Paris, Grez, Monterey, Europe, Honolulu, Sydney, San Francisco.

Act I

(BELLE is in the Vailima Space.)

BELLE: Vailima, the sound of it is a murmur, a sweet murmur that stirs memory. It is hard to believe that eighteen years have passed since I last looked from these windows across the wide lawn, over the hillside forest to the harbor and the sea. The first day I ever came to Vailima and saw the sharpness of the horizon from this vantage, I thought about how people used to believe ships could sail too far and fall off the edge of the world. Maybe that's what we were all doing here, sailing, reaching out for an edge of something. Eighteen years since my mother and I left, and now I bring her back, to lie forever next to Louis. I never realized how much I was like my mother until after she died. I'd catch my own eyes in the mirror and see her staring back. I'd say something and hear the sound of her voice. It is so still tonight. I think I can hear the rustle of the sheets in the next room as my husband moves in his sleep. I remember nights like this—quiet and clear. We would lie out on the lawn and stare at the night sky so full of southern stars it left a brightness in your mind long after you had gone inside and fallen asleep. Tomorrow we will leave my mother on that beautiful hilltop called Vaea, which couldn't be more unlike the place in which her life began in 1840.

WOMAN 1:	See Fanny.
WOMAN 2:	See Fanny Van de Grift.
WOMAN 3:	See Fanny seed the gardens.
WOMAN 1:	Plant the trees.
WOMAN 2:	Grow the flowers.
WOMAN 3:	Bring in the sheep.
WOMAN 1:	Milk the cows.
WOMAN 2:	Tend the poultry.
WOMAN 3:	Pick the berries.
WOMAN 1:	Bake the pies.
WOMAN 2:	Keep accounts.
WOMAN 3:	And sew the dresses with lace and ruffles and ribbons.
WOMAN 1:	And see Fanny Van de Grift on horseback.
WOMEN 2 & 3:	Ride and ride and ride.
WOMAN 1:	Over Indiana fields.
WOMEN 2 & 3:	Chasing the wind.
MOTHER:	Fanny!
FANNY:	I'm busy, what do you want?
MOTHER:	Fanny, would you come here for a moment?
FANNY:	Father's counting on me to—
MOTHER:	Fanny!
FANNY:	(*Wearily*) Yes, mother. I hope this doesn't take too much time.
MOTHER:	Listen to the girl!
FANNY:	I have things to do!
MOTHER:	(*Turning her around*) Well, you're not blond or fair, and you don't have straight hair. You're not tall and willowy, and you

don't have pretty blue eyes. What shall
we do with you? First, this hair, dark,
wild, frizzy—

(*MOTHER slaps a bonnet on FANNY.*)

MOTHER: There now. That's it, cover it up. And this amber-
colored skin. I swear, your father must have some
queer blood in his family. No one in *my* family has
skin this dark, or eyes like midnight. If we scrub
you with this, it might lighten you up.

(*MOTHER starts to scrub FANNY harshly. The other WOMEN
join in.*)

WOMAN 1:   Here, Mrs. Van de Grift, try this—

WOMAN 2:   No, try this, my grandmother swears by this.

WOMAN 1:   Land sakes, she's dark, let's try this.

FANNY: (*Yelling*) Stop! Just stop it! Leave me alone, would
you?

(*The WOMEN and MOTHER back off, staring at her.*)

FANNY: (*Throws away bonnet and stamps her foot*) Look,
I don't care if my hair is frizzy. (*Wiping off her
skin*) And I don't care if my skin turns amber in
the sun. And I don't care if I have eyes like black-
berries. This is what I look like!

(*FANNY freezes in a pose with the other WOMEN. BELLE is in
the Vailima Space.*)

BELLE: Yes, my mother had a look so unlike anyone else—
they'd wonder if she had gypsy blood, or Spanish
blood, or Indian blood, or who knows what.

(*FANNY moves to the Vailima Space.*)

BELLE: And she used to say—

FANNY: Now remember what I tell you, Belle. Always strike a personal note in your dress and the way you do your hair. Don't try to look like other people. If you succeed in that, you are nowhere, only a plain pudgy dark woman. Keep to the slightly oriental, the rather unusual, and you are a houri.

FATHER: That's my Fanny.

MOTHER: Jacob, you spoil those girls. You don't know how people talk.

WOMAN 1: Wild girls.

WOMAN 2: Heads in the clouds.

WOMAN 1: Unmanageable!

WOMAN 2: Bold, saucy manners.

WOMAN 1: Talkers!

WOMAN 2: Tomboys, every one of 'em.

MAN 1:   Prettiest damn women in Indiana.

FATHER: Let 'em talk. Our Fanny has instinct, feeling, insight, character!

MOTHER: Girls don't need character.

FATHER: Fanny will have it anyway.

(*FANNY and her sister JO eat apples and play on stilts.*)

JO: George Marshall is coming to visit.

FANNY: So?

JO: I want to marry him.

FANNY: You want to get married?

JO: To George Marshall.

FANNY: You're not old enough, Jo.

JO: You are. Daddy says you'll get married first.

FANNY: Who wants to get married?

JO: (*Getting off her stilts*) Me, I do. Quick, get down, here he comes. Good afternoon, George Marshall.

GEORGE: Good afternoon, Miss Jo.

FANNY: (*Munching her apple, still on stilts*) Hey, George.

GEORGE: (*Happily as he walks on*) Hey, Fanny!

(*SAM approaches. FANNY sees him.*)

FANNY: Who's that?

JO: Sam, George's friend. Good afternoon, Sam Osbourne.

SAM: Good afternoon, Miss Jo.

FANNY: (*Tossing him a half-eaten apple*) Hello, I'm Fanny.

SAM: (*Laughs, takes a bite of the apple*) Hello to you, Miss Fanny.

(*SAM walks off eating the apple. FANNY watches and gets off stilts.*)

FANNY: You can have George Marshall, Jo. I'm marrying Sam Osbourne.

BELLE: They were married in 1857. She was sixteen. He was eighteen.

(*SAM walks to BELLE.*)

SAM: You were a honeymoon child, Belle. That's why you're so joyful.

(*SAM fades back. Both BELLE and FANNY speak directly to audience.*)

BELLE: When I'm four, my father buys a silver mine way out in the wild west.

(*FANNY packs a suitcase.*)

FANNY: Sam loves adventure.

BELLE: We're going to be with him!

FANNY: Well, we've spent our savings, my dowry.

BELLE: My father isn't afraid of anything.

FANNY: Sold our house.

BELLE: And he is so *handsome*.

FANNY: Sam says some mines yield a hundred thousand a day.

BELLE: And charming.

FANNY: And prospectors wear diamond buttons.

BELLE: My father knows everything.

FANNY: Have houses like marble sculptures.

BELLE: He tells me I'm pretty.

FANNY: And their women take baths in champagne.

BELLE: (*Aside, but FANNY hears*) My father likes women.

FANNY: Stop dawdling, Belle! It's almost time.

(*FANNY snaps the suitcase shut. All move in to say goodbye.*)

MOTHER: Fanny, it's not right.

FANNY: You know I'd follow him anywhere, Mother.

MOTHER: A young woman with a child, traveling alone.

FANNY: We'll be all right.

FATHER: Watch out for the riffraff, dear. The west is promising, but dangerous.

FANNY: I'll miss you so much, Papa.

(*FATHER gives FANNY a derringer.*)

FATHER: You're going to run into the best and the worst. I know you're courageous, Fanny, but be careful too.

FANNY: The train moves out and down the track, and for the first time in my life I have a—what is it I have? Is it a feeling? A sensation? A knowing? (*Pause*) It's something deeper, it's moving away. I am leaving. I am leaving a whole life behind me.

(*BELLE moves to the Vailima Space.*)

BELLE: In this house at Vailima, I think I hear the rustling of my mother's holokū (*Hawaiian gown*). I feel her passing, just passing outside my door.

FANNY: But soon the town fades, moving back, and that part of me starts its slow and swaying dance into memory.

BELLE: Only a year, and already things about her I can't remember.

FANNY: And now before me, everything begins to open up, everything becomes clear, and the track stretches out and takes me flying along, flying on this train, with my little Belle, into the future.

BELLE: I don't want it all to slip away. Mama, I'm scared.

(*FANNY moves over to BELLE.*)

FANNY: Now come on darling, don't be frightened. We'll have a great adventure, you and I. One we'll never forget.

BELLE: Chicago, the busiest place I ever saw.

(*WOMEN and MEN make a crowd and bustle by.*)

FANNY: New York, the crowds! If we're not careful, we'll miss the ship for Panama.

(*WOMEN and MEN bustle another way.*)

BELLE: On the ship, everyone watches us.

(*WOMEN form a gossip group.*)

WOMAN 1:   How could she? It's a scandal to travel alone.

WOMAN 2:   She's certainly asking for it, whatever she gets.

WOMAN 1:   And the little girl! It's just plain foolhardy.

WOMAN 2:   Have you noticed how she plays up to all the men?

(*MEN are in a group.*)

MAN 1:   Now there's a brave little woman.

MAN 2:   Plenty of pluck.

MAN 1:   None of that female nonsense.

MAN 2:   And not bad looking either.

BELLE: Aspinwall, Panama, swirls with heat and malaria, with desperation and death. Days and days of waiting for a train to take us across the isthmus, waiting for a train that we think might never come.

FANNY: Belle, darling, come with me now. Hello? Hello!?

(*STATIONMASTER comes out. A SHADOWMAN appears and watches.*)

STATIONMASTER: Afternoon, ma'am.

FANNY: You're the stationmaster?

STATIONMASTER: Yes, ma'am.

FANNY: Any word about the train?

STATIONMASTER: Still some trouble, ma'am.

FANNY: (*Nervous, twists at her bracelet*) Well, I was wondering about the train, when it comes, I mean, the fare—

STATIONMASTER: Yes?

FANNY: (*Now fingering her locket*) Well, you see, it's cost so much waiting. It's already been a week. I was just wondering—

STATIONMASTER: Wondering?

FANNY: Never mind, come on Belle.

(*FANNY and BELLE move away. The SHADOWMAN follows. FANNY sets her bag down on a bench and begins to re-pin her hair.*)

SHADOWMAN: Excuse me, ma'am.

FANNY: Yes?

SHADOWMAN: Well, ma'am, it's just that, I've seen people in your predicament before.

FANNY: Oh?

SHADOWMAN: Yes, so you see, I thought I could advise you, give you some advice.

FANNY:	That's very kind of you.
SHADOWMAN:	See now, your jewelry won't interest anybody.
FANNY:	No? I thought surely—
SHADOWMAN:	No, ma'am, I'm afraid not. It's worthless here.
FANNY:	(*Crestfallen*) Oh, dear. I see.
SHADOWMAN:	Now there are other things people are interested in buying.
FANNY:	What is that?
SHADOWMAN:	If it's of quality, that is.
FANNY:	Quality?
SHADOWMAN:	You're real quality, ma'am.
FANNY:	(*Getting it, not quite believing it*) What?
SHADOWMAN:	Don't play coy, it doesn't suit a woman like you.
FANNY:	You think I'm that way, do you?
SHADOWMAN:	(*Steps boldly toward her*) I've seen the way you are. And I like it well enough.

(*BELLE has become frightened and hides behind the bench.*)

FANNY:	I think you better leave me alone.
SHADOWMAN:	I think you better be smart and use your best asset, ma'am.

(*The SHADOWMAN closes in on FANNY. He grabs her and tries to make advances. BELLE pulls out her mother's revolver, points it at the SHADOWMAN, and cocks the trigger. She is nervous, but determined.*)

BELLE:	You leave my mother alone!
SHADOWMAN:	(*Jumps away, terrified*) Look, little girl, now don't do—

BELLE: Shut up!

SHADOWMAN: Okay, okay. (*To FANNY*) I was just fool-
                    in,' ma'am, honest—tell her!

(*FANNY takes the gun from BELLE, but keeps it pointed at the
SHADOWMAN.*)

FANNY: Just shut up, you hear? Now get out of here, and
                    never come near us again.

(*SHADOWMAN runs off.*)

FANNY: (*Hugging BELLE*) There, there now, darling, we
                    learned something today, didn't we? (*Kisses her
                    forehead*) We can certainly defend ourselves if we
                    have to.

(*BELLE moves to the Vailima Space.*)

BELLE: Then hundreds of miles later, away from Panama
                    on a ship off the coast of Mexico bound for San
                    Francisco.

BELLE: (*To FANNY*) I don't like it here, Mama, I want to
                    go back.

FANNY: I wish you could see it the way I do, Belle. The
                    deep blue, the endless horizon, the light.

BELLE: It's too big. We'll get lost.

FANNY: If you could only see how far things go on.

BELLE: No, I want to go back!

FANNY: (*Tenderly*) We can't go back, darling, we can only
                    go forward.

BELLE: And on we went into the loneliness of Nevada and
                    the desolate landscape of Reese River, where
                    everything looked bleak, rocky, and sulfurous.
                    After months of traveling, danger, and worry, to
                    come to this, you'd have thought . . . (*she would
                    have sat down and wept*)

(*FANNY flings herself into SAM's arms. SAM whirls her around as BELLE watches.*)

FANNY: Sam, oh Sam, I'm so glad to see you. I missed you so much. Just look at how you've had to live without me.

BELLE: My mother made a home out of anywhere.

(*FANNY rolls up her sleeves.*)

FANNY: Some nice curtains and a little paint, we'll start to cheer things up. You'll see!

BELLE: And she could learn whatever she wanted—

(*PROSPECTOR 1 shows FANNY how to roll a cigarette. He hands her papers with two piles of tobacco.*)

PROSPECTOR 1:   Now, ma'am, you see, you make two piles of tobacco, so when you roll it up it spreads out.

FANNY: (*Rolling up a cigarette*) Oh, I see.

PROSPECTOR 1:   You'll get the hang of it.

FANNY: (*Lighting up her smoke*) I will.

(*PROSPECTOR 2 stands, and FANNY walks over to him, with her cigarette hanging from her mouth and her revolver in her hand.*)

PROSPECTOR 2:   Now you sight down the barrel, ma'am, right straight down the barrel 'cause that's where that bullet comes flying out. You do it enough times, and you'll get a kinda feel for it. Like the gun is part of your hand or something.

FANNY: (*Sighting down the barrel of her gun*) I see.

PROSPECTOR 2:   Now it's one thing to know how to use a gun, but it's another thing to use it. If you don't make up your mind to use a

	gun when you have to out here, well, you might as well roll over and die before you get out of bed.
FANNY:	I see.
PROSPECTOR 2:	Mountain lions, men gone crazy, rattlesnakes—
PROSPECTOR 1:	The rattlesnakes, they always warn you with their rattlin'.
FANNY:	(*Sighting around with revolver*) I see.
PROSPECTOR 2:	They love that afternoon sun too. You watch out now.
FANNY:	I will.

(*FANNY puts her gun near a laundry basket and starts to fold her laundry.*)

BELLE:	My mother made a home while my father chased dreams of silver and gold hidden in the earth. My mother learned, and my father chased—

(*A rattlesnake noise. FLIRTING WOMAN 1 goes to SAM.*)

FANNY:	Belle, don't move.

(*FANNY fires her pistol near BELLE's feet.*)

BELLE:	In Reese River, my father chased—
FANNY:	Be still, Belle.

(*A rattle as FLIRTING WOMAN 2 goes to SAM. FANNY fires the gun.*)

BELLE:	In Virginia City, my father—

(*Another rattle as FLIRTING WOMAN 3 goes to SAM. FANNY fires the gun.*)

FANNY:	Watch out! There's another one.
BELLE:	And when we finally settled in San Francisco, in East Oakland, my father—

(*Many rattles as FLIRTING WOMEN begin to caress SAM.*)

FANNY: They're all over!

(*FANNY fires the gun several times, puts it down, and resumes folding laundry. FLIRTING WOMAN 2 strolls over, and makes a knocking sound.*)

FANNY: See who's here, Belle.

(*BELLE looks at FLIRTING WOMAN 2, and runs to FANNY.*)

BELLE: Mama, it's a woman.

FANNY: Well, did you ask her in, Belle? Where are your— (*FANNY sees who it is, pauses, and stares at the woman*) Just what do you mean by coming here?

FLIRTING WOMAN 2:

              (*Sassy*) Why, I've just decided to make a friendly call on you, that's all.

FANNY: A friendly call?

FLIRTING WOMAN 2:

              (*Taunting*) That's right. I'm a friend of Sam's. I have a right to make a friendly call.

FANNY: Well, here's a friendly welcome.

(*FANNY looks at her, smiles, and slaps her in the face. FLIRTING WOMAN 2 recoils.*)

BELLE: Mama!

FLIRTING WOMAN 2:

              You, you, you're no lady like they all said. You're just a beast!

(*FLIRTING WOMAN 2 runs away.*)

BELLE: My father loved my brothers, Lloyd and little Hervey, but he loved me best. On Sundays, when everyone slept late, he and I would go on glorious walks, and he would talk about everything.

(*SAM takes BELLE's arm, and they walk.*)

SAM: The Bible is only a book, Belle. It's a fine historical record, but it's a book to be read like literature, and today more people than ever know it. See those church steeples? They'll be obsolete when you're grown up.

(*SAM and BELLE reach home, where FANNY is waiting.*)

SAM: (*Hanging up his hat*) Enjoy the moment, Belle. Learn to enjoy the moment. Yesterday's gone and tomorrow hasn't come yet.

(*SAM sits and picks up a book. BELLE sits with her head on his knees.*)

BELLE: Go on Papa, read.

SAM: Now, what were we—

BELLE: (*Pointing to the place*) *Vanity Fair,* right here.

SAM: Oh, right, "So Mr. Osbourne, having a firm conviction in his own mind that he was a woman killer, did not in any way run from his fate. And as Emmy did not say much, he chose to fancy that she was not suspicious of what all his acquaintances were perfectly aware."

FANNY: (*Icily*) I wonder, Captain Osbourne, that you dare read your own story to your daughter.

SAM: (*Raising his voice*) God Almighty, woman! You can't forget *anything.*

FANNY: (*Matching him*) You mean *everything.* No, I can't forget *everything.*

BELLE: My father moved to the city, and my mother threw herself into photography, cooking, and her garden. She rode her horse, shot a rifle, sewed clothes more beautiful than any in a store window. When I was sixteen, I began to go to the

School of Design in San Francisco to study art. My mother thought she would be an artist too, and joined me.

(*FANNY gets ready, grabs her drawing board in a flurry. She wears a silver medal on a chain.*)

FANNY: Come on, Belle, we're going to miss the ferry! Why, Belle, what's wrong?

BELLE: Your drawings, your paintings!

FANNY: You don't like them?

BELLE: You do everything better!

FANNY: Nonsense.

BELLE: You won the class prize, the silver medal.

FANNY: This was just luck, dear. You're the one with real talent, you'll see.

(*Men walk past looking at FANNY. BELLE looks at men looking at FANNY. MAUD approaches.*)

MAUD: (*Faintly jealous*) Why, Fanny Osbourne, how smart you look.

FANNY: Why, thank you, Maud.

MAUD: And is this your little girl?

FANNY: Yes, this is my daughter, Belle.

MAUD: Anyone might think she was your sister.

BELLE: How do you do, ma'am.

MAUD: What lovely big eyes you have, my dear.

BELLE: (*Flattered*) Thank you, ma'am.

MAUD: Oh, but you'll never be as good-looking as your mother.

(*MAUD leaves. BELLE moves to the Vailima Space. FANNY watches.*)

BELLE: Even now, I remember how pretty she was.

FANNY: Now, Belle, snap out of it. You're young and lovely, with everything before you.

BELLE: All my life, I've seen people always comparing.

FANNY: And just look at me! Thirty-five, three children, a husband in name only, drying up like an old stick.

(*SAM struts on another part of the stage with FLIRTING WOMAN 2. BELLE watches.*)

FANNY: Well, my children are beautiful—my steady Lloyd, my darling baby Hervey with the golden curls, and Belle.

BELLE: I loved my father. But—

FANNY: It doesn't have   **BELLE:**   It shouldn't have
         to happen to her.   happened to her.

(*A beat. FANNY looks at SAM and FLIRTING WOMAN 2, and then looks away, thinking.*)

FANNY: (*Excited*) Belle, I have an idea!

BELLE: What? What is it?

(*SAM leaves and FLIRTATIOUS WOMEN become UNDERMINING WOMEN.*)

UNDERMINING WOMAN 1:
         You're not thinking of leaving Sam, are you? At your age, a woman doesn't leave her husband.

FANNY: We could go—

UNDERMINING WOMAN 2:
         Charming as you are.

BELLE: Go where?

UNDERMINING WOMAN 3:
         Your youth is behind you.

UNDERMINING WOMAN 1:
         The clock is ticking.

UNDERMINING WOMAN 2:

    Soon you'll be gray.

FANNY: Belle, we could go to Europe to study art!

BELLE: What?!

UNDERMINING WOMAN 3:

    It's 1875. It's just not proper.

UNDERMINING WOMAN 2:

    A scandal, everyone will condemn you.

(*SAM enters, defiant.*)

SAM: It's a crazy idea.

FANNY: Think of Belle and the training she'll get.

SAM: You just want to get away.

FANNY: Of course I want to get away.

SAM: Then go alone!

FANNY: I will not leave my children.

SAM: I will not have them traipsing all over Europe after their crazy mother.

FANNY: We are going to study art. And you don't even live with us.

SAM: Do you think you're pleasant company? I can't stand it here.

FANNY: You love that other woman.

(*Silence.*)

FANNY: At least you admit we can't go on like this.

SAM: I admit nothing.

FANNY: Give us a year, Sam, just a year. It will be so good for Belle and me. You'll be so proud of her accomplishments.

SAM: The expense.

FANNY: You can send us the same check every month. We'll live very simply.

(*SAM fades, and FANNY turns her attention to BELLE.*)

FANNY: We could, Belle. It would be an adventure for Lloyd and Hervey too.

BELLE: What about Daddy?

UNDERMINING WOMAN 1:

If you turn your back on your obligations—

UNDERMINING WOMAN 2:

You're thirty-five. If you leave Sam at your age—

FANNY: He doesn't even live with us, and—

UNDERMINING WOMAN 3:

You're done for.

FANNY: I'm suffocating, Belle.

(*FANNY looks at her silver medal. BELLE watches from the Vailima Space.*)

BELLE: She struggled with what to take and what to leave behind. But she always kept that silver medal with her.

FANNY: Some dreams you never let go of.

BELLE: When she died, I looked everywhere for it.

FANNY: Others just fade away.

BELLE: Where, Mother? Where did it go?

(*Lights change. MEN and WOMEN stroll, humming a romantic French song.*)

BELLE: She didn't speak a word of French, but there we were, all settled in the Rue de Naples in Paris.

FANNY: If we live very modestly, we'll manage.

(*FANNY and BELLE set up easels as three ARTIST WOMEN join them.*)

BELLE:	We're both enrolled at Julian's L'Atelier des Dames.
FANNY:	Said to be the best in Paris.

(*M. FLEURY poses a MALE MODEL.*)

FANNY:	On Mondays, M. Fleury poses the model.
BELLE:	Mother, it's a man!
FANNY:	Portraits in the morning.
BELLE:	Oh my god!
FANNY:	In the afternoon—
BELLE:	He's taking off his clothes!
FANNY:	(*Trying to be composed*) Nude figures.
BELLE:	Mother, you can see his—
FANNY:	Now, Belle, well, just don't draw that part, just make a little smudge or something.
BELLE:	(*Laughing, tantalized*) Oh-là-là! I'm in Paris!

(*M. FLEURY begins his critique. BELLE concentrates.*)

FLEURY:	Bonjour, ladies!
WOMEN:	Bonjour, M. Fleury.
FLEURY:	(*To ARTIST 1*) You call this thing an arm? Why, it looks like a chicken leg! Again, do it again! Do it again! (*To ARTIST 2*) No, no, no, look at his face. Does he look like he is smelling the horse droppings? NO! Again, do it again. (*FLEURY looks at ARTIST 3's drawing and bursts out laughing*) Please, don't let our model see this. He is very good, and we wish him to come back. (*To BELLE*) Liar, liar, liar. You cannot see eyelashes. Do not lie, draw what is there, please. (*To FANNY*) Hmm, hmm, perhaps you have some talent, *if* you care to develop it.

(*ARTIST WOMEN stare a little jealously at FANNY. M. FLEURY snaps his fingers, and the model changes poses. Everyone draws.*)

BELLE: But my youngest brother, Hervey, got sick, and my mother couldn't come anymore.

(*FANNY moves to her own space and puts away her drawing.*)

FANNY: I sent for the best doctor in Paris. (*To BELLE*) He says Hervey has scrofulous consumption.

BELLE: (*Not acknowledging*) Oh, but I love the atelier!

FANNY: (*Sadly*) He says I must not expect much improvement.

BELLE: Every morning I walk to the atelier, the city just waking.

FANNY: All of our money goes to Hervey's medicine. He is ill, gravely ill.

BELLE: I save my bus fare to buy things to eat.

FANNY: We're poor, and I can't manage to keep Belle and Lloyd properly fed.

BELLE: I love to visit the marketplace.

(*WOMEN form marketplace and BELLE strolls in.*)

FANNY: Hervey can't swallow anything.

BELLE: The market women are so nice to me. (*To MARKET WOMAN*) Confecture, s'il vous plâit.

FANNY: The market women think Belle is a little housemaid.

MARKET WOMAN:
            No, no, chérie.

BELLE: They don't laugh at my French.

MARKET WOMAN:
            Confiture, chérie, confiture.

FANNY: And they give her food. While all the time, Hervey's eyes grow bigger and brighter. He trembles all the time.

BELLE: (*Watching FANNY*) At Christmas, they give me presents.

FANNY: Day or night, I do not leave him. He has a rasping cough and his appearance is dreadful. People cannot bear to look at him. (*To BELLE*) Please, Belle, he asks for you every day—

BELLE: (*Scared*) Please, Mama, I can't. I can't look—

FANNY: It's his birthday—

BELLE: (*Turning away, as she's going to be sick*) I'm sorry, I can't. I just can't look. (*Pause*) To this day, I cannot write or speak about my little brother's last illness. But we all knew, long before the day came . . .

(*FANNY alone in a pool of light.*)

FANNY: Toward the end, I dared not leave him, for every few hours he would bleed in a new place. He would close his eyes and clench his teeth, but he never cried, even once, though the pain made him deathly sick. In his most violent convulsions, his bones snapping in and out of joints like the crack of a whip, he lay, in my arms, silent, looking into my eyes. All I could do was let him hear the sound of my voice speaking words of love and comfort. And so it went, day after day, until finally his bones cut through his skin and lay bare, but from his lips, never, never one word of complaint. On the last day, I smelled blood. I searched and searched him over and over, even burning my hair with the candle I held for light, but I could not find it, for he was bleeding internally. He woke and asked me to sing him a song. "Now lie down beside me, Mama," he said, softly, and so I lay down with him on the white sheets and put my head on the pillow close to his, encircling him in my arms. He never woke again. (*Turning to SAM OSBOURNE*) You, Sam, you, you spent all your money on your mistresses. If we hadn't been so hungry, if we hadn't been so cold—

SAM: You're the one, dragging him off! You! If you'd just stayed home!

BELLE: My mother has the first of her "illnesses." She spends hours staring into space.

FANNY: As I follow, walking behind the little white coffin, I want to call Hervey's attention to the pretty, pitiful sight.

BELLE: She floats around the house like a ghost.

FANNY: He must be so tired of lying on his back. I should turn him over.

(*A DOCTOR enters and BELLE speaks to him.*)

BELLE: Her eyes are hollow orbs and every day she wastes away. Doctor, she hardly speaks.

(*DOCTOR approaches FANNY, but she is oblivious.*)

DOCTOR: You must do something Mrs. Osbourne. You must have a change of scene, or there will be more suffering.

(*FANNY does not respond. DOCTOR takes FANNY by the shoulders.*)

DOCTOR: Listen, you may care nothing for yourself, Mrs. Osbourne, but you have a son and a daughter who have been neglected through this ordeal. If you do not turn your attention to them, you will lose another child.

(*DOCTOR turns and leaves. After a pause, FANNY motions BELLE to come to her. She embraces her as the lights fade. Lights rise again on FANNY alone.*)

FANNY: Grez-sur-Loing is a lost place, tucked away in the folds of rolling hills. Meadows sink into deep shadows, the hills grow ghostly white, and the darkness bleeds out, a little at a time.

(*BELLE enters.*)

BELLE: (*Bored*) Everything here is so quiet. My mother and I paint and draw, and draw and paint, while

Lloyd fishes and fights with the innkeeper's sons.

FANNY: Every night I dream of things, big things: a great rush of water or a wall of snow moving toward me. In the darkness, I see veiled forms that move just beyond the world of light.

BELLE: Mother! Mother! I've met them!

FANNY: They want to come in, into the light!

BELLE: Mother, I've seen them, talked with them. They're charming. They come here every summer.

FANNY: (*Panicky*) Maybe they don't want us here! Maybe they don't want us here!

BELLE: Mother! They were smiling and talking in a friendly way. They're *artists*.

FANNY: (*Back in reality*) Artists?

BELLE: Yes! They're like us, they love art! (*A beat, exhilarated*) Now the summer air of Grez is something strange and new. It is full of real artists! And I love everything about them: their deep talk and rumpled clothes, their knapsacks of paint and brushes, fingers scented with linseed oil and turpentine, the stubs of cigarettes in the ash trays, drawings everywhere, and the smell of brandy and wine. I love to see them change when I enter the room, the way their eyes pay close attention to my every move, the way they try to see who will make me laugh or smile first. And how is it I hardly seemed to notice myself before—this way I feel now, as if every moment I am becoming something different, folding out a thousand petals, one by one, in a slow and dazzling dance.

FANNY: My eyes shine outward, the mask nods and smiles, speaks politely and sometimes, with more than a little insight, drops a witty remark or two. I try always to be calm, because now I feel the underboil as I remember with hatred and shame that for years my husband has preferred the beds of cheap whores to mine, preferred vulgar drunken company to that of our own children. And then come the blank hours, when I think I hear Hervey calling, and the emptiness in my arms spreads over me. . . . From the shadows, I watch life. I feel it swirling by, and see Belle lit up like a candle. So it passes, this first summer at Grez.

MALE ARTIST 1:

(*To BELLE*) Wait until you meet him!

BELLE: Who?

MALE ARTIST 2:

He's a genius.

BELLE: Who's a genius?

MALE ARTIST 3:

He's the best of us—the most talented of us all.

MALE ARTIST 2:

He's going to be a famous writer.

MALE ARTIST 1:

Generous, openhearted—

MALE ARTIST 3:

He lights up the room—

MALE ARTIST 2:

And his talk holds you spellbound for hours.

BELLE: Who are you talking about?

FANNY: It's never quite what you think. One moment you can be sitting quietly in the evening, trying to leave things behind, ready to leave everything to younger, less damaged souls, when an image comes out of the night. You might see it in the half-light, through the French doors of a country inn.

(*Soft light rises on LOUIS.*)

LOUIS: The ideal story is that of two people who go into love step for step . . . like a pair of children venturing together into a dark room.

FANNY: And in the back of your skull, you hear the sound of shattering glass.

LOUIS: The essence of love is kindness, passionate kindness.

FANNY: As if you hear window after window, a thousand windows breaking and falling away.

LOUIS: Kindness run mad, kindness run violent.

BELLE: (*Looking at him*) Who is that?

(*LOUIS moves to FANNY and takes her hand.*)

LOUIS: My name is Louis, Robert Louis Stevenson.

(*Lights fade on FANNY and LOUIS.*)

BELLE: That summer, I had my own ideas of love. Love was an angel with a paintbrush and a voice that called you home.

(*One of the ARTISTS becomes O'MEARA, and sings an Irish ballad directly to BELLE. They move together and sit, sketching each other.*)

BELLE: (*To audience*) We had three wonderful summers at Grez.

O'MEARA: Did you really have an Indian friend?

BELLE: (*Cheerfully*) Yeah, I did. There were lots of American Indians in Nevada.

O'MEARA: (*Mimicking her*) Yeah.

BELLE: (*With an Irish accent*) Would you be making fun of me now, Mr. O'Meara?

O'MEARA: (*Puts down his work, moves next to her*) Yeah.

BELLE: (*Continues with accent*) I can see you're a great one for teasing the ladies.

O'MEARA: (*He turns her face to his*) Yeah.

BELLE: You're not sweet on me, are you?

O'MEARA: (*Kissing her*) Yeah.

(*Lights dim, and rise on FANNY and LOUIS.*)

FANNY: Oh, Louis, you can't be serious.

LOUIS: I was never more serious. Fanny, we're practically man and wife.

FANNY: (*Nervous, to herself*) No, stop it. Don't think about what can't be.

LOUIS: You don't have to stay married to him.

FANNY: No one, my own family—who would speak to us after such a thing? He could take my children away from me!

LOUIS: Don't you love me?

FANNY: Don't you know it by now?

LOUIS: Then, we should be—

(*FANNY puts her fingers over his lips to quiet him.*)

FANNY: Please, please don't spoil these moments.

(*FANNY kisses him. Lights dim, and rise on BELLE and O'MEARA, who walk as if looking at paintings.*)

BELLE: Two more seasons in Paris. We want to see everything—

O'MEARA: Velázquez, a seventeenth-century master.

BELLE: But this isn't Spain.

O'MEARA: Villa Medici, Rome.

BELLE: It looks so modern.

O'MEARA: It's the brushstrokes, Belle, so thin and delicate, in some places he has let the canvas show through.

We see the nature of all moments in life here, transient, passing, nothing to stay the same—so unlike the other work of Velazquez, but just like the world of the artist.

BELLE: You think so?

O'MEARA: (*Melancholy*) We see everything so closely—see that every second the world is altered, and something goes by that will never come again, that nothing's for holding on to.

BELLE: You make it sound so sad.

(*O'MEARA looks at BELLE. He laughs, picks her up, whirls her around, and kisses her.*)

O'MEARA: Of course I do! I'm Irish.

(*Lights dim on BELLE and O'MEARA, and rise on FANNY and LOUIS.*)

FANNY: He's forcing me. He won't send me any more money. I'll have to go.

LOUIS: I could help you.

FANNY: You're penniless.

LOUIS: Why won't you marry me?

FANNY: Be practical. I'm already married.

LOUIS: Divorce him.

FANNY: Besides the scandal, which could kill us both, your father would disown you.

LOUIS: I know you love me, Fanny.

FANNY: Love isn't everything.

LOUIS: How can you say that?

FANNY: I'm frightened. Louis, you're ten years younger than I am!

LOUIS: Please, please marry me.

(*Lights rise on BELLE and O'MEARA. FANNY looks at them.*)

FANNY: No! I—I can't. I'm scared. I have to go back. (*To BELLE*) We're going. We have to go back to America.

(*BELLE and FANNY move to their own space. LOUIS and O'MEARA remain in dim light, watching.*)

BELLE: You're not serious, Mother.

FANNY: (*Agitated*) I'm very serious. We have to go back.

BELLE: But why? All of a sudden? Why now?

FANNY: Because it's been three years now. We had an agreement with your father!

BELLE: You're lying!

FANNY: (*Now mad*) Don't talk back to me!

BELLE: You know I love O'Meara! You just want to take me away!

FANNY: So, you think you love O'Meara?

BELLE: I *know* I love him.

FANNY: He loves you?

BELLE: Yes.

FANNY: You want to stay?

BELLE: Yes!

FANNY: Then marry him.

BELLE: What?

FANNY: If you love him and you want to stay here, then you'll have to marry him.

BELLE: But—

FANNY: Has he asked you?

BELLE: Not in so many—

FANNY: Speak with him.

BELLE: He's poor!

FANNY: More than one couple has started out that way.

BELLE: He's just beginning! He—

FANNY:	I'm telling you, either you marry him, or you come home with me!

(*BELLE turns to O'MEARA, and FANNY turns away.*)

BELLE:	Frank, my, my mother says that if we don't—
O'MEARA:	I'm living on an allowance. I've no money. I'm living for my work.
BELLE:	But I thought you—
O'MEARA:	I do, I do, but I can't. I love you, Belle, but I'm just not ready.

(*Lights fade on O'MEARA. BELLE turns to FANNY.*)

FANNY:	Well?
BELLE:	You. It's you, you're jealous, aren't you?
FANNY:	Be careful, Belle.
BELLE:	Louis doesn't love you, does he?
FANNY:	You know nothing!
BELLE:	It's going nowhere!
FANNY:	Shut your mouth.
BELLE:	You're too old, and he doesn't want you!
FANNY:	I'm warning you—
BELLE:	And you just can't bear to see me happy.
FANNY:	(*Grabbing her by the shoulders*) Shut up! Just shut up!
BELLE:	You can't stand it that someone loves *me*.
FANNY:	(*Pushing her away*) So go ahead! Make a mess of your life. Marry him!
BELLE:	(*Yelling*) He won't! Are you happy? He won't marry me!

(*BELLE breaks, crying. FANNY turns, hesitates once, and goes to her.*)

FANNY:	Belle, I'm so—

BELLE: (*Venomous, pushing her away*) Don't! Don't touch me! Don't ever touch me again!

(*FANNY, stunned, backs away. BELLE is in the Vailima Space.*)

FANNY: Sometimes we don't see things until it's too late.

BELLE: You didn't have to. Why did you take him away from me?

FANNY: Some things we just can't see.

(*Transition. Lights rise on FANNY and BELLE.*)

FANNY: I went back to America.

BELLE: I never saw him again.

FANNY: I went back to more death and parting. In Indiana, my father—

BELLE: In California, *my* father is so happy to see me!

(*SAM gives FANNY a cold look, but BELLE flings herself into SAM's arms, and he whirls her around.*)

FANNY: I went back to—Sam, maybe it's time we thought about—

SAM: Belle and Lloyd will not be the children of divorced parents.

BELLE: (*Callously*) My mother has another one of her "illnesses."

SAM: Your eccentric behavior is a shame to us.

BELLE: And for no good reason, she loses her voice.

SAM: You're lucky I don't have you committed.

BELLE: Papa, Papa, come and see my drawings.

SAM: These are beautiful. I always knew you were extraordinary! I'm going to show you off to all of San Francisco!

FANNY: I see a long string of empty days laid out before me.

BELLE:	My father installed us in a lovely hacienda in the old Spanish town of Monterey.
FANNY:	So he could carry on with his women in San Francisco.
BELLE:	In 1879, it was a lovely place, and except for a few artists, undiscovered by the outside world.

(*Enter Nellie Van de Grift.*)

FANNY:	My youngest sister, Nellie, comes from Indiana.
BELLE:	My father mostly stays away. I see him in the city.
NELLIE:	Fanny's health improves.

(*NELLIE helps FANNY set up an easel. FANNY draws.*)

BELLE:	To the horror of her family in Indiana, Nellie becomes engaged to a Spanish aristocrat, Adulfo Sanchez.

(*ADULFO enters, bows to NELLIE, and they dance to a romantic Spanish song.*)

NELLIE:	Belle meets the young artist Joe Strong.

(*Enter JOE STRONG. He bows to BELLE, and they dance while FANNY draws and watches.*)

FANNY:	Don't, Belle.
BELLE:	Why not?
FANNY:	It's so soon since you left—(*O'Meara*)
BELLE:	Don't talk to me about him.
FANNY:	I just don't think Joe is . . .
BELLE:	What?
FANNY:	Well, he always drinks just a little too much.
BELLE:	I don't care.
FANNY:	Just don't make a foolish choice.
BELLE:	It's my choice, Mother.

FANNY: Don't fall for the first pretty face to flatter you.

BELLE: (*Singsong*) I can't hear you.

FANNY: For something shallow and insipid. (*Pause*) He'll be just like your father!

BELLE: (*Stops dancing*) My father is very good to me.

FANNY: I'm telling you what I see.

(*The music ends, and BELLE walks over to look at FANNY's drawing.*)

BELLE: No matter how you draw me, you always make me look hideous.

(*ADULFO and JOE exit. BELLE moves to the side with NELLIE while FANNY continues to draw.*)

BELLE: She won't ruin things for me again.

(*BELLE moves to a spot of light and meets JOE. They stand together.*)

NELLIE: One afternoon, in secret, Belle and Joe Strong went to a minister in Pacific Grove and became man and wife.

(*BELLE moves back near NELLIE, and JOE exits.*)

BELLE: In a few weeks, when I'm twenty-one, I'm leaving to live with Joe. He and Papa are getting a place for us.

NELLIE: Then a few weeks later—

(*LOUIS appears, disheveled, with a rucksack.*)

LOUIS: Fanny.

(*FANNY looks up to see him, and her whole being lights up. They embrace.*)

FANNY: Louis!

BELLE: See what a hypocrite she is?

NELLIE: Belle!

BELLE: She didn't want me to be with Joe, and all the time she was waiting for him.

LOUIS: Have you made up your mind, Fanny?

FANNY: I know I love you, Louis. I know you and Lloyd are the only two people who have any deep affection for me.

BELLE: Listen to her!

LOUIS: What do you want?

FANNY: Time, just a little more time.

BELLE: She's thinking of divorcing *my* father.

NELLIE: She wouldn't dare.

FANNY: It could ruin us.

LOUIS: How could we be more ruined than we are now? We'll never be happy unless we can live together as man and wife.

BELLE: See!

(*BELLE exits.*)

FANNY: But I'm still afraid of so many things. Think of the disgrace that would fall on Belle. I'm hoping she'll make a good marriage. I don't want to spoil her chances.

LOUIS: I'll take some time to see the countryside.

FANNY: Not far away.

LOUIS: Please, Fanny, don't condemn yourself to this joyless prison.

(*LOUIS exits. NELLIE moves quietly to FANNY.*)

NELLIE: Is he gone?

FANNY: For a while. Where's Belle? I haven't seen her all day.

NELLIE:	She's— I don't exactly know.
FANNY:	What?
NELLIE:	I mean, she—
FANNY:	Nellie, where is she?
NELLIE:	She's going. I mean packing—
FANNY:	Going where?
NELLIE:	She's going . . . away.
FANNY:	With Joe?
NELLIE:	I think so.

(*Lights on BELLE and JOE. BELLE is packing. SAM stands apart, observing. FANNY moves to JOE and BELLE.*)

FANNY:	(*Furious*) Just what do you think you're doing!?
BELLE:	I'm leaving, Mother. I'm leaving with Joe!
FANNY:	I won't allow it. I won't allow you to elope with him.
BELLE:	We're already married. Last month.
FANNY:	You went behind my back?
BELLE:	You heard me!
FANNY:	You're only twenty. You need my consent. It can't be legal.
BELLE:	I had Papa's. Papa knew all along.
FANNY:	(*Slaps BELLE in the face*) You selfish, ungrateful little witch—
BELLE:	(*Shoves FANNY away*) Papa cares about me. He loves me.
FANNY:	(*Glaring at SAM*) You've made your choice, Belle. Now you live with it.

(*Lights rise on NELLIE writing a letter.*)

NELLIE:	To Mrs. Jacob Van de Grift, Clayton, Indiana. Dear Mama, you wrote about me hiding things

from you, and now I must confess that I am
guilty. The scandal of Fanny's divorce, as if it is
not enough, is compounded by her intention to
marry another man quite soon, a Mr. Robert
Louis Stevenson, who under other circumstances
could be seen as a very decent man from a good
family. It pains me to tell you that in her present
situation, the scandal would be unbearably worse
for all if she does not marry him. But to tell you
the truth, Mother, though her conduct humiliates
me, I can't say a word against my sister. She has
been more generous and kind to me than
anyone—especially concerning my engagement
to Adulfo Sanchez. Our old friend Mr. Orr will
not allow me in his house because I am engaged
to a Spaniard. I know my sister to be good. Perhaps her unhappy life has led to her weakness of
character. Your loving Nellie.

(*Lights rise on FANNY and LOUIS.*)

FANNY: It's settled, Louis, and final. (*Pause*) It won't mat-
           ter so much for a boy, will it? If his mother's been
           divorced, I mean.

LOUIS: (*Coughing*) No, no, Fanny, it won't.

(*LOUIS continues coughing.*)

FANNY: Louis, are you alright?

(*LOUIS continues to cough until he can hardly breathe. He sits,
and FANNY rushes to him.*)

LOUIS: Oh please, not now.

(*LOUIS coughs. FANNY holds him.*)

LOUIS: Blood. Fanny, oh God, I can taste the blood.

FANNY: No, Louis, it won't be now. I won't let it. Do you
           hear me? I won't let you go now.

(*BELLE in the Vailima Space.*)

BELLE: Maybe we should, maybe we should just try to let go, like some things never happened.

FANNY: What are you saying, Belle?

BELLE: Those of us who are still alive. We have to go on.

FANNY: You decide. You decide what you want to keep, and what you want to leave behind.

(*Lights rise on LOUIS standing alone.*)

LOUIS: Forgive me if I take this opportunity to remind you that, to divorce her husband and marry me, Fanny risked being shunned by her friends and family. She risked the loss of her dear son Lloyd, and when she finally decided to have me, I was penniless, most likely to be disinherited, and no one had heard of me. I was deathly sick and it looked probable that I would make her a widow in only a few short months. If not, she certainly knew she would be saddled with an invalid for as long as I might live. We married for one reason, for one reason only, because we deeply loved each other, and had no greater wish than to be man and wife.

(*FANNY joins LOUIS.*)

FANNY: We married on May 19, 1880. We spent our honeymoon squatting in an old mining camp up north in Silverado. Clean air, warm days, and soon Louis was well enough to travel. Accepted by his family, we then left for Britain.

(*Lights to BELLE, standing alone.*)

BELLE: Joe and I stayed in San Francisco for two years. We had a son, Austin. Joe got several good commissions for work in the Hawaiian Islands, so off we went. (*Pause*) At the time, I wanted to leave everything behind me, but even though oceans and continents separated us, even though infrequent letters were our only link, sometimes I felt like she was right there, watching everything.

(*A divided stage. FANNY and BELLE sometimes cross-relate for emphasis. FANNY writes while BELLE sits sketching.*)

FANNY: My dear Belle, how are you and your dear son, Austin?

BELLE: We're fine, Mother.

FANNY: Oh, and how is Joe?

BELLE: (*Icily*) He's fine, Mother.

FANNY: For Louis's health, the doctors have ordered Davos, a sanatorium high in the Swiss Alps. It is very cold, but I'm glad to be away from Britain and Louis's so-called friends. To tell you the truth, I found it hard to think much of that crème de la crème.

(*HENLEY stands in a spot of light.*)

HENLEY: My God! She's from America!

FANNY: Especially that brute, Henley.

HENLEY: She belongs in a log cabin, making bread.

FANNY: Disgustingly overbearing.

HENLEY: How can we take her seriously? She's a woman with no intellect.

FANNY: With no regard for Louis's health, he keeps him up all night, drinking and gossiping.

HENLEY: Purely the instinctual type.

(*HENLEY turns toward FANNY. He coughs, then blows his nose. FANNY observes this on her way toward him.*)

FANNY: Good afternoon, Henley.

HENLEY: Good afternoon, is Louis about?

(*HENLEY sneezes.*)

FANNY: Do you have a cold?

HENLEY: A small, bothersome sniffle sort of thing. I—

FANNY: I'm sorry. I've asked you before. I've asked all Louis's friends, no one must come with a cold or other symptoms of illness.

HENLEY: See here, woman, you—

FANNY: Please understand, the smallest sniffle to you could mean death for Louis. When you're completely well, Henley, you'll be most welcome.

(*FANNY turns away and leaves him.*)

HENLEY: Do you see?! Do you see how she is? She's worse than these women who take up spiritualism! She actually believes in that utterly *ridiculous* theory of germs!

(*HENLEY exits.*)

FANNY: (*Back to writing*) I keep a constant watch over Louis, never knowing when another hemorrhage will come. But he's getting some of his writing published, and is always working. Oh, by the way, how is Joe?

(*BELLE speaks from her sketching place. Behind her, JOE is at an easel, drinking. He puts on his coat.*)

BELLE: You're not going out, are you?

JOE: I'm going out.

BELLE: It's almost supper.

JOE: I can't work anymore today.

BELLE: Then relax.

JOE: I'm meeting Jules.

BELLE:	Austin's going to be home any minute, and look at you, you're in no condition to—
JOE:	(*Loud*) I'm bored, Belle, b-o-r-e-d.
BELLE:	(*Hurt*) I see.
JOE:	(*Exiting*) I'm going out.
BELLE:	As I said, Joe is fine. His painting goes on very well. At first, he was confused about how to treat the tropical landscape, but now I think he is quite inspired by it.

(*Light dims on BELLE and rises on FANNY.*)

FANNY:	Well, Louis and I have quit our cottage in France—such a joy after the cold and bleak of Davos. *Treasure Island,* I hope you've heard, is Louis's first great success. I hated to leave my perfect dollhouse, but—
LOUIS:	You don't have to sulk about it.
FANNY:	And I don't have to like them either.
LOUIS:	Baxter and Henley are my best friends. I invited them here to Hyeres.
FANNY:	They exhaust you with food, drink, and vicious gossip, and they make *you* pay for everything.
LOUIS:	Very well, if you don't like their company, we'll remove ourselves to Nice.
FANNY:	Louis, you can't!
LOUIS:	I'm not listening to your bossing.
FANNY:	You're not well, Louis.
LOUIS:	And I'm not your prisoner either.
FANNY:	In Nice, he caught a cold, which rapidly became a lung congestion. Then, he developed a kidney infection. Of course, at the first sign of illness, Baxter and Henley deserted him, long gone before I could arrive.

LOUIS: (*Very ill*) I'm a stupid, sorry wretch, Fanny.

FANNY: Stop it. Just stop that kind of talk now.

LOUIS: You should just have done with me.

FANNY: (*Kindly, with a laugh*) Hah! Don't I just wish I didn't love you. (*Pause*) For days, it was uncertain. Then, word came of a cholera epidemic. So of course we had to flee. I can't tell you, Belle, how fortunate you are, not to be plagued by the shadow of death.

(*Crossfade to BELLE.*)

BELLE: Something happens to me that I do not tell her until many years later. While I am in Honolulu, I have another child, a beautiful baby boy with sweet golden curls. I call him Hervey. When he is eleven months old, I am invited by my dear friends to visit them at 'Ulupalakua on the island of Maui. 'Ulupalakua is like a jewel set high on the slopes of Haleakalā. It is so beautiful I can hardly bear it— as though I had seen it before, or been waiting for it all my life. It was a shock that one day during our visit, I noticed Hervey's head was drooping and his eyes looked languid. I felt his cheeks and found them burning hot. The doctor arrived late that evening. By morning, we thought Hervey was a little better, and the doctor, who had been holding him, lay him down on the bed, saying "Let him sleep." My baby slept, but never woke again. As the Hawaiian women mourned, with the most heartbreaking sounds I have ever heard, we laid him to rest in a small grave strewn with white gardenias. (*Pause*) And strangely, underneath the black weight of grief, there is only one person I want . . .

(*BELLE looks as lights rise on FANNY, who is writing.*)

LOUIS: (*Calling*) Fanny!

FANNY:	My dear Belle, we have for some time now been at Bournemouth, installed in a charming house called Skerryvore.
LOUIS:	(*Calling*) Fanny!
FANNY:	Louis has made another successful recovery from a hemorrhage, and now is insisting that I listen to him read a story that has furiously occupied him for several days. It started with a dream he had—
LOUIS:	Fanny, I'm waiting!
FANNY:	(*Going to LOUIS*) Here I am.
LOUIS:	I've just finished, and I want you to be the first person to hear this.
BELLE:	(*From her space*) There was only one person whose presence I would have given anything for.
LOUIS:	"Here then, as I lay down my pen and proceed to seal up my confession, I bring the life of that unhappy Henry Jekyll to an end." (*Pause*) Well, how do you like it? It's good, isn't it?
FANNY:	If you say so.
LOUIS:	A real shilling shocker. I'm sure I can sell it.
FANNY:	I suppose you could.
LOUIS:	You suppose . . . You know it's good. Don't give me that look. You have to see, this is good work!
FANNY:	I think you've made a story and missed the point.
LOUIS:	(*Very irritated*) What did you say?
FANNY:	I said, I think you've missed the point.
LOUIS:	I missed the point? I can't believe you'd say a thing like that. It's a thoughtless remark.
FANNY:	Still, I say it. I think you missed the point.
LOUIS:	(*Raising his voice*) The point! Just what point is it you think I missed?

FANNY:	The allegory, you've missed it.
LOUIS:	No, you've missed it. This is a crawler, madam!
FANNY:	Well, it should be something more than just a crawler.
LOUIS:	You know nothing about writing.
FANNY:	You've made Jekyll a bad man pretending to be good.
LOUIS:	Just as he should be.
FANNY:	No, he should have a good self and a bad self, just like all of us.
LOUIS:	That's the most ignorant idea I've ever heard.
FANNY:	Then don't read to me. Don't ask me what I think.
LOUIS:	I work and work and this is what I get in return. Well, I just won't waste my time anymore.

(*LOUIS throws down the story and leaves.*)

FANNY:	Yes, it started with a dream he had. He read the manuscript and, after a painful revision, has produced a story that I think is his most brilliant: an allegory about the good and evil nature inherent in the human condition. My love to Austin and yourself, and tell me, how is Joe?

(*Lights to BELLE. JOE is in the background painting a WOMAN MODEL in a pareo.*)

BELLE:	Everything here couldn't be better. Austin is growing so quickly, and Joe's career continues to flourish.

(*JOE moves to the MODEL.*)

BELLE:	He is very popular and has so many—

(*JOE is kissing the MODEL.*)

BELLE:	Commissions he can hardly—

(*BELLE turns to them.*)

BELLE: Joe!

(*MODEL looks at BELLE, giggles, and runs out.*)

JOE: Why do you have to bother me when I'm working?

BELLE: Working?

JOE: That was nothing. It meant nothing.

BELLE: This is where we live!

JOE: (*Moves to her*) Come on, Belle, don't be mad.

BELLE: (*Pushes him away*) Stop it, how could you?

JOE: Well, maybe if you weren't so cold.

BELLE: Cold? After the things you do all over town?

JOE: You can't forget. You just can't forget anything, can you?

BELLE: *Everything!* I can't forget *everything!*

JOE: Suit yourself. Sulk if you want to, but this is my life, and I'm going to enjoy it. I'm going to enjoy every moment.

(*JOE exits. BELLE goes back to writing, struggling to keep control of her emotions.*)

BELLE: He has so many commissions he can hardly keep up. We continue to be so happy.

(*Light on FANNY.*)

FANNY: While *Jekyll and Hyde* has brought Louis fame and fortune, the doctors say Louis cannot pass another winter in Britain. Perhaps we will try America. Leaving this house will nearly break my heart. How is Joe?

(*Lights to BELLE. Enter DR. RICHARDS.*)

BELLE: (*Lying*) Joe has had a slight cold.

DR. RICHARDS:

> Do you understand, Mrs. Strong? He's had a breakdown, a serious breakdown.

BELLE: I understand.

DR. RICHARDS:

> He's ready to leave the sanatorium, but he's weak. You'll have to watch him carefully.

BELLE: I'll do my best.

DR. RICHARDS:

> You may need help. Is there someone you can write to, your family? I know your mother is—

BELLE: I can take care of him.

DR. RICHARDS:

> I'm worried about you.

BELLE: I'll take care of myself.

(*Lights to FANNY.*)

FANNY: New York has been exhausting for Louis. If I am not careful, insistent to the point of appearing a shrew, success could quickly be the death of him. Let them call me names. It's his life and I don't intend to give up. We are going to try the Adirondacks.

(*BELLE and DR. RICHARDS are helping JOE to sit at his easel.*)

DR. RICHARDS:

> (*To JOE*) Remember what I said. Leave off the drink or it'll kill you.

FANNY: Sorry to hear Joe was under the weather.

BELLE: Joe is just fine. You would hardly know he was ill at all.

(*Lights to FANNY.*)

FANNY: For all the doctors' advice about cold air and altitude, Louis's health does not improve. We have decided to take desperate measures, and to do the exact opposite of what the doctors have ordered all these years.

BELLE: Joe, Fanny, and Louis are going on a sea voyage to the South Pacific.

FANNY: I'm going to San Francisco to hire a yacht. I thought if I—

BELLE: She's sending the passage for Austin and me. She wants us to see them off.

FANNY: Do you realize, Belle, it's been nearly eight years?

(*FANNY and BELLE face each other from a distance.*)

BELLE: In San Francisco, I first see her as she steps off the train.

FANNY: As I step off the train, I see her!

BELLE: Time has always been good to her, but I see she looks older.

FANNY: And I see she is no longer the young girl who ran off with an artist.

BELLE: (*Waving, running to her*) Mother!

FANNY: Belle!

BELLE: We walked, sat in cafés, talked and talked for hours about everything. (*To FANNY*) Your painting, are you still—

FANNY: No, I don't have time, Louis's illness . . .

BELLE: Drawing?

FANNY: I can't. There's always so much to arrange for Louis.

BELLE: Your stories, are you still writing?

FANNY: No. Louis is the writer, Belle. *His* writing is important.

BELLE: We talked for hours about everything except—

(*Pause.*)

| BELLE: | You heard about Papa. | FANNY: | Of course, I was shocked about Sam. |

(*Silence. Lights on FANNY and BELLE dim as SAM looms behind them in hazy light.*)

SAM: It was late. I'd been working late when I left the courthouse. I walked out whistling. It was a dark night, no moon. The fog was rolling in. I went to a house, a house near the waterfront. He asked me to meet him there, said it was urgent. When I got there, the front door was wide open and all the lights were on. I walked in but no one was there, not a soul. I waited awhile, then decided to leave. And strangely, as I stepped out into the street, the lights in the house went out all at once. The fog was now very thick. I was walking away when I heard someone behind me. Someone with a quick, swift step and then—

(*Lights rise again on FANNY and BELLE.*)

BELLE: He just vanished! Disappeared! No one's seen him since that night.

FANNY: No trace at all?

BELLE: None.

FANNY: (*Agitated*) Perhaps he's run off with another woman.

BELLE: He could have been shanghaied.

FANNY: Maybe suicide.

BELLE: Or robbed and murdered.

FANNY: (*Really irritated*) He couldn't even die a decent death!

BELLE: (*Defensive*) People respected him! People liked him! He never said a cross word to me!

FANNY:	I'm sorry. I'm sorry, Belle. I'll never mention it again.

(*BELLE in the Vailima Space.*)

BELLE:	Their South Sea voyage ended in Honolulu, and we were all reunited. (*A beat*) Eight years ago, Louis and Fanny were poor nobodies, their marriage a scandal. Now they were wealthy international celebrities, still happy and in love. The thought of my life with Joe—
FANNY:	Belle.
BELLE:	Why have you come here?
FANNY:	I can see you're suffering.
BELLE:	Don't look at me like that.
FANNY:	I know—(*something is troubling you*)
BELLE:	You always knew, didn't you?
FANNY:	Are you sure, Belle, sure you're not *using* marriage?
BELLE:	You have no right to say that to me.
FANNY:	Using it to prove something to me?

(*Enter LOUIS.*)

FANNY:	We've had a serious talk with Joe, and he's signed a paper placing himself and his financial affairs absolutely in Louis's hands.
LOUIS:	We've decided to take him with us on our cruise to the Gilbert Islands. We think it would help him.
FANNY:	We know you don't want to leave Austin and come with us, so I've made arrangements for both of you to wait for us in Sydney. You'll leave Honolulu on the next steamer for Australia.
BELLE:	Leave Honolulu? I've lived here for seven years. This is my home. I don't know anyone in Australia.

LOUIS: You can wait just as well in Australia.

BELLE: Wait for what?

LOUIS: Wait until you're called for.

BELLE: I waited for months in Sydney. Fanny and Louis arrived full of enthusiasm. They had fallen in love with Sāmoa, and for the sake of Louis's health planned to settle there. They went back to begin their house, but one day, Louis returned to Sydney, alone.

(*LOUIS and BELLE alone.*)

BELLE: No, Louis, I don't want to go. The *Sydney Bulletin* has even offered me a steady job writing a theatrical column, and I could teach drawing and dancing. I've made a life here.

LOUIS: And Joe? He's right back to his old ways.

BELLE: I just don't have the heart to turn him out.

LOUIS: He'll ruin you, Belle. Come to Sāmoa, where we can watch out for you, and help you to manage him.

BELLE: We'd just be a burden.

LOUIS: One I'm happy to bear. Please let's talk it over.

BELLE: We didn't talk over me coming to Sydney.

LOUIS: I know. I'm sorry. That's why I want you—I want you to come of your own free will. The truth is, I have to face things. If I want to live, I can never go back to Britain again. Fanny, Lloyd, you, and Austin, you're my family now, and all that I have. Oh, look here, I've brought you something.

(*LOUIS takes out a ring and gives it to BELLE.*)

LOUIS: It's topaz, my birthstone. I got one for your mother and myself too.

BELLE: Louis, it's beautiful.

LOUIS: I know I'm not old enough to father you, Belle, but if you could, you might come to look on me as a guardian and protector. Your mother wants it very much, but it would mean a great deal to me too.

(*LOUIS touches BELLE on her cheek and exits. BELLE moves to the Vailima Space.*)

BELLE: On very still nights like tonight, the sound of the waves folding over the reef rises up the hill and floats across Vailima. My mother was the island that gave me life, the homeland from which I'm sure I've departed—that is, until I look at my body, this body of evidence. My body, her body, the remains of her body, which tomorrow I will carry up the hill called Vaea, and tuck safely away in the earth.

End ACT I

Act II

(*BELLE in the Vailima Space.*)

BELLE: If you ever come here to Sāmoa, you will immediately be influenced by the virulent growth and decay of nature, which simultaneously and relentlessly permeates everything. Growth and decay, out of control, side by side, here on the edge of the earth, as if there is no difference in one or the other, only the endless cycle of life and death, only the ashes to ashes and the dust to dust.

(*FANNY enters near BELLE and looks around.*)

FANNY: I loved everything. Why did I have to leave?

BELLE: So, our years here at Vailima began, in this house that they built together, in a life we all made, carving out a place for ourselves, one day tumbling into the next.

FANNY: I remember things so vividly. If you came visiting, from the town of Apia, you would climb slowly up the forest path to our red gate.

(*FANNY walks busily on and off with tools.*)

BELLE: When the red gate opens for the first time, you see the big house, with the sweeping green lawn, and very fine it looks. If you come unexpectedly, you will find us all scattered. Aunt Maggie, Louis's mother, is in charge of our spiritual life.

(*Enter AUNT MAGGIE.*)

AUNT MAGGIE:

It's not right that only the help comes to morning and evening prayers. The family should set the example!

(*Enter LLOYD.*)

BELLE: My brother Lloyd does the books.

LLOYD: (*To BELLE*) Look, they just don't understand. We can't keep spending like this.

(*Enter LOUIS.*)

BELLE: Louis, who is now in better health than he has ever been, is either riding Jack, his horse, or upstairs working in his big room that faces the sea.

LOUIS: Fanny! Fanny! Where is my volume of Spenser? I know I saw it just the other day!

BELLE: As the head housekeeper, I'm feeding over fourteen people a day. And Fanny? She could be anywhere.

AUNT MAGGIE:

Fanny, I would like to speak to you. You haven't come to morning prayers once this week.

FANNY: I have over fifty vanilla vines. If I don't plant them now, they'll be dead by tomorrow, Aunt Maggie.

AUNT MAGGIE:

Belle, why don't *you* come to morning prayers with the rest of us?

BELLE: I'm sorry, but breakfast is so complicated!

LLOYD: My God, Mother! Who ordered twenty cases of champagne?

FANNY: Not now, Lloyd. I'm trying to get this pipe laid in from the spring. Do you want to keep carrying water forever?

LOUIS: Fanny! I can't find the damn book! Fanny!

BELLE: Mother, there's worms in the new flour.

FANNY: Pick them out!

AUNT MAGGIE:

What's your excuse, Lloyd, for not coming to prayers?

LLOYD: Uh, actually, I'm thinking of taking up Buddhism.

AUNT MAGGIE:

Louis, I will not stand for this!

LOUIS: Fanny! Where the blazes are you?

FANNY: Laying out the lawn tennis court you insist we need, dear!

AUNT MAGGIE:

It's disgraceful, all the servants present and none of the family.

LLOYD: Louis, we can't go on spending like this.

BELLE: (*Whacking with a broom*) Help! There's a centipede crawling under the table!

LLOYD: We're going to go broke!

AUNT MAGGIE:

We're all going to hell!

BELLE: We're being attacked by insects!

LOUIS: Fanny, for God's sake, help me!

(*Pause. FANNY enters.*)

FANNY: Why is everyone standing around like this? Do you need me to give you something to do?

(*All exit quickly except LOUIS.*)

LOUIS: Sit down, love, you look exhausted.

FANNY: There's so much to do if we want to make it work.

LOUIS: Sit down and watch the sunset with me.

FANNY:	It is beautiful, isn't it?
LOUIS:	The sky is about to catch on fire.
FANNY:	All this land.
LOUIS:	And the sea looks like a flaming lake.
FANNY:	And it's ours. All ours.
LOUIS:	Look, Fanny! A fruit bat scanning for a meal.
FANNY:	Finally, our own piece of earth.
LOUIS:	I haven't seen Joe all day.
FANNY:	He's drinking again.
LOUIS:	He doesn't do a stitch of work, does he?
FANNY:	No, and I think he's sleeping with the girl who does the wash.
LOUIS:	Are you sure?
FANNY:	I'm sure.
LOUIS:	I feel sorry for him, but he *is* incorrigible.
FANNY:	He's a monster.

(*Lights to BELLE strolling with a basket. She meets VIA.*)

VIA:	Tālofa (*Greetings*), Belle!
BELLE:	Tālofa lava, Via.
VIA:	You haven't come to town for so long.
BELLE:	There's so much to do at Vailima.
VIA:	Where's Austin?
BELLE:	He stayed at home today.
VIA:	The British consul is having a dance this month— his daughter's birthday.
BELLE:	Yes, we'll be there.

(*Enter LAGI. She looks BELLE over.*)

VIA:	Everyone is talking about it. There's going to be fireworks.
BELLE:	Really?

VIA:	Maybe they're coming on the next boat from Fiji.

(*LAGI walks up to BELLE and taps her sharply on the shoulder.*)

LAGI:	Tālofa.
BELLE:	Tālofa.
LAGI:	My name is Lagi.
BELLE:	How do you do? I'm—
LAGI:	I know who you are.
BELLE:	You do?
LAGI:	You think you're such a smart pālagi (*Caucasian*) lady who lives up on the hill.
VIA:	(*To LAGI*) E, salapū! Alu 'ese! (*Shut up! Go away!*)
LAGI:	I bet you think you're so pretty too.
BELLE:	Why are you talking like—
LAGI:	Hah! You can't even keep a husband.

(*LAGI pinches BELLE hard on the arm and laughs. BELLE screams and drops her basket. LAGI runs away. VIA rubs BELLE's arm in a comforting way. She helps BELLE gather up the basket things.*)

VIA:	That woman has no shame.
BELLE:	Who *is* she?
VIA:	(*Cagey*) You really don't know her?
BELLE:	No.
VIA:	She's no one. Just a bad woman. No one.
BELLE:	Please, tell me who she is.
VIA:	You should bring Austin down to the horse races at the beach.
BELLE:	Via, I thought we were friends.
VIA:	Well, she's the one your husband lives with.
BELLE:	Lives with!
VIA:	At the house he got her in Tauese.

BELLE:	They have a house?
VIA:	You didn't know?
BELLE:	Not that he was *living* with a woman! Not that he got her a house!
VIA:	Oka (*Oh*)! Poor Belle! Everyone in Apia knows.

(*Lights to LOUIS and FANNY.*)

FANNY:	Do you hear me? I'm going to kill him!
LOUIS:	Fanny, lower your voice. She'll hear you.
FANNY:	He's vermin. Filthy vermin.
LOUIS:	He's a sick person.
FANNY:	He's a drunk. He won't work. He's made Belle's life hell. And he's been supporting a mistress on *your* money!
LOUIS:	For God's sake, be quiet.
FANNY:	If he sets one foot on this—
LOUIS:	I'll take care of it. But for now, can you think about Belle?
FANNY:	You *know* who encouraged her to marry him.
LOUIS:	Look, her life is damaged. But we can help her make a new one.
FANNY:	I hope he dies in the gutter.

(*Crossfade to BELLE, who has been crying. LOUIS approaches carefully. BELLE senses him before she sees him.*)

BELLE:	You don't have to creep around me. I won't break.
LOUIS:	Your mother is in a temper, you know.
BELLE:	The whole house knows.
LOUIS:	I'm worried that if she sees Joe . . .
BELLE:	Don't worry. I had one of the boys take his things to Apia and tell him not to come back.
LOUIS:	Thank you, Belle. You've saved us all from a mountain of grief.

BELLE: I know she's always hated him.

LOUIS: Do you? Hate him?

BELLE: I'm disgusted with him and myself, for marrying him.

LOUIS: Divorce him.

BELLE: But Austin—

LOUIS: From now on, I'll be his legal guardian.

BELLE: You would do that?

LOUIS: He's a joy to me.

BELLE: (*A beat*) I feel so dirty.

LOUIS: Stop thinking like that.

BELLE: Like a used rag, with spots that won't ever wash out.

LOUIS: It's him, not you.

BELLE: Just the thought, the thought that I ever gave myself to him makes me sick, sick to my stomach!

LOUIS: He's worthless baggage, and you'll never have to see him again. Tomorrow I'm going to Apia to file for a divorce on your behalf. I won't see you trapped in a joyless prison.

(*Exit LOUIS. BELLE watches him and then moves to the Vailima Space.*)

BELLE: I'm ashamed that I once resented him so much.

(*FANNY enters.*)

FANNY: Sometimes it startles me, Belle, how you look so much like me.

BELLE: I'll never be as good-looking as you.

FANNY: And you were divorced at the same age I was.

BELLE: I remember.

FANNY: And Lloyd was just about Austin's age.

BELLE:	What?
FANNY:	Just about the same age as when I met Louis, and we got married.
BELLE:	Yes, I remember.
FANNY:	And you and Louis . . .

(*LOUIS is trying to write. His fingers cramp. LLOYD watches.*)

LOUIS:	Damn pen. Damn fingers. What the hell's the use?
FANNY:	(*Walks to him*) What's wrong?
LOUIS:	Writer's cramp.
FANNY:	Rest.
LOUIS:	Rest? Look at this stack of unanswered letters. And the mail steamer is due next week.
FANNY:	I'll help you.
LOUIS:	No, you're far too busy.
FANNY:	I will.
LOUIS:	I'd be keeping you from more important work.
LLOYD:	How about my typewriter?
LOUIS:	The click and clack of it drives me crazy.
LLOYD:	Everyone uses them now.
BELLE:	Maybe I could help. I mean, I could try.
FANNY:	That's an idea.
BELLE:	But you'd have to go slowly and help me with the spelling.
LOUIS:	Well, let's try it.

(*BELLE takes dictation. FANNY moves to the side, gardening, watching.*)

LOUIS:	My dear Barrie, that's B-a-r-r-i-e, got it? My dear Barrie, comma, I give you on request a thumbnail sketch of myself, colon, name in family, The Tame Celebrity, period. Exceedingly lean, comma,

beginning to be grizzled, comma, crow's-footed, comma, general appearance of a blasted boy, period. Drinks plenty, period. Curses some, period. Temper unstable, period. If accused of cheating at cards, comma, would feel bound to blow out brains, period.

(*BELLE and LOUIS laugh. FANNY turns to observe them.*)

LOUIS: And Fanny, colon, insane black eyes, comma, boy's hands, comma, wild blue dress usually spotted with garden mold—

(*BELLE and LOUIS laugh while FANNY looks at them, then at her dress.*)

LOUIS: And Belle, colon, runs me like a baby in a pram.

(*LOUIS and BELLE laugh again as FANNY watches and lights fade and rise on a table. LOUIS walks in and rings a bell. LLOYD, AUNT MAGGIE, BELLE, and FANNY join him, standing.*)

LOUIS: Let us pray. Lord, thou sendest the rain upon the uncounted millions of the forest, and givest the trees to drink exceedingly. Teach us the lesson of trees. The sea around us, which the rain recruits, teams with fishes, teach us, Lord, the meaning of fishes. Let us see ourselves for what we are, one out of the countless clans of thy handiwork. When we would despair, let us remember that these also please and serve thee. Amen.

(*All sit.*)

LOUIS: Well, I trust we all had a full day.

LLOYD: Miracle of miracles, I've almost got the books to balance for last month.

AUNT MAGGIE:

I've made great progress as to the death and destruction of my bête noire: the lantana bushes.

FANNY: The vanilla plants have really taken off. And the cocoa trees, healthy beyond my greatest expectations. We'll have a botanical showplace. And today, just by the bathing pool, I heard the most extraordinary bird singing.

LLOYD: I think I heard that too. It was haunting.

FANNY: I hope to attract all kinds of birds. Wouldn't it be something? Our land, a bird sanctuary.

AUNT MAGGIE:

I think I know the bird you mean. It has three kind of short sounds and then a long melodious sound like a mournful wail.

FANNY: Exactly.

BELLE: The Sāmoans think that bird sings in sorrowful events. They think it's evil.

FANNY: (*Irritated*) Don't spoil it for me.

LOUIS: (*Like he's had a great revelation*) Why, Fanny! Of course! I never realized it before!

FANNY: What?

LOUIS: Why, you, my dear, have the soul of a peasant!

LLOYD: (*Aside to BELLE*) Oh-oh.

(*A silence. Everyone stares at LOUIS.*)

FANNY: What did you say?

AUNT MAGGIE:

What did he say?

LOUIS: You have the soul of a peasant.

FANNY: Are you saying that because I love to work in the earth?

LOUIS: No, because you're wonderfully intoxicated by the *ownership* of it.

FANNY: And I suppose that possession, no, the stupidity of possession, has no power over an *artist* like yourself.

LOUIS: (*Perplexed*) Why, Fanny, I meant no insult. I hugely admire the peasant class.

FANNY: Do you think me so unsophisticated that I can't see exactly what you mean?

LOUIS: You misunderstand—

FANNY: You, the lofty artist, looking down from your upper class at me, the intoxicated dirt digger.

LOUIS: I say it because an artist wouldn't—

FANNY: Artist! Artist! Artist! Don't talk to me about being an artist. I gave up everything for you—for your *art*. It was built on my back! Your artistic idealism would crumble around you if it weren't for me. And this is how you repay me, with these contemptible pronouncements?

BELLE: Mother, calm down.

LLOYD: He didn't mean—

FANNY: Shut up, both of you! All of you! I do everything to make this place work, and what for? For a pack of worthless ingrates.

(*FANNY storms off.*)

AUNT MAGGIE: I think you upset the lass, Louis.

(*Lights fade on the table, and rise on FANNY, alone.*)

FANNY: I plant a seed or a root, and I plant a bit of my heart. I see tender shoots rise toward the sun, and I don't feel so far removed from God. In a way, I *am* an artist. I'm creating this garden, this house, the land, things I've bound all together in good faith and love. But now he's hacking at the strings, trying to make it fall apart.

(*Enter LOUIS.*)

LOUIS:	Where have you been? I was worried.
FANNY:	I want to be alone!
LOUIS:	But it's late and damp out here.
FANNY:	(*Darkly*) I said, leave me alone!

(*Lights on BELLE and LLOYD.*)

BELLE:	I'm telling you, Lloyd, something's wrong with her.
LLOYD:	You're such a worrier.
BELLE:	You saw what she did last Sunday.
LLOYD:	Well, he shouldn't have called her a peasant.
BELLE:	She's staring all the time, and walking around like a ghost.
LLOYD:	She's just tired, that's all.
BELLE:	She's been like this before, in Grez and Monterey. Don't you remember?
LLOYD:	I remember she's always had nervous spells.
BELLE:	I can't believe you and Louis! You just refuse to see!

(*LOUIS calls from his desk.*)

LOUIS:	Belle, I'm ready!
BELLE:	I'm coming! (*To LLOYD*) I'm telling you to pay attention to her. It's getting serious.
LOUIS:	Belle!
BELLE:	I'm on my way! (*To LLOYD*) Are you listening to me?
LLOYD:	Okay, okay, I will.

(*BELLE marches into LOUIS's space. LOUIS is trying to open a letter with a big knife.*)

BELLE:	Louis, what are you doing?
LOUIS:	Opening letters.

BELLE: (*Taking knife away*) You could slice off a finger.

LOUIS: That knife belonged to Bully Hayes.

BELLE: We're not on a pirate ship.

LOUIS: Yes, Mum.

BELLE: Let's get started. I thought you were ready.

LOUIS: Very good, Mum. Oh, by the way, Mum, I scribbled a little verse for your mother and yourself.

BELLE: Oh?

LOUIS: Yes, would you care to hear it?

BELLE: Please.

LOUIS: High as my heart the quip be mine
That draws their stature to a line
My pair of fairies plump and dark
The dryads of my cattle park.
From European womankind
they are divided and defined
the nobler gait, the naked foot
the indiscreeter petticoat.

(*FANNY watches. She is disheveled and her hands are bleeding.*)

One with a crop-halo wild
And one more sedulous to please
Her long dark hair deep as her knees.

(*FANNY enters.*)

LOUIS: Fanny, what is this?

FANNY: Just a little break from my peasant occupations.

BELLE: Mother, look at your hands. They're bleeding.

FANNY: I was clearing out some prickly grass.

BELLE: Why didn't you wear gloves?

FANNY: You know why.

BELLE: What?

FANNY:	Don't play the innocent!
BELLE:	What are you—(*talking about?*)
FANNY:	You hid them from me.
BELLE:	No, they're right on the shelf in the shed.
FANNY:	You hid them from me on purpose.
BELLE:	(*Upset*) I didn't!
FANNY:	(*Nasty*) Are you calling me a liar?
BELLE:	No.
LOUIS:	Fanny, please . . .
FANNY:	Are you trying to make me seem crazy?
BELLE:	No.
FANNY:	Then admit it. You hid the gloves. You want me to bleed!
BELLE:	(*Exits in tears*) No, I didn't. I don't.
LOUIS:	Fanny, what are you doing?
FANNY:	She's scheming against me.
LOUIS:	She's not.
FANNY:	She is!
LOUIS:	Don't torture her.
FANNY:	Oh, I forgot. You're enthralled with her. You prefer her shallow company to mine.
LOUIS:	We work. She's been a great help getting my *work* done.
FANNY:	(*Mimicking him*) "Her long dark hair deep as her knees."
LOUIS:	Fanny, for God's sake!
FANNY:	Well, I won't bother the *artist* and his little assistant. I'll just go on about the business of the *peasant* class.

(*Exit FANNY. BELLE enters.*)

BELLE:	Is she gone?
LOUIS:	Yes.
BELLE:	Can't you see what's happening?
LOUIS:	(*Pause*) I don't want to believe it.
BELLE:	I found the gloves.
LOUIS:	Where were they?
BELLE:	On the shelf where they always are.

(*LLOYD is working at his books. FANNY enters.*)

LLOYD:	Mother.
FANNY:	(*Agitated*) Lloyd, you have to do something.
LLOYD:	What's the matter?
FANNY:	It's Baxter and Henley.
LLOYD:	What about them?
FANNY:	I just spoke to them, down at the red gate.
LLOYD:	Mother, they're in Britain!
FANNY:	No, they're here, and they want to take Louis to Apia to celebrate.
LLOYD:	Don't you see? That's just impossible.
FANNY:	Of course, it's impossible. Remember what happened the last time? They almost killed him.
LLOYD:	That's not what I mean.
FANNY:	You have to put them off. Don't let them take him. Don't let him go.
LLOYD:	Don't worry. He's not going anywhere.
FANNY:	I'm the one. I'm the one who won't let him go.
LLOYD:	Look, look out the window. There's nobody there.
FANNY:	They're just hiding.
LLOYD:	Don't worry.

FANNY: Oh, but I do, because I'm the one who's watched all these years. I'm the one who won't let him go. (*Pause*) Why are you looking at me like that? Is there something wrong with me? With my dress or my person?

LLOYD: Why, no, no, nothing, nothing at all.

FANNY: Then don't expect me to sit here and gab all day. I don't know about you, but I have work to do.

(*BELLE in the Vailima Space.*)

BELLE: December signals the tropical summer. The weather turns silent and still.

FANNY: Nothing moves or breathes.

BELLE: It's unbearably hot.

FANNY: And the air turns thick and humid.

BELLE: Days of gray.

FANNY: And the dark sky presses down on you, pushing you until you can't think.

BELLE: And the body labors just to breathe.

(*FANNY moves away, alone.*)

FANNY: Until you feel you've been shoved to the edge, the edge of the world, and any moment the ground could give way, and you could fly apart—explode into a million pieces.

(*BELLE goes to meet LOUIS at the table.*)

LOUIS: Where could she be?

BELLE: Lloyd and the men are looking for her.

LOUIS: Why is this happening now?

BELLE: The doctor said she was under strain.

LOUIS: Now that we have everything, money, fame . . .

BELLE: That she's been under tremendous strain for years.

LOUIS: Now, just when we've begun to be well.

BELLE: No, Louis, *you're* the one who's famous, and *you've* just begun to be well.

LOUIS: Is it me? Do you think it's me? That I've done this to her?

BELLE: I didn't mean that.

LOUIS: Caring for me, always worried that the next hemorrhage will kill me.

BELLE: I didn't mean anything like that. The Sāmoans say it's ma'i aitu (*spirit sickness*).

LOUIS: Ghosts?

BELLE: They think she's possessed by a ghost.

LOUIS: Possessed?

BELLE: They say she's disturbed something in the bush, that she'll have to pay.

(*FANNY alone.*)

FANNY: Here I am, standing at the top, at the edge of this place, where the water falls over the long drop, and the sight of it turns the stomach, and lets loose a whirl in the mind. This far, so sad to come this far, and only one way now but down. I thought there would be more than this. . . . But I am not a cow! Louis, I am not a milk cow waiting in your shed! I am something. I am something more.

(*LLOYD enters at a distance.*)

LLOYD: Mother, stay where you are and don't move. I'm coming for you.

(*FANNY takes a small step forward.*)

FANNY: Oh, don't worry, Lloyd, I'll be right there.

(*The lights go to black as FANNY moves forward.*)

LLOYD: (*With lights*) No! Stop! Move back!

(*LOUIS and BELLE.*)

LOUIS: She's quiet for now. I'll go and get her powders.

BELLE: Lloyd went off for Dr. Mueller.

LOUIS: I think she only has cuts and bruises.

BELLE: He said she didn't fall very far.

LOUIS: If she hadn't landed on that ledge . . .

BELLE: I'll sit with her while you get her medicine.

(*BELLE moves to FANNY, who is lying down. FANNY perceives BELLE, but pretends not to notice.*)

BELLE: Mother? Mother, how are you feeling?

FANNY: Belle?

BELLE: Yes, I'm right here.

FANNY: I feel a chill. I'm cold.

BELLE: I'll get you a wrap.

(*BELLE exits. FANNY gets up and grabs the Bully Hayes knife, hiding it in the folds of her dress as she lies down. BELLE returns with a blanket.*)

BELLE: Here you are.

(*As BELLE nears her, FANNY quickly jumps up and grabs BELLE, and holds the knife to her neck. LOUIS enters.*)

LOUIS: (*Calmly*) Fanny, darling, what are you doing? Put the knife down.

FANNY: But Louis, she—

LOUIS: Come on, darling, put it down.

FANNY: But I caught her trying to steal. She's always wanted everything that's mine—my looks, my silver medal. She wanted Sam to herself. Now she wants you. Who knows what she'll try to take next?

LOUIS:	Please, Fanny, put the knife down.
FANNY:	She has to be stopped!
LOUIS:	Fanny, Austin was having a very bad dream. He's crying. He needs his mother. So put the knife down so she can go to him.
FANNY:	(*After a beat*) Oh, poor Austin. Is he all right?

(*FANNY lowers the knife, and BELLE breaks free. LOUIS moves to FANNY. He takes away the knife and holds her.*)

LOUIS:	(*To BELLE*) Are you hurt?

(*BELLE shakes her head. No.*)

BELLE:	I'm sorry, Mother.
FANNY:	Sorry for what, dear?
BELLE:	I'm sorry I'm so hateful to you.
FANNY:	Why are you saying that? Why would she say such a thing, Louis?
LOUIS:	It's all right, dear, she doesn't mean anything. Dr. Mueller is on his way up to see you.
BELLE:	I'll wait outside.

(*BELLE exits.*)

FANNY:	Is something wrong? Did I say something to upset her?
LOUIS:	No, nothing, my love. Come, come and lie down, you're tired.
FANNY:	I am, Louis. I'm so tired.

(*BELLE sits by herself. DR. MUELLER enters.*)

DR. MUELLER:

A penny for every thought.

BELLE: Dr. Mueller. How is my mother?

DR. MUELLER:

It's a beautiful night here.

BELLE: Yes, almost always.

DR. MUELLER:

    Nowhere but Sāmoa have I seen such stars.

BELLE: Nowhere.

DR. MUELLER:

    Are you alright? Louis told me about . . . the incident.

BELLE: I'm fine.

DR. MUELLER:

    Your mother is very sick.

BELLE: Is she going mad?

DR. MUELLER:

    All this tropical luxury. It is like a drama or a story your stepfather made up. The wife of a famous author succumbing to madness in the jungle.

BELLE: It's not such a great story if you're in it.

DR. MUELLER:

    The small things can become so magnified in your mother's mind.

BELLE: But is she . . .

DR. MUELLER:

    Mad? For now, yes, she exhibits signs of madness. If you ask me the cause, I don't know. But the tension, the strain of creating all of this out of nothing—only six months to build a house like this in the middle of the bush in Sāmoa. Not to mention the extensive gardens. Isn't it through her work that all of this came about? Enough to exhaust anyone's mind *and* body. On the other hand, it could be the symptoms of a change of life multiplied many times by the largeness of her inner world. If it is either one of these, the madness will pass.

BELLE: If not?

DR. MUELLER:

Also possible is a more serious matter, dementia praecox, true madness, in which case she will simply get worse.

BELLE: Tonight was frightening.

DR. MUELLER:

She is not herself, my dear. (*Pause*) May I ask, do you like it here?

BELLE: Like it here?

DR. MUELLER:

Yes, you see, frankly, I'm puzzled that two lively young people like yourself and your brother choose to live in this isolation. I would think Sydney or Honolulu would be more to your liking.

BELLE: I don't know why we're here. Maybe we're like moths.

DR. MUELLER:

Moths?

BELLE: Yes.

DR. MUELLER:

Ah, yes, I see, spellbound by the two bright flames.

(*Exit DR. MUELLER. BELLE moves into the Vailima Space, where FANNY stands.*)

FANNY: Did I seem like that to you?

BELLE: Like a flame?

FANNY: Like a bright flame gone mad.

BELLE: You were always more brilliant than I was.

FANNY: I can't thank you enough, Belle.

BELLE: You would have done the same for me.

FANNY: Don't imagine I think it a small thing. You helped me to recover.

BELLE: Mother—

FANNY: No, let me finish—and you and Lloyd were the greatest comfort to Louis. I'm grateful for your love and loyalty.

BELLE: Are you just saying all this to embarrass me?

FANNY: Why would I need to embarrass you?

(*LOUIS and LLOYD enter.*)

LOUIS: Fanny, we've invented a game!

LLOYD: It's called truth.

(*FANNY and BELLE join in.*)

FANNY: That sounds dangerous.

LOUIS: No, no. We write different traits on scraps of paper and put them in this jar.

LLOYD: Like, humor.

LOUIS: Or kindness.

LLOYD: Or neatness.

LOUIS: Then we score each other, truthfully, from one to ten.

FANNY: It *is* dangerous.

BELLE: It doesn't sound like a game.

LOUIS: We'll tell the truth, and find out how we see each other.

LLOYD: Just try it once before dinner.

FANNY: I can't believe I'm going along with this.

(*They all write something and put it in the jar. LLOYD picks one.*)

LLOYD: Beauty? Belle, this is your writing!

BELLE: (*To LLOYD*) We'll see how truthful you can be and still stay alive.

LOUIS: Now, you go first, Fanny.

FANNY: I give Belle an eight, Lloyd a seven—

LLOYD: Favoritism.

FANNY: She combs her hair, dear. And Louis, you get a six, until you take an interest in your appearance.

LOUIS: I have inner beauty, Fanny.

LLOYD: Well, I gave you all a seven.

BELLE: What?

LLOYD: You all look the same to me.

BELLE: I give Louis a six, slightly above average. And Lloyd six and a half on account of his youth. And mother, a seven.

LOUIS: Lloyd, old friend, seven. I've always envied your height. Belle an eight, and Fanny a ten.

FANNY: Louis! You're supposed to tell the truth.

BELLE: (*Laughing*) Yes. That's the name of the game, truth!

LOUIS: (*To BELLE, almost admonishing*) But I am telling the truth. Your mother is the most vivid, fascinating, and beautiful woman I have ever met. I thought you knew that.

(*BELLE looks at him and moves away to the Vailima Space.*)

BELLE: Monday, December 3, 1894, began as usual. Tea, breakfast, my mother busy distilling her perfumes. Lloyd was typing something, and Louis was dictating to me—*The Weir of Hermiston*—the novel he considered his masterpiece. At noon, we met for lunch.

(*They all gather at the table.*)

LOUIS: Go with each of us to rest
And when day returns
Call us up with morning hearts
Eager to labor

Eager to be happy if happiness be our portion
And if the day be marked for sorrow
Strong to endure it. Amen.

Fanny, you've got to cheer up.

LLOYD: Two days of brooding is enough.

FANNY: I told you. I just can't shake this feeling.

LOUIS: That doom and gloom and danger are about to befall us!

FANNY: Don't make fun of me. I don't *want* to feel like someone we love is in danger.

LOUIS: I just want to see you happy, love.

FANNY: Well, let me be a black cloud now, and later we can laugh about it.

(*BELLE moves back to the Vailima Space.*)

BELLE: We moved into the afternoon. Louis went to read, Fanny to her perfumes, Lloyd rode down to Apia, and returned late in the afternoon. I think he went for a swim in the stream.

(*LOUIS is whistling. He meets FANNY, who carries a bowl and some bottles to the table.*)

LOUIS: (*Kisses FANNY on the forehead*) You're happy.

FANNY: Let's make something special, Louis.

LOUIS: What's that?

FANNY: Our Vailima mayonnaise.

LOUIS: And how can a gentleman help?

FANNY: By finding a bottle of good Burgundy.

LOUIS: At your service.

(*FANNY happily pours and measures, humming to herself. LOUIS returns with the wine.*)

LOUIS: You know this is my favorite.

FANNY: It hasn't escaped me. Here, cut this lemon.

(*LOUIS holds up the lemon, places it down and cuts it in half with a clean slice. His hands shoot immediately to his head.*)

LOUIS: Fanny, do I look strange?

FANNY: Louis!

(*LOUIS walks unsteadily to lie down.*)

LOUIS: Oh my god, what a pain!

FANNY: Louis, what is it?

LOUIS: It's in my head!

FANNY: Lloyd! Belle! Hurry!

LLOYD: (*Running in*) What happened?

FANNY: I don't know!

LOUIS: My god! This pain.

(*LOUIS loses consciousness. FANNY shakes him, opens his shirt, and starts to rub his chest.*)

FANNY: Dr. Mueller. Get Mueller!

(*LLOYD runs out.*)

FANNY: Louis, come back! Please come back to us.

(*BELLE is in the Vailima Space, with a dim light still on FANNY.*)

BELLE: There isn't much to say. He left us so quickly. The center around whom we all had found an orbit. Our small band, our little tribe, our patchwork family was irreparably damaged. Our heart had been ripped away from us.

(*FANNY is on her knees, her head buried where LOUIS died. LOUIS has quietly risen and moves to one side.*)

LOUIS: (*As a spirit, to FANNY*)

Take thou the writing, thine it is

For who burnished the sword, blew on the
   drowsy coal
Held still the target higher, chary of praise
And prodigal of counsel—who but thou?
So now in the end, if this be the least good,
If any deed be done, if any fire
Burn in the imperfect page, the praise is thine.

(*LOUIS exits. BELLE is in the Vailima Space. FANNY joins her.*)

BELLE: The chiefs of many villages came and cut a pathway up to the top of Mt. Vaea just behind this house.

FANNY: It's such a distance, Belle.

BELLE: I know it is, Mother, but we have to.

FANNY: I tried so hard.

BELLE: Yes, you did, but our lives just take certain turns.

FANNY: Some dreams are so hard to let go of.

BELLE: We tried to hang on to Vailima by ourselves, but it became obvious that it was impossible, so we packed up and found ourselves back in our old city, San Francisco. My mother built a house at the corner of Hyde and Lombard. It was a big house with a rough exterior, like a fortress overlooking the Pacific. (*To FANNY*) I still don't see why we have to turn out all the lights.

(*FANNY is at a table with a Ouija board. BELLE goes to sit down as the lights dim.*)

FANNY: Atmosphere! We have to create an atmosphere.

BELLE: I don't think this is a good idea.

FANNY: But just think if we could talk to him. Now, put your hands like this.

(*BELLE puts her fingers on the board.*)

BELLE: (*Exasperated*) If I have to.

FANNY:	Try to relax and be positive, or it won't work.
BELLE:	I'm trying.
FANNY:	There, now what do you feel?

(*MEN and WOMEN as spirits move around the stage.*)

BELLE:	Well, I guess I feel something.
FANNY:	Now fingers lightly, only lightly touching.
BELLE:	(*Getting into it*) Lightly.
FANNY:	Now I'm going to ask. Are there any spirits present?
BELLE:	(*A beat*) It's moving. I feel it moving.
FANNY:	Remain calm. Now just be calm.
BELLE:	It's moving to yes.
FANNY:	Do you wish to speak to us?
BELLE:	N-o-w. Now, it spelled now.
FANNY:	Speak, you're welcome to speak.
BELLE:	It's moving again. I don't like this.
FANNY:	We're waiting to hear you.
BELLE:	It's scaring me.
FANNY:	H-e-a-r. Hear me. Yes, yes, we hear you.
BELLE:	(*Scared*) Something's wrong. Something in the air.
FANNY:	(*Watching the board intently*) C-o-l—you're cold. Out—outside. You're outside and it's cold.
BELLE:	Yes. It's way too cold in here.
FANNY:	M-a-m-a. Mama. Who is mama?
BELLE:	So cold. I can't let go.
FANNY:	Mama. Cold. Who is mama, child? Who are you?
BELLE:	Mother, please, I'm freezing, and I can't let go!
FANNY:	Who are you? Please tell us!
BELLE:	Her-Her-Herv—

FANNY: Is it you? My baby? Hervey, is it you?

BELLE: (*As if possessed*) Her-, Her-, Her-, Hervey. Stop. Hervey. Stop, stop it, Hervey. Stop! STOP! STOP!

(*BELLE jumps away. FANNY stays.*)

BELLE: I can't do this! I'm suffocating! I need my own life!

(*BELLE moves to the Vailima Space.*)

BELLE: But here, at Vailima, in this house, I wonder what my life is all about.

FANNY: What is it, my darling?

BELLE: Sometimes I wonder if what I really want—(*is everything back*)

FANNY: What? What do you want, child?

(*Lights to CLARA, a young office clerk.*)

CLARA: Belle! Belle!

(*BELLE moves into CLARA's space.*)

BELLE: Clara, don't shout in the reception room.

CLARA: (*As if looking out a window*) But look, he's coming.

BELLE: All of San Francisco will see you peeking out the window.

CLARA: But it's Ned Field!

BELLE: Come away from the window. It's rude.

CLARA: I can see why you like him.

BELLE: Oh?

CLARA: He's like the sun coming into a dark room.

BELLE: He's silly.

CLARA: Don't pretend you don't care. I've seen you flirt.

BELLE: Clara, he's my son's age.

CLARA: I bet you'd just like to marry Mr. Ned Field anyway.

BELLE: Be quiet, Clara! He's at the door.

(*NED FIELD enters. He is young, bright, and charming.*)

CLARA:	Good morning, Mr. Field.
NED:	Good morning, Clara. Ah, Mrs. Strong—
BELLE:	Belle.
NED:	Belle, back from—where this time?
BELLE:	Italy by way of London.
NED:	Find any priceless first editions?
BELLE:	Some.
NED:	Ah, the life of the avant-garde and antiquarian booksellers.
BELLE:	You're here to meet with the layout editor, aren't you?
NED:	Have you heard anything? Are they using my illustrations?
BELLE:	Sit down and read a magazine, Mr. Field.
NED:	A cruel teaser.
BELLE:	I think you'll be happy.
NED:	I was wrong, an angel.
BELLE:	Just go and sit down.

(*NED sits, and CLARA is looking out the window.*)

CLARA:	Belle, look, here she comes!
BELLE:	Clara, get away from the window!

(*FANNY enters. She pauses. NED looks up. FANNY smiles and nods. NED is riveted. He stands.*)

CLARA:	(*Going right to FANNY*) Mr. Doxey said you were to come right in, ma'am.
FANNY:	Thank you, Clara.

(*CLARA moves to escort FANNY.*)

FANNY:	Belle, dear, I'll see you after my meeting.

BELLE: I'll be here.

(*CLARA and FANNY exit.*)

NED: Good Lord, who was that? Belle, who *was* that?

BELLE: Mrs. Stevenson.

(*NED gives her a blank look.*)

BELLE: Dr. Jekyll? Mr. Hyde? R-L-S?

NED: His wife?

BELLE: Widow.

NED: (*Excited*) Why, I've had her card in my pocket for months. To think I've put off visiting her. She's an acquaintance of the family!

BELLE: Your family?

NED: From Indiana.

BELLE: I guess you'll be calling on her *now*.

NED: So, you *know* her?

BELLE: She's my mother.

NED: You're her daughter?

BELLE: Always, her daughter.

(*BELLE turns away, and NED moves to a space by himself.*)

NED: First, let me tell you that at twenty-three, I was neither a dreamer, an innocent, or a sponger. I was educated, independently wealthy, and had known the excesses of bohemian life. Furthermore, I had no presentiment, no intuition that as I slipped behind the curtain of trees concealing the stair-way to her house, I toyed with fate.

(*Light rises on FANNY.*)

FANNY: Come in, Mr. Field.

NED: Ned, please, call me Ned.

FANNY: Come in, Ned.

NED: What a magnificent view.

FANNY: I needed to have a view of the sea.

NED: It's amazing. It feels like . . .

FANNY: Like what?

NED: It feels as if I were looking at the Pacific for the very first time.

FANNY: I like to watch the sea.

NED: Yes, it's beautiful.

FANNY: In fact, my life, sometimes I think my life has been a wild ride on the crest of a wave that runs on and on, but never breaks.

(*NED moves to a space by himself.*)

NED: What I did not know was that after walking through Fanny's door, I would never leave her side, even for a single day, for the next eleven years—that every moment near her would always be intense and amusing.

(*NED looks over at FANNY and extends his hand. FANNY hesitates and looks away.*)

NED: Fanny.

FANNY: There's so much work to do, making sure Louis's work is properly handled.

NED: I can help you. You know the respect and regard I have for his work.

(*FANNY moves to NED and takes his hand. Silence, as they look at each other.*)

FANNY: Are you sure you want to do this?

NED: Of course!

(*Pause. NED kisses her forehead. A transition as FANNY laughs.*)

FANNY: Well, I'm just not sure if I want to *see* it.

NED: But she'll be so disappointed if you don't show up.

FANNY: All these women making such a fuss.

NED: It's an honor for her to be asked. Look! Here she comes.

(*BELLE enters with SUFFRAGETTE WOMEN. They escort BELLE to a lectern. They are waving signs and cheering.*)

BELLE: Sixty years ago, in 1848, the demands for the enfranchisement of women were formulated at Seneca Falls. What we demand now, we demanded then, for the same sensible reasons: that we are citizens of this country, full and free; that we are native born; that we are taxed as any citizen is taxed; that we are subject to and obey the laws of this land; that the burdens and responsibilities we have had in shaping this country are by no means small or lesser than those of men. And yet, still, we are deprived of one of the central rights of citizenship—the right to vote. Should California women still be denied this right? (*Loud cries of No! No! No!*) There are no logical arguments against the ballot for women—only some portentous fossils whose historic prejudice has reached mastodon proportions. Please tell all senators: VOTE YES FOR WOMEN!

(*SUFFRAGETTES cheer and congratulate BELLE as she steps down from the platform. BELLE moves to meet NED and FANNY.*)

NED: Belle, what a speech. You were marvelous! Charismatic!

BELLE: Thank you, Ned.

FANNY: Of course she was. She's my daughter.

BELLE: (*Kisses FANNY*) I'm glad you came, Mother.

(*They walk together.*)

FANNY:	Although you know how I feel, Belle. I can't understand you and your friends making such a commotion over voting.
BELLE:	What are we hearing, Ned?
NED:	I don't know.
BELLE:	You don't see why women should vote? Mother, you are the most independent and adventurous woman I know.
FANNY:	I may look that way on the outside, but on the inside I'm nothing but a clinging-vine sort of woman who longed to be taken care of. It just never worked out that way.
NED:	(*With a laugh*) Oh, Fanny, you don't expect us to believe that, do you?

(*NED moves off. FANNY and BELLE remain together.*)

BELLE:	How is Ned's new play?
FANNY:	Oh, it's lighthearted, some of it's quite funny.
BELLE:	I hear it's doing very well.
FANNY:	I'm sure he'd like it if he was paid more.
BELLE:	It's not as if he needs the money.
FANNY:	Even young men with family money have a longing to prove themselves.

(*BELLE and FANNY sit.*)

BELLE:	Do you love Ned, Mother?
FANNY:	Why are you asking? Is it because of the talk?
BELLE:	(*A laugh*) No. I'm just wondering.
FANNY:	You know, people still say, "What a comfort Louis's fame must be to you." But I'd give it all up in a second to have him back—poor and unknown.
BELLE:	But Ned.

FANNY:	I think he stays because he enjoys my company.
BELLE:	He's *devoted* to you.
FANNY:	I don't know why.
BELLE:	Well, do you have plans?
FANNY:	Time ahead looks like a long series of empty rooms. I have no . . . plans. What about you?
BELLE:	Me?
FANNY:	Over the years, you've had so many admirers.
BELLE:	No one I've really wanted.
FANNY:	(*As she walks to lie down*) I want you to be happy.

(*BELLE moves to the Vailima Space. FANNY will now be older.*)

BELLE:	My mother was always very pretty, but when she aged, she became truly beautiful. (*To FANNY*) That day, you never answered my question.
FANNY:	What, dear? What was it you were asking?
BELLE:	Ned. I was asking you if you loved Ned.
FANNY:	What does it matter now anyway?
BELLE:	You *know* why—(*I want to know*)
FANNY:	Forward, Belle, we can only go forward. I'm tired now.
BELLE:	I think you should—(*tell me how you felt about him*)
FANNY:	All this stuff and nonsense about love. I said I'm tired, Belle, so stop bothering me about it.

(*FANNY moves away, lies down, pulls a blanket over herself, and sleeps.*)

BELLE:	Part of her always stayed so young, we hardly noticed how old she'd become.

(*Enter NED.*)

NED:	Fanny! Great news! They want me to do a screenplay!

(*FANNY doesn't move.*)

NED: Fanny?

(*NED gently shakes her.*)

NED: Fanny? Fanny, wake up. Fanny! (*Pause*) Oh my god! Belle! Belle!

BELLE: (*Rushing in*) What?

NED: Belle, come quick. It's Fanny.

(*NED and BELLE both kneel on either side of FANNY.*)

BELLE: Mother? Mother, wake up. Wake up!

NED: Is she? Is she? Should I get the doctor?

BELLE: (*Feeling for a pulse*) Mother, please, Mother.

(*FANNY wakes up, very groggy and grumpy.*)

FANNY: Fuss, what's all this fussing over me. I told you I'm tired. Now leave me alone, and let me sleep. A person can't even take a nap around here without being fussed over.

(*NED looks over at BELLE, who is both shocked and relieved. He takes her hand. They stand over the sleeping FANNY and then move together downstage. NED puts his arm around the frightened BELLE.*)

BELLE: Oh, Ned, I thought she—I thought—

NED: It's all right. She's fine.

BELLE: I—I don't know what I would do. She's always been there.

NED: I'd be lost too.

BELLE: The things we've done and been through together.

NED: It's okay, she's still here. She's still here.

(*A beat. BELLE steps away from NED and looks at him.*)

BELLE: (*Quietly, seriously*) She's still here now, but she won't always be. Then what will we do?

(*BELLE moves alone to the Vailima Space.*)

BELLE: It happened a few weeks before her seventy-fourth birthday, in February of 1914. A winter storm bore down with relentless winds and sheets of rain. That afternoon, around a glowing fire, with a few friends, Ned read his new play. After dinner, they played cards until ten thirty. The next morning, Agnes, her maid, could not wake her. She died peacefully, feeling no pain. She was not sick and did not suffer. She died surrounded by love and devotion. Rain and wind continued for several days. Streams and rivers overflowing their banks. (*Pause*) In August, I married, and then, in the spring, my husband and I left San Francisco to fulfill my mother's final request. We brought her back, back to the crescent harbor of Apia, back to this house at Vailima, back to the hill where *he* lies waiting.

(*FANNY stays at the edge of BELLE's light, circling her.*)

FANNY: And, now, have you finally gotten what you've wanted all these years?

BELLE: That's not fair, Mother, you always had more.

FANNY: Like Psyche, stealing from the box.

BELLE: More beautiful, more talented, more everything.

FANNY: Dying for something just out of reach.

BELLE: Why shouldn't I have what I want? You're gone now.

FANNY: Is that what you've been waiting for?

BELLE: Go away now! You can't interfere anymore. You're dead!

FANNY: Am I?

BELLE: You're just a dark shadow!

FANNY: Whose dark shadow?

BELLE: Go away!

FANNY: You'll never get rid of this shadow!

BELLE: Get out! Get out of my life and leave me alone!

VOICE: (*Offstage*) Belle!

BELLE: (*Pulls herself together*) Yes?

VOICE: (*Offstage*) Belle, where are you?

BELLE: I'm in here.

(*FANNY fades back as NED FIELD enters in a robe.*)

NED: Belle, I thought I heard voices.

BELLE: It's just me, Ned, thinking out loud. You should go back to sleep.

NED: (*Going to her, kissing her*) I want to sleep with my wife. With you, Mrs. Ned Field.

BELLE: I'll be in soon.

(*NED turns to go, stops, takes something from his robe pocket, and turns back.*)

NED: You know, I'm not sure if this is the right time, but as I was packing, I found something, and I remembered Fanny always said that she wanted you to have it.

BELLE: What is it?

(*NED gives her FANNY's silver medal.*)

BELLE: Her silver medal.

(*Silence as BELLE turns over the medal in her hands.*)

NED: She used to say it was the first thing that made her realize that she was really herself—that she could step outside of everyone's *idea* of her, draw her own image, and be something new. I thought you might like to wear it tomorrow.

BELLE: Thank you, Ned. I will.

(*Exit NED. BELLE holds the silver medal. She puts it on. FANNY moves into the light, but BELLE speaks as if she can't see her.*)

FANNY:	I'm not so really dark as you imagine, my darling.
BELLE:	Mother, if I could just make you see why—
FANNY:	Out here, we *can* see clearly, so clearly—
BELLE:	If you could hear me, I'd want you to know—
FANNY:	How everything works in a circle.
BELLE:	He remembers, everything.
FANNY:	Like a coconut frond arching back on itself.
BELLE:	He's loved the same things I have.
FANNY:	Belle, my best companion.
BELLE:	He loves me because I'm part of you.
FANNY:	Tomorrow is another day.
BELLE:	And I love him because he's part of you, of us.
FANNY:	We'll have a great adventure you and I—
BELLE:	And I didn't want to lose everything.
FANNY:	One we'll always remember!
BELLE:	I couldn't let it all slip away.

CURTAIN

THE HOLIDAY OF RAIN

FOREWORD

The Holiday of Rain was commissioned by Kumu Kahua Theatre and was first produced by Kumu Kahua Theatre in Honolulu, Hawai'i, in March of 2011. The director was Harry Wong III, with Katherine Aumer as assistant director. In order of appearance, the cast included:

William Somerset Maugham	Tony Nickelsen
Gerald Haxton	Tyler Tanabe
Tinamoni/Mrs. Horn/Adonai	Kiana Rivera
Blake Von Elsner/Sefo	Shawn Anthony Thomsen
Effie Von Elsner/Sadie	Eleanor Svaton
Aleister Crowley/Rev. Davidson	Craig Howes
Charmian Drake/Mrs. McPhail	Lauren Ballesteros
Reed Edmond/Dr. McPhail	James Keawe Bright
Theo Von Elsner/Mrs. Davidson	Danielle Zalopany

THE CAST OF CHARACTERS (WITH ETHNICITY, AGE, AND DOUBLE CAST ROLES/ETHNICITY FOR PLAY WITHIN PLAY)

William Somerset Maugham: British, 40s
Gerald Haxton: American, 20s
Tinamoni/Mrs. Horn: Polynesian, 30s–40s
Blake Von Elsner/Sefo: 'afakasi, looks Sāmoan, 30s–40s
Effie Von Elsner/Sadie: American, 30s

Aleister Crowley/Rev. Davidson: British/American, 40s

Charmian Drake/Mrs. McPhail: 'afakasi, looks pālagi, American/British, 30s

Reed Edmond/Dr. McPhail: 20s–30s, 'afakasi, looks pālagi, Scottish

Theodora Von Elsner/Mrs. Davidson: 'afakasi, looks pālagi, American

THE SET

There are three *Playing Areas*: 1) the *Sitting Room* of a classy inn called the Sadie Thompson Bed and Breakfast in Pago Pago, American Sāmoa. In the rear center of the *Sitting Room* is a door that leads outside. There are also hall exits to the right and left. 2) *Downstage Left* (*DL*) and 3) *Downstage Right* (*DR*). These two *Playing Areas* change uses.

THE TIME

The time is 1916, briefly, and the present.

THE PLACE

The place is Pago Pago, American Sāmoa.

Act I

(*The sound of heavy rain. In the DL Playing Area, ALEISTER CROWLEY stands over a small smoking cauldron. He has a beard and wears a hooded robe. He is mumbling a magical spell in a strange language. In the DR Playing Area, SOMERSET MAUGHAM stands with an umbrella and two suitcases. He is crouching, obviously nervous about the weather. Enter GERALD HAXTON. He ducks under the umbrella.*)

MAUGHAM: There you are at last. This is the worst rain I've ever seen.

GERALD: And this thick soupy cloud. I had trouble finding you.

MAUGHAM: It's him. I know it.

GERALD: Willy, this is 1916, not the Dark Ages!

MAUGHAM: He's after me.

GERALD: Just stop! Aleister Crowley is not after you.

(*CROWLEY throws something in the cauldron. It flares, and there is lightning and the sound of thunder. CROWLEY, MAUGHAM, and GERALD react.*)

MAUGHAM: The tram accident in San Francisco? The ceiling fan crashing on our dinner table in Honolulu? And this morning, centipedes in my shoe!

GERALD: You need a rest.

MAUGHAM: He's after me for writing that book.

GERALD: Start working. It always makes you feel better. Where *is* the help they promised us?

MAUGHAM: A week to make sure no one has measles on the ship. I don't want to stay here a week, damn it!

GERALD: You'll feel better when we get to the inn.

MAUGHAM: (*Worked up*) This is Pago Pago, for God's sake! What kind of an inn do you think they'll have? And we'll be stuck with those dreadful people.

GERALD: How would you know they're dreadful? We hardly saw any of them. We spent almost the whole time in the cabin, remember?

MAUGHAM: I didn't want them bothering me.

GERALD: Not *everyone* is a fan of William Somerset Maugham.

MAUGHAM: You needn't be hurtful, Gerald.

GERALD: You're so negative about people.

MAUGHAM: Some missionaries and a tart.

GERALD: I never said tart.

MAUGHAM: A tart, that's what you said.

GERALD: You know, I don't think anyone is coming for us.

MAUGHAM: This year has been so confusing.

GERALD: That's what you get for sleeping with *women*.

MAUGHAM: My life is a muddle.

GERALD: Well, it's almost over.

MAUGHAM: What?!

GERALD: The *year*. I meant the *year*.

(*CROWLEY looks into the cauldron and chuckles. Lights go to half in the DL Playing Area and rise on the Sitting Room. TINAMONI goes downstage to pour a cup of tea. CROWLEY throws something again into the cauldron, making bigger lightning and thunder. This time he is knocked a little from the cauldron. MAUGHAM and GERALD cringe again. TINA also reacts.)*

GERALD: It's getting worse.

(Enter BLAKE VON ELSNER, carrying part of a sign that says "Sadie Thompson.")

BLAKE: Well, Tina, I guess we can put this back up next to the "Bed and Breakfast" on our sign.

TINA: Not in this weather.

BLAKE: Jerry left just in time. They've closed the roads outside of town.

TINA: I'm worried, Blake. This sudden storm is so strange.

BLAKE: Did the couple say why they canceled?

TINA: No, I just got an email from the agency.

BLAKE: And the *Superior Inns of the Pacific* reviewer?

TINA: Coming next week, thank God! He could really put us on the map. (*Looks under the table*) Oh-oh, I forgot to put away my Martha Stewart magazines. Well, it doesn't matter now.

BLAKE: Our no-refund, pay-in-advance rule for fantasy visits was a brilliant move.

TINA: They're so much work—hiding the electrical outlets and the overhead lights, hours of research. It's so different from our mystery packages.

BLAKE: It's kind of a letdown not to do this one. I mean, this is the real building where they all stayed: Sadie Thompson, Somerset Maugham. I wonder what they were really like.

TINA: I'm not sure if it was a good idea to give Theo that part. I think she's taking a turn for the worse.

BLAKE: It was a great idea. It's the only thing that's inter-
          ested her since . . . since she came home.

TINA: Now, what happened to Charmian and your dear
          aunt Effie?

BLAKE: They went to the Island Moon Bar with John Hall.

TINA: Hmm, John better be careful.

BLAKE: Effie's turned into the merry widow—drinking and
          flirting are her favorite pastimes.

TINA: She was so young when she married your uncle
          Nordhoff.

BLAKE: And he was way too old for a Barbie doll.

TINA: But he wasn't too old to be chronically unfaithful,
          was he?

BLAKE: (*Gives her an affectionate kiss*) Something I prom-
          ise I will never be. (*Short pause*) I think you would
          have made a great Mrs. Horn, Tina. Did you ever
          find out who these people were?

TINA: The agency just said they were a rich gay couple who
          were dying to pretend they were Somerset Maugham
          and Gerald Haxton. I wrote a scenario based on
          Maugham's short story "Rain," and they accepted.

(*Lights fade on the Sitting Room. CROWLEY again invokes
lightning and louder thunder. He is knocked to the ground by
the blast. MAUGHAM, GERALD, TINA, and BLAKE are all
startled. MAUGHAM goes into a panic.*)

MAUGHAM: Gerald! Gerald! I feel so odd!

GERALD: Come on now, don't get all worked up. We've got to
          help ourselves.

MAUGHAM: My chest! My lungs! I feel I'm suffocating!

GERALD: We're about to be washed away here!

MAUGHAM: He's trying to kill me!

GERALD: (*Yelling*) For God's sake! There is no such thing as black magic!

(*CROWLEY invokes a deafening blast of thunder and lightning. He is knocked unconscious. Lights flash on MAUGHAM and GERALD and on TINA and BLAKE. All four scream. MAUGHAM and GERALD are knocked off their feet. TINA and BLAKE grab on to each other as the lights go black. Then lights slowly rise on the Sitting Room.*)

BLAKE: Oh my God.

TINA: Are you okay?

BLAKE: Yeah, you?

TINA: Yeah.

BLAKE: I thought we were hit by lightning.

TINA: I think it was right outside. (*Runs to the window and looks out, gasps*) Blake, Blake, look, look at those two men!

BLAKE: Look at those clothes.

TINA: The steamer trunks.

TINA AND BLAKE:
 Oh shit!

TINA: It said they canceled.

BLAKE: Three of our role players are gone and the road's closed.

TINA: How could they have gotten here in this storm?

BLAKE: What shall we do?!

(*Lights on MAUGHAM and GERALD.*)

GERALD: (*Helping MAUGHAM*) Okay, you're okay. Take a deep breath. That's it.

MAUGHAM: This is worse than the war!

GERALD: Willy, it's all right. Just breathe. Don't panic.

(*Lights to TINA and BLAKE.*)

TINA: Okay, okay, don't panic, one thing at a time, take away the dirty cups.

BLAKE: Dirty cups.

TINA: Oh, the sign. Get the sign out of here.

BLAKE: (*Takes the sign and starts to exit*) The sign.

TINA: (*Calling after him*) Warn Theo and get the others at the bar! (*Running for the coffee table*) Martha, get rid of Martha Stewart.

(*Lights flicker out in Sitting Room. TINA jumps.*)

TINA: That's right! The kerosene lamps. Thank you, universe.

(*Lights to DL while TINA lights several kerosene lamps, and the Sitting Room takes on a soft and romantic look.*)

MAUGHAM: Oh, look at my suit! What a mess.

GERALD: Why, look, Willy, there's the inn. It's been right there all this time.

MAUGHAM: The . . . Bed and Breakfast? That's an odd name.

GERALD: Who cares what it's called, for Christ's sake. Let's get out of this storm.

SCENE 2

(*DL in the Playing Area. A dim light. ALEISTER CROWLEY lies sprawled out. Enter EFFIE, slightly tipsy. She falls over CROWLEY and they become entangled. Lights rise as they straighten up.*)

EFFIE: (*Confused*) What the hell? Cool raincoat, dude.

CROWLEY: (*Groggy*) What happened?

EFFIE: Oh shit, now I'm muddy *and* drunk.

CROWLEY: My God! I must have transported with them.

EFFIE: Maybe you've been drinking too.

CROWLEY: Ow! I think I hit my head.

EFFIE: (*Waves her hand over his eyes*) Do you know what day it is? I do!

CROWLEY: Remind me.

EFFIE: Tuesday, March 3, 2023. (*Substitute the reading or performance date*)

CROWLEY: Incredible.

EFFIE: What are you doing out in this weather anyway?

CROWLEY: I could ask you the same question.

EFFIE: I'm looking for a husband.

CROWLEY: (*Laughs*) Good Lord! Ouch, my head.

EFFIE: Not a real husband, silly. I've had one of those. Better let me see your head. I'm looking for a pretend husband for Theo, for their Somerset Maugham thing.

CROWLEY: What are you talking about?

EFFIE: I had one, but I kicked him in the nuts back at the bar, and now he refuses to do it. (*Looks at his head*) Hmm, nasty cut.

CROWLEY: What Somerset Maugham thing?

EFFIE: (*Ignoring his question, looking at his injury*) I guess I didn't have to kick him *there*. But he shouldn't have pawed at me.

(*EFFIE touches his wound.*)

CROWLEY: That hurts!

EFFIE: Oh, don't be such a baby. I meant to say the Maugham *and* Haxton thing—mustn't forget Gerald Haxton. It's at the B&B.

CROWLEY: B&B?

EFFIE: They weren't supposed to, but they showed up anyway.

CROWLEY: I wasn't supposed to either. (*Looking at her*) But I'm glad I did.

EFFIE: Okay, mister, don't try any tricks. I know who you are.

CROWLEY: (*Proudly*) Oh, so you recognize me?

EFFIE: You're the reviewer from the *Superior Inns of the Pacific*. That must be a cushy job, travel writing.

CROWLEY: (*Deflated*) You think I'm a travel writer?

EFFIE: Trying to sneak in undercover, aren't you?

CROWLEY: (*Pause*) Do you think I could?

EFFIE: (*Calculating*) So you want to get in there with no one recognizing you?

CROWLEY: Especially if *you're* going there too.

EFFIE: (*Talks to herself*) Why did I have to kick him? (*To him*) Okay, okay, what's your name anyway?

CROWLEY: Um, Crow, my name is Peter Crow.

EFFIE: Effie Von Elsner. Listen, can you act?

CROWLEY: I love the theatrical.

EFFIE: If I do this, would you try to write something nice about the inn—well, at least promise not to write anything bad?

CROWLEY: Darling, if I get to be part of the "Maugham thing," I'll write whatever you want.

EFFIE: We'll have to change your appearance a little bit. The beard has to go.

CROWLEY: Who exactly will I be portraying?

EFFIE: Do you know anything about missionaries?

CROWLEY: It just happens I was raised by narrow-minded religious fanatics.

EFFIE: Perfect!

(*Set note: From this point on, the DR becomes the Guest Room and DL is the Veranda. In the Guest Room are two comfortable chairs with ottomans and two small tables: one with paper and pens and one with a typewriter. On the Veranda is a pune'e [platform daybed], two rattan chairs, and an old coffee table.*)

SCENE 3

(*Sitting Room.*)

GERALD: Mr. Maugham is settled and resting. Thank you for being so patient with him, Mrs. Horn.

TINA: My name is Tinamoni, but please call me Tina. I hope your room is alright.

GERALD: Oh! The room! This inn! He just couldn't—I just couldn't believe it. What luck! We never expected to be this comfortable in Pago Pago.

TINA: I'm sorry you won't meet Mr. Horn. He's gone to Swains Island.

GERALD: Business?

TINA: Ah, yes, copra interests.

(*Offstage giggling.*)

GERALD: Who's that?

TINA: Oh, just the girls. They help with the cleaning.

GERALD: Well, I think I better check on Will—Mr. Maugham.

TINA: You're a very loyal friend.

GERALD: I'm actually his secretary. He's a famous writer, you know.

(*More giggling.*)

TINA: Of course, dear. Now tea is in a couple of hours. That's when things will begin—when you'll meet the other guests, I mean.

GERALD: Just enough time for a good rest.

TINA: I'll knock on your door when everything is ready.

GERALD: Well, thanks, you've been very kind.

(*GERALD exits. EFFIE calls from offstage.*)

EFFIE: Is he gone?

TINA: Yes, Effie.

(*Enter EFFIE and CHARMIAN DRAKE.*)

TINA: Giggling in the hall does not help, ladies.

CHARMIAN: Sorry, Tina.

TINA: Well, thank you for doing this, Charmian. You've only been here a day and we're asking you for favors.

CHARMIAN: You know I'd do anything for you and never feel like I'd repaid you.

TINA: I know you had other plans for your sabbatical. And I'm sure if "Rain" isn't on the Pacific Island literature blacklist at your university, it deserves to be.

(*EFFIE starts searching for something.*)

CHARMIAN: Ah, Maugham! One of the crowned pricks of the colonial canon—but like I said, for you, I'd take a bullet.

EFFIE: I think it'll be fun.

CHARMIAN: Effie picked up a man on the way home from the bar to play the reverend.

TINA: What?!

EFFIE: Where's the chocolates?

TINA:	Never mind the chocolates. Who is this guy?
EFFIE:	Crow. Peter Crow, and the costumes fit him perfectly.
TINA:	What happened to John Hall?
EFFIE:	He's injured.
CHARMIAN:	He made the moves on her, and she kicked him in—
EFFIE:	It's my new all-purpose solution to unwanted male behavior. You just take really good aim and—
TINA:	Don't tell me any more!
EFFIE:	(*Finding the chocolates and helping herself*) Don't worry, this guy will work out. Especially when he sees how wonderful this place is.
TINA:	And where is Mr. Crow right now?
EFFIE:	Studying his part and shaving.

(*Enter BLAKE in a burst.*)

BLAKE:	We made it back just in time. We're totally blocked. The stream is overflowing on one side and there's a landslide on the other.
TINA:	Oh, no!
BLAKE:	I found a doctor, thank God.
CHARMIAN:	Is someone sick?
BLAKE:	For "Rain." I found a Dr. McPhail. And you'll never guess, it's Reed Edmond!
TINA:	Reed? I thought he was in the States.
BLAKE:	He travels back and forth to Apia. He was on his way over here looking for a place to hole up for the night since all the flights to Upolu are canceled.
TINA:	Did you tell Theo?
CHARMIAN:	How come I haven't seen Theo yet, our brilliant artiste?
EFFIE:	She likes to be alone.

TINA: Internal injuries—of the heart.

EFFIE: As in, broken.

CHARMIAN: I heard about the accident.

EFFIE: She was driving home from the gallery.

CHARMIAN: Wasn't her professor in the car or something?

EFFIE: Dead.

TINA: And she blames herself for everything.

CHARMIAN: I understand they were very close.

EFFIE: Having an affair.

BLAKE: Effie!

EFFIE: Face it, Blake. Your little sister was sleeping with a married jerk.

BLAKE: It was finished!

TINA: Okay, stop this now.

EFFIE: Yeah, don't talk to your aunt in that tone of voice.

BLAKE: You're five years *younger* than me, Auntie F.!

CHARMIAN: (*Laughing*) This *is* going to be fun.

TINA: 'Aua le pisa (*Be quiet*)! We don't have time for this! You two go get dressed for the meeting before tea.

(*TINA ushers EFFIE and CHARMIAN out and turns to BLAKE.*)

TINA: Listen, something's wrong.

BLAKE: You're telling me.

TINA: No, I mean *really* wrong.

SCENE 4

(*MAUGHAM sits in the Guest Room in one of the chairs, writing in his notebook.*)

MAUGHAM: Gerald is right of course. Beginning something new, even if it's just sketching things out, is always like a tonic for me. I'm thinking of setting it right here in Pago Pago. Everyone's fascinated by exotic locations that they would never dare visit, places that take them away from the humdrum, places that feel a little dangerous. I could set it in a boarding house like this one: wood framed, veranda on both floors. But no one would ever believe it could be this nice or this clean, and that's not what the public wants in a Pacific scenario. People want grit, flies, and heat. Yes, that's it, a rumpled bed, a ragged mosquito net, a rickety washstand, and rain, endless rain.

SCENE 5

(*THEODORA [THEO] VON ELSNER is on the Veranda in her "Rain" costume.*)

THEO: I had broken it off with him the week before. I didn't even want him in the car that day. There were dozens of people who could've given him a ride. But no, he was on a mission. He sat there next to me as we glided through traffic, launching an arsenal of nasty words, aiming them straight for my heart. I received them as we sat at the stoplight. I received them with the sound of the truck roaring in behind me. I received them in a vision in the rearview mirror. First, the cartoon grin of the metal grill, then the impact of the hit, and flying like stars, we exploded into the intersection. The intersection, the crossroad, the point in time. The point from which I returned in fragments and pieces, the point where he veered off, went in another direction, and vanished, completely.

(*TINA calls from outside the light.*)

TINA:	Theodora?
THEO:	Yes.
TINA:	(*Short pause*) Are you sure you're up to this?
THEO:	Yes.
TINA:	Darling, I know things seem dark to you. But it's like crossing on a very narrow plank over a deep chasm. It's risky and frightening, but you *will* come to the other side.
THEO:	(*Turns away*) I don't know what you're talking about.
TINA:	I think you do.
THEO:	I like being a missionary woman.
TINA:	At the eleventh hour, Blake's found someone to be the doctor.
THEO:	Who?
TINA:	Reed Edmond.
THEO:	Oh.
TINA:	Will it be okay?
THEO:	He's from another lifetime.
TINA:	I don't want you to feel uncomfortable.
THEO:	I won't feel anything.

(*TINA goes to hug her as the lights fade.*)

SCENE 6

(*EFFIE, REED EDMOND, BLAKE, CROWLEY, and CHARM-IAN are gathered in the Sitting Room talking to each other. They are all in their "Rain" costumes. BLAKE wears a lavalava as the "native" helper. TINA and THEO are looking in from the*

*Veranda and about to enter the Sitting Room as the lights rise.
TINA takes a step forward when CROWLEY looks up at her.
TINA gasps and is visibly shaken. CROWLEY is also shocked at
first, then grins to himself and turns to talk to someone. Only
BLAKE sees this exchange.)*

THEO: *(Immediately struck by CROWLEY)* Who is that
               man?

TINA: What? What did you say?

THEO: I said, who is he?

(TINA and THEO enter the Sitting Room.)

TINA: *(Ignoring THEO's question)* Has everyone met
               each other?

BLAKE: *(Suspicious)* But *you* haven't met Peter yet, have
               you?

TINA: Ah, yes, Mr. Crow, is it? I'm Tina. How can we
               thank you for rescuing us? Effie tells us you've had
               some acting experience.

CROWLEY: I have.

TINA: And, Reed, thank you so much.

REED: Anything for you, Tina.

CHARMIAN: What if they walk in?

BLAKE: I have their door rigged. Every time it opens, out
               here you'll hear a sound like a clock chime. Of
               course, *they* won't hear it.

TINA: So, whenever you hear that sound, be prepared to
               be in 1916, and from now on, stay in the period
               clothes we've given you. I think everyone has at
               least one change. Peter, Charmian, and Reed, did
               you have time to read the short story and go over
               the scenario?

REED:	(*With a Scottish accent*) I've read it so many times before, lass, I could recite it to you.
TINA:	Reed, that's amazing.
REED:	All my life, I've been listening to Charlie MacDonald, my father's best friend.
CHARMIAN:	I'll have to work to put aside Maugham's condescension, his racism, and his misogyny, but other than that, I'll do my best.
TINA:	Thank you, Charmian. Peter?
CROWLEY:	I have a photographic memory. It's an interesting tale. I wonder if it's plagiarized, like some of Maugham's other work.
TINA:	Don't worry about knowing the lines word for word. The main thing is to remember who you are, the general ideas that we have to get across, and how we're moving the action forward. And if they ask questions, try to deal with it as best you can. Just take it one moment at a time. Questions? Okay, so an hour until teatime. And break a leg, everyone.

(*All exit but BLAKE and TINA.*)

BLAKE:	Something weird *is* going on here.
TINA:	Yes, and it's going to get worse.
BLAKE:	This doesn't sound good. Do you know Peter Crow from somewhere else?
TINA:	What makes you ask that?
BLAKE:	A hunch.
TINA:	(*Ignoring the question*) Look, I'm sorry, darling. I'm going to have to ask you to go out in the rain one more time.

SCENE 7

(*REED approaches THEO on the Veranda.*)

REED: Will you say hello, Theo?

THEO: If you like.

REED: It's been a while.

THEO: Over six years.

REED: I've heard you've had some rough times.

THEO: You might know.

REED: Well, I hope things are better.

THEO: Yeah.

REED: I happened to be in San Francisco, and I saw your *Outrageous Fortune* show.

THEO: You did?

REED: I thought it was brilliant.

THEO: Why?

REED: Other than your perfect composition? I'd say the things I found most compelling were the poetic and understated ways you communicated a sense of urgency and pain while at the same time holding the eye with your superb use of color and motion.

THEO: Oh.

REED: And I liked the repeated images of the sega birds.

THEO: I'm glad someone recognized them.

REED: I'm surprised you're giving me the time of day.

THEO: That was ages ago.

REED: Was it?

THEO: Does it matter?

SCENE 8

(*The sound of a chime. We hear TINA's voice in the dark.*)

TINA: Okay, get ready.

(*Lights rise on the Sitting Area. There is a fancy setup for after-noon tea. Present are THEO, REED, CHARMIAN, and TINA. They are chatting amongst themselves as GERALD and MAUGHAM enter.*)

TINA: Ah, Mr. Maugham and Mr. Haxton, did you have a pleasant rest?

GERALD: Yes, thanks.

TINA: Let me introduce you to your fellow lodgers. Dr. and Mrs. McPhail, this is Mr. Somerset Maugham and Mr. Gerald Haxton.

REED: I believe I saw you on the ship. Pleased to meet you.

CHARMIAN: Yes, so pleased.

TINA: And this is Mrs. Davidson. Her husband, Reverend Davidson, will be with us shortly.

THEO: How do you do?

TINA: Let me get you some tea. Cream and sugar?

GERALD AND MAUGHAM:

                Please.

THEO: I suppose you're waiting for the boat to Apia too?

GERALD: Yes, we are.

MAUGHAM: You're a medical man, Dr. McPhail?

REED: That's right. My wife and I will settle in Apia for twelve months or so.

CHARMIAN: My husband needs a rest. He was wounded in the front.

GERALD: We were at the front. Flanders.

REED: I could never get used to the sound of shells hur-
               tling over the trenches as I operated.

MAUGHAM: Deplorable conditions. I need a rest myself.

CHARMIAN: (*To THEO*) You and Reverend Davidson must be
               anxious to get home.

THEO: Oh yes, we left things in the hands of native mis-
               sionaries. They are very devout, but—

CHARMIAN: But?

THEO: They give in so easily to pressure.

GERALD: Are your islands like these?

THEO: Oh no, ours are low islands, not volcanic like this
               one. We're thankful not to be stationed on an
               island like this.

MAUGHAM: And why is that, may I ask?

THEO: Too many steamers touch here—that makes the
               natives unsettled—and then there's the naval sta-
               tion, that's bad for the natives too. We've had
               enough trouble as it is eradicating native dancing
               and getting the people to dress decently.

REED: (*To THEO*) I used to like dancing when I was
               young. Didn't you?

THEO: Native dancing is indecent and leads to immorality.

CHARMIAN: How do they dress, your islanders?

THEO: The women wear Mother Hubbards, and the men
               wear pants. Reverend Davidson always said that—

(*Enter CROWLEY as DAVIDSON.*)

MAUGHAM: (*Scared, frozen*) It's him!

GERALD: Oh my God! Aleister Crowley!

CROWLEY: Please! Don't mention that name in my presence!
               To my everlasting embarrassment, I do resemble
               the despicable person you speak of.

THEO: (*Thinking fast*) Oh yes, my husband is often mistaken for . . . for . . .

CROWLEY: You see, my delicate wife cannot even bring herself to mention the name of the beast.

TINA: Are you all right, Mr. Maugham?

MAUGHAM: (*To GERALD*) It's, it's not him?

GERALD: No, no it's not. It just *looks* like him.

TINA: I can assure you this is the Reverend Alfred Davidson.

MAUGHAM: My lord. If you had a beard—I beg your pardon, but the resemblance is uncanny.

CROWLEY: Unfortunately, unfortunately.

TINA: Won't you have some tea, Reverend? More tea, Mr. Maugham?

MAUGHAM: (*Composing himself*) Yes, thank you. Haven't seen such a lovely tea since I left London.

GERALD: Your wife was just telling us about your work. About making your flock wear pants.

CROWLEY: Ah, yes, it's my belief that Christianity would never take hold unless we got rid of the lavalava. How can you expect people to be moral when their only garb is a thin strip of cotton cloth?

(*A sharp knock on the door. Enter EFFIE as SADIE THOMPSON. She is dressed in a very flashy way.*)

EFFIE: I'm looking for Mrs. Horn.

TINA: Can I help you?

EFFIE: The quartermaster sent me. He said yah'd have a room for me.

TINA: Well . . .

EFFIE: Do yah or don't yah? I ain't got all day here.

TINA: There is one room left. Downstairs off a storage area.

EFFIE: I don't need much.

TINA: It's a dollar fifty a day.

EFFIE: I can only pay a dollar.

TINA: I would have to think about it.

EFFIE: Don't pull that stuff with me. I'll pay a dollar a day and not one bean more. No one else is coming in all this rain!

TINA: Well, all right.

EFFIE: That's the goods.

TINA: Sefo will show you where it is.

EFFIE: Listen, I got some swell hooch in my bag. I'd be glad to give you a shot. And anyone else is welcome too.

TINA: Sefo—

(*Enter BLAKE in a lavalava.*)

TINA: Sefo, take Miss—

EFFIE: Thompson. Sadie Thompson.

TINA: Take Miss Thompson to the downstairs room.

(*Exit BLAKE and EFFIE.*)

THEO: Wasn't that the woman on the ship?

CHARMIAN: She looks rather fast to me.

MAUGHAM: Cheap is how I would describe her.

THEO: I hope we won't have to eat our meals with her.

TINA: I'll arrange for her to eat on her own.

REED: The founder of Christianity wasn't so exclusive.

CHARMIAN: Alec!

REED: It was a jest, dear.

MAUGHAM: That is an interesting philosophy, Reverend Davidson, to instill moral behavior by changing a person's garb.

THEO: Oh, but we changed much more than that.

CROWLEY: Yes, you see, when we first arrived, these people had no sense of sin. They constantly broke the commandments without even knowing it. So, we had to make a sin out of their most commonplace activities. Not just adultery and thievery, no. I made it a sin for a woman to show her bosom in public, for a man not to wear trousers.

GERALD: But how did you get them to obey?

CROWLEY: Fines. We fined them if they did not obey.

MAUGHAM: And if they refused to pay?

CROWLEY: (*Hedging, looks around*) Well, ah, if they refused to pay, such an interesting question.

THEO: (*Saving him*) If they refused to pay, we expelled them from the church. And if we expel someone from the church, no one will purchase their copra, or anything else they might produce. People shun them. They get excluded from normal village life.

MAUGHAM: How very efficient.

THEO: We are doing the work of the Lord!

CROWLEY: Yes, we are doing the work of the Lord, sir! When I see the need to act, I act promptly. If the tree is rotten, it should be cut down and cast into flames.

MAUGHAM: I see, yes, well, this has been most pleasant. But we have some work to do so—if you will excuse us.

SCENE 9

(*GERALD and MAUGHAM walk to the Guest Room.*)

MAUGHAM: Oh, this is perfect. It couldn't be better if I'd arranged it myself. Missionaries right out of a book. A cheap prostitute. A ramshackle inn in Pago Pago.

GERALD: This place is hardly ramshackle.

MAUGHAM: Of course, no one would believe a missionary wife could be young and pretty.

GERALD: Why not?

MAUGHAM: I'll make her older, give her a sheepy face, and an irritating voice.

GERALD: Well, I did notice one odd thing about her.

MAUGHAM: What's that?

GERALD: She's quite tan. She looks as if she could be part native herself. And so do those other two—the doctor and his wife.

MAUGHAM: She's been out in the sun for years. They've all been out in the sun on deck. Honestly, Gerald, I don't know where you get these ideas.

GERALD: Mrs. Horn is lovely, don't you think?

MAUGHAM: Very nice woman, but she'll have to go. Too intelligent, too refined to be a native wife. She's probably horribly unstable, and we just haven't seen it yet.

GERALD: I don't know where *you* get these ideas.

MAUGHAM: Native women, mixed-blood women, just aren't like her!

GERALD: I think you're envious.

MAUGHAM: Well, well, I didn't know women appealed to you, Gerald, dear.

GERALD: (*Irritated*) You're the one who's gotten a woman pregnant and had a child. You're the one who's going to get married. So, I guess I can be attracted to a woman if I want to.

MAUGHAM: Please, I'd like to get to work.

GERALD: Fine.

MAUGHAM: I've already written something of an introduction for you to type. And what time is supper?

GERALD: I think she said eight.

MAUGHAM: Well, I don't want to miss a minute with those people. "We had to make a sin of their most commonplace activities. If a tree is rotten, it should be cut down and cast into flames." It's perfect.

SCENE 10

(*In the Sitting Room, TINA is setting up for the next "Rain" scene. CROWLEY enters.*)

CROWLEY: Adonai.

TINA: I have a different name now, Aleister.

CROWLEY: It *is* you. *And,* you're a woman.

TINA: Yes, and I like it better, thank you. What are you doing here?

CROWLEY: You're just as beautiful, my darling.

TINA: I am not your darling.

CROWLEY: I couldn't believe it when you left.

TINA: You made it impossible for me to stay.

CROWLEY: I was young and foolish.

TINA: You weren't ready.

CROWLEY: If I wasn't ready, why did you come to me?

TINA: You were able to perform the Abra-melin ritual, so I had to appear. But still, you were a mistake, a miscalculation.

CROWLEY: Huh! I thought *you* were the miscalculation.

TINA: What?

CROWLEY: Face it, my dear, you aren't very angelic . . .

TINA: I told you, I'm a working-class daemon, no wings, no choir, no bullshit.

CROWLEY: It was cruel of you to leave me like that.

TINA: After you tried to trap me? Misuse me? Turn our lives into *The Tempest?* I didn't leave you. I escaped.

CROWLEY: I wouldn't do it again, Adonai, I swear.

TINA: Because you won't have another opportunity. Now, how the hell did you get here?

CROWLEY: Where exactly is Pago Pago anyway?

TINA: (*Realizing*) You didn't plan to come here, did you? This is a mistake.

CROWLEY: I don't know what you mean.

TINA: What was it? Revenge?

CROWLEY: Why do you say that?

TINA: Female intuition.

CROWLEY: I was bored. Maugham was always such a snot with his ascot and his affected manners. I wasn't really sure what would happen. I was just experimenting.

TINA: *You* brought them here. That's the real Somerset Maugham and Gerald Haxton!

CROWLEY: Who did you think they were?

TINA: Never mind who I thought they were! I'll explain later. Listen, you need to do what I tell you.

CROWLEY: You can't tell me what to do.

TINA: You go and try the most elementary spell. It won't work here for you. So, you bloody well better do what I tell you, because you're powerless.

CROWLEY: (*With a smile*) You've underestimated me before, haven't you, Adonai?

(*CROWLEY exits, TINA sighs, shakes her head, and addresses the audience.*)

TINA: Yes, you heard right. And I know what you're thinking, that I'm nothing like I'm supposed to be—it's all that medieval church imagery that's stuck in your mind. Here's how it is. We're sent to live among you, assigned according to our strengths and weaknesses. You see, we're learning too. We don't just flutter in and make everything rosy. We serve by example and encouragement, nudging people toward spiritual growth. Divine intervention is only for emergencies.

(*BLAKE enters, frantic.*)

BLAKE: Tina! Tina! I did what you said. I went to the landslide, the streambed, and across the street to the bay!

TINA: And?

BLAKE: I whacked the tennis balls with the racquet at every place, and they bounced right back. We're trapped inside some kind of barrier.

TINA: Yeah, I can guess why too.

BLAKE: Tina, are you okay?

TINA: Yes. No.

BLAKE: (*Suspicious*) Was that Crow guy bothering you?

TINA: No, no. I'm fine, really.

BLAKE: What's going on?

TINA: Blake, I need you to trust me and help me. Can you do that?

BLAKE: Yes, but—

TINA: I need you to help me by staying calm and by carrying on as usual.

SCENE 11

(*CHARMIAN stands alone.*)

CHARMIAN: You wonder why I'd do anything for her? Because I was a piece of garbage before she plucked me out of the gutter. Because I was doing drugs and drinking for days at a time before she helped me clean up. Because she gave me food, shelter, and compassion when no one else gave a shit. Because she held my hand like a child, and walked me through things step by step until I could do them on my own. Because she had faith and confidence in me before I had any for myself. Because she made me believe I could survive my past and transform myself into something new.

(*CHARMIAN moves to the Veranda. EFFIE is there. They pick up nail files and lounge around filing their nails.*)

EFFIE: Do you think things happen for a reason, or do you think everything is a coincidence?

CHARMIAN: You mean, do I think there's order in the universe, or do I think everything is random?

EFFIE: Do you think it was providence that I met Peter Crow in the rain or just luck?

CHARMIAN: Why do you ask?

EFFIE: Why did the perfect person for the part just appear out of nowhere?

CHARMIAN: Don't you think he came from somewhere?

EFFIE: Are people thrown together by fate or by accident?

CHARMIAN: Are you attracted to him?

EFFIE: (*Laughs*) Wouldn't *you* like to know?

CHARMIAN: I wonder why he wanted to do this so badly?

EFFIE: Don't you think it's because he's a writer?

CHARMIAN: With an interest in Somerset Maugham?

EFFIE: Yeah, what was he saying about Somerset Maugham?

CHARMIAN: Didn't he accuse him of plagiarism?

EFFIE: And hasn't Tina told us about that Aleister Crowley character before?

CHARMIAN: Wasn't he some kind of alchemist, some occult weirdo from a really long time ago?

EFFIE: Do you think Peter really looks like him?

CHARMIAN: Didn't she say Maugham wrote a book making fun of him?

EFFIE: Was it called *The Magician?*

CHARMIAN: Yes, and didn't Crowley get really pissed off?

EFFIE: I wonder if we could find a picture of him?

CHARMIAN: But don't you think that guy playing at being Maugham is great?

EFFIE: And what about that Haxton person?

CHARMIAN: You're not attracted to him too, are you?

EFFIE: Do you really think he's gay?

CHARMIAN: (*Chuckles*) Don't you think that's a little desperate?

EFFIE: Have I turned into a maladjusted widow?

CHARMIAN: Are you starved for male attention?

EFFIE: Am I so transparent?

CHARMIAN: Haven't I known you forever?

(*The chime sounds.*)

EFFIE: Yikes, is it time already?

SCENE 12

(*Lights on the Sitting Room. TINA, REED, CHARMIAN, THEO, CROWLEY, MAUGHAM, and GERALD are all sitting around after dinner.*)

GERALD: That was a splendid meal.

MAUGHAM: Excellent.

TINA: (*Placing a tray and glasses in the center*) Please help yourselves to the port.

GERALD: (*Touches her hand*) You're absolutely marvelous.

(*Both MAUGHAM and CROWLEY notice the physical contact. Loud scratchy jazz music starts playing, and BLAKE and EFFIE can be heard laughing.*)

THEO: There's that annoying music again.

CHARMIAN: It sounds as if she has some male visitors. I don't see how she could have made friends so quickly.

THEO: I thought I saw a couple of sailors sitting outside her room earlier.

CHARMIAN: I guess she's not very particular.

GERALD: It sounds harmless, really.

CROWLEY: (*Standing*) Of course! Why didn't I see it!

THEO: What's the matter, Alfred?

CROWLEY: Why, she's from Iwilei!

CHARMIAN: What is Iwilei?

CROWLEY: It is a plague upon the earth, the crying scandal of the Pacific, the red-light district of Honolulu.

REED: Yes, women of every nationality and the police know all about it. I believe their philosophy is that vice is inevitable and the best thing to do is to localize and control it.

CROWLEY: That is until the very day we arrived in Honolulu. The sinful population of women was brought before the magistrates that morning.

CHARMIAN: Now that you mention it, I saw her coming on board at the very last minute before we sailed.

CROWLEY: She must have escaped prosecution.

TINA: Perhaps I should go down and ask her to be quiet.

GERALD: You shouldn't have to do that. I'll tell her for you.

(GERALD rises.)

TINA: (*Nervous*) Wait. I mean, finish your port first, Mr. Haxton.

CROWLEY: How dare she come here. I'll put a stop to this myself!

REED: Get a hold of yourself, sir.

CROWLEY: I won't stand for this house to be turned into a brothel! When the tree is rotten, it should be cut down and cast into the flames.

MAUGHAM: There may be three or four men down there.

CROWLEY: Someone such as yourself might be afraid, but a *real* man—

(TINA clears her throat loudly and gives CROWLEY a "look.")

CROWLEY: A real man of God, that is, will not shrink from his duty.

(CROWLEY storms out.)

THEO: The fear of personal danger never stops him in what he sees as his duty.

(We hear the door below flung open and the sound of the gramophone needle ripped off the record. We hear CROWLEY shouting, EFFIE shouting back, and then the sounds of a scuffle.)

GERALD: Oh my God! Should we help him?

MAUGHAM: No. Best to stay out of it, Gerald.

CHARMIAN: Do something, Alec!

REED: Why? What has she done to us?

(*We hear what sounds like CROWLEY being thrown out. The gramophone starts again, but not as loudly as before. CROWLEY enters and passes through toward his room. He looks roughed up. THEO rises.*)

THEO: Oh, Alfred!

CROWLEY: (*Dramatically*) Please, leave me alone.

(*CROWLEY exits. THEO sits back down.*)

THEO: That creature will be sorry. Alfred is most kind and charitable when a troubled soul needs comfort, but he has no mercy for sin.

MAUGHAM: What do you suppose he'll do?

THEO: I don't know, but I wouldn't be in that woman's shoes for anything in the world. (*Pause*) I must go to him now.

(*Silence as THEO exits.*)

REED: I don't see why he couldn't mind his own business.

MAUGHAM: Well, that was a bit of excitement. I think I've got some notes to sort out.

GERALD: Do you need—

MAUGHAM: No, no, Gerald. Enjoy another glass of port.

REED: We should really retire too, my dear.

CHARMIAN: Oh yes, good night.

(*MAUGHAM, REED, and CHARMIAN exit. GERALD pours himself a huge glass of port.*)

SCENE 13

(MAUGHAM is in his chair in the Guest Room.)

MAUGHAM: Oh, it's just too delicious. "A plague upon the earth, the crying scandal of the Pacific." But the dinner tonight was far too sophisticated. No one would believe cheese soufflé in Pago Pago. Let's see, hamburger steak, that's more like it. Yes, hamburger steak every night. And now, the perfect conflict, a righteous man of God set up against a prostitute. But, she's much too appealing. I'll have to make her more whore-like, give her ugly bulging calves and cheap shiny clothes. He's perfect, however. Yes, there's even something attractive and alluring about his nature, so strong and powerful, almost seductive in his unflinching will. All that virility must be thoroughly wasted on his mousy wife. I must try to get to know him a little better.

SCENE 14

(In the Sitting Room, GERALD is pouring himself another large glass of port. He is now slightly tipsy. EFFIE enters. She doesn't see GERALD at first and is going to help herself to the port. She has a box of chocolates.)

GERALD: Grabbing a short one?

EFFIE: God, you scared the bejesus out of me.

GERALD: *(He pours her way too much)* Oh, please, allow me. You probably aren't supposed to be here.

EFFIE: Probably not. Want some chocolate?

GERALD:	MMM. Thanks. So, *are* you from Iwilei?
EFFIE:	So, what if I was? Would you hate me?
GERALD:	No, but that minister might.
EFFIE:	I can handle him.
GERALD:	Why didn't you just pretend you weren't a call girl, pretend you were something else?
EFFIE:	What?
GERALD:	You know, like a nurse, a shop girl, a secretary.
EFFIE:	But then there wouldn't be any story.
GERALD:	Story?
EFFIE:	"Rain"!
GERALD:	I know it's raining. Anyway, you look too cute to be a hooker.
EFFIE:	Cute?
GERALD:	I mean, you have that girl-next-door look.
EFFIE:	Oh, how sweet of you.
GERALD:	(*Upset*) It's that, you seem so nice. (*Almost crying*) Sorry, I shouldn't drink alone.
EFFIE:	Why, Gerald, what's wrong? Come on now, you can confide in me. I'm very discreet.
GERALD:	(*Sniffling*) Well, this person I love, you see, is getting married, and I know that they love me, not the person they're marrying, but they're getting married because, because . . .
EFFIE:	Because they want to seem respectable? Because they think they need to keep up appearances? Because social climbing is more important than loyalty?
GERALD:	How do you—
EFFIE:	We, uh, we girls in the profession have seen it all. I had no idea Mr. Maugham was getting married.

GERALD: He's made a woman fall in love with him. She's had his child.

EFFIE: I'm sure he'll be very sorry.

GERALD: He doesn't really even *like* women.

EFFIE: Do you?

GERALD: I don't know. Sometimes . . .

EFFIE: Sometimes?

GERALD: (*Cuddles up to her*) Sometimes.

EFFIE: Well, I'll bet you a hundred smacks Maugham's making a mess of his life and yours and hers.

GERALD: I guess he's afraid. A lot of us are afraid, especially after what happened to Oscar.

EFFIE: Who's Oscar?

GERALD: Oscar Wilde. He—never mind, it's too depressing.

EFFIE: Whatever it is, there's no excuse for dumping someone you love.

GERALD: (*He starts to get over-friendly and kisses her cheek*) You're so kind and—

EFFIE: Hey, hey, listen, I think you've had one too many. You should go to bed now, kid.

GERALD: Couldn't we just—

EFFIE: (*Standing*) No, no! My bad. Professional habit, you know. Just go to bed.

(*GERALD exits. EFFIE pours another and exits. CROWLEY, who has been listening in the shadows, enters. TINA, who has also been watching, meets him.*)

CROWLEY: She was splendid, don't you think? A whore with a heart of gold.

TINA: Shut up. The poor boy is hurt.

CROWLEY: I was hurt and you didn't care.

TINA: Too little, too late.

CROWLEY: I couldn't believe you walked away.

TINA: (*Ignoring the topic*) Did you do what I told you?
            Did you try?

(*A silence.*)

TINA: Hah. You did, didn't you? See, you have no power
            here.

CROWLEY: I don't think I'll tell you what happened.

TINA: You don't have to.

CROWLEY: Are you going to help me?

TINA: Are you going to help *me*?

CROWLEY: What do you want?

TINA: First, I want to know exactly what you did to get us
            all trapped in this place.

CROWLEY: Trapped?

TINA: Yes, we are definitely trapped. And I am not spend-
            ing eternity in the same house with *you* and
            Somerset Maugham.

(*The chime sounds.*)

TINA: Oh Jesus, what now!

(*Exit TINA, fast. CROWLEY, who was about to pour himself a
drink, stops and pretends to be reading his Bible as MAUGHAM
enters.*)

MAUGHAM: Oh, Reverend Davidson.

CROWLEY: I couldn't quite sleep, so I decided to sit out here
            for a bit.

MAUGHAM: I just came for a nightcap of port.

CROWLEY: I suppose liquor might help one to sleep, but I feel
            it is a very bad habit.

MAUGHAM: I have many bad habits, I'm afraid.

CROWLEY: Do you?

MAUGHAM: Oh, yes.

CROWLEY: Perhaps you'd like to discuss them sometime. I'm always ready to offer comfort and counsel to those in need.

MAUGHAM: Your faith must be very strong, Reverend. You simply radiate confidence and strength.

CROWLEY: I burn, Mr. Maugham, with passion and devotion, and with that comes a submission to his will.

MAUGHAM: (*Admiringly*) You don't strike me as the submissive type at all.

CROWLEY: I submit to *his* will only. I am in his joyful bondage. Are you a churchgoing man?

MAUGHAM: No, not really, but I suppose my wife, my future wife, that is, might make me one.

CROWLEY: Marriage? Oh, it's an excellent institution. A wife can save a man from a multitude of worldly sins.

MAUGHAM: That's my thought exactly.

CROWLEY: (*Singing, enchanting him*)

There is a balm in Gilead
to make the wounded whole . . .

(*Not singing*) Do you wish to be saved from worldly sin?

MAUGHAM: (*Standing*) I don't know.

CROWLEY: (*Singing*)

There is a balm in Gilead
to heal the sin-sick soul.

MAUGHAM: Perhaps I do. Perhaps I do and just didn't know it.

CROWLEY: (*Taking MAUGHAM's hands*) I suggest you return to your room and pray for guidance right now. I sense you are on the brink, Mr. Maugham, on the brink of discovering something wonderful.

MAUGHAM: (*Mesmerized*) I—I—well I, well—yes, I will, yes. I will try it. I'll try it right now.

(*MAUGHAM exits. CROWLEY waits for the chime, pours himself a glass of port, smiles to himself, drinks it down, and pours another.*)

CROWLEY: I never thought I would see Adonai again, my holy guardian angel. Adonai, Tina, boy, woman, what does it matter? It's the same *soul* I loved. I didn't appreciate that presence in my life, but I knew when it was gone. Believe me, I knew when it was gone. And now, through fate or accident, I have another chance. Yes, I will get Adonai back.

SCENE 15

(*BLAKE and REED are on the Veranda.*)

REED: So, how long has Theo been here?

BLAKE: About three months. Tina went up right after the accident.

REED: Was she badly hurt?

BLAKE: She broke her collarbone. She had a concussion. She took her teacher's death pretty hard.

REED: Effie said he was much more than her teacher.

BLAKE: His wife blamed Theo for everything. But it wasn't the first time he'd been messing around. He'd made it a constant habit. And Theo had already broken it off with him. She was just giving him a ride when it happened. Anyway, the wife brought the kids to the hospital. She said she wanted to show the children their father's murderer. The wife was screaming, the kids were crying. They had to call security to get her out of there. And she sent hate mail, lots of it, but Tina was able to intercept most of it. She had to have the phone disconnected too. It was a mess.

REED: The lady sounds psychotic.

BLAKE: I don't know what I would have done without Tina.

REED: She's the best thing that ever happened to you, brother.

BLAKE: She stepped in just like she did when we first met.

REED: Wasn't that just after your folks died?

BLAKE: Theo was still a kid. We were floundering around like lost sheep.

REED: Well, something must have been watching over you.

BLAKE: Yeah, but this messy business—it's nearly broken Theo.

REED: I can see that.

BLAKE: Some days she just stays in her room, stares out at the bay, and doesn't say a word.

REED: She doesn't seem to have any problem pretending to be Mrs. Davidson.

BLAKE: It's the first thing that's brought any life into her. It's great.

REED: Is it?

BLAKE: What do you mean?

REED: Something about it bothers me. It's like she's a little *too* good.

SCENE 16

(*It is the next morning. In the Sitting Room, TINA and BLAKE are clearing the breakfast things for THEO, CHARMIAN, MAUGHAM, and GERALD.*)

MAUGHAM: Another day of this monotonous rain.

GERALD: And another delicious meal.

TINA: Why, thank you.

MAUGHAM: (*To BLAKE*) Boy, a fresh pot of tea, if you please.

(*BLAKE gives him a dirty look as he takes the teapot and cup.*)

CHARMIAN: I believe his name is Sefo.

GERALD: Where are the doctor and the reverend?

CHARMIAN: My husband is visiting the hospital.

THEO: Reverend Davidson is making a call on the governor.

MAUGHAM: I hope that woman didn't insult him terribly last night.

THEO: She threw beer on his clothes and they were stained and stinking of her—

(*EFFIE enters suddenly. She is wearing a sexy Chinese dressing gown. Everyone stares.*)

EFFIE: Morning, all!

(*No one answers her. THEO is livid.*)

EFFIE: Here's your rent, Mrs. Horn—seven bucks for the whole week, and I expect a return on my money if we're lucky enough to leave this burg sooner.

TINA: Don't worry, Miss Thompson. If you leave early, you'll get a refund.

EFFIE: (*Mockingly*) And how is the man of God this morning, any better?

CHARMIAN: (*To THEO*) Don't answer her.

THEO: How dare you speak to me, you tramp!

EFFIE: Huh! Did I ask him to visit me?

THEO: I'll have you turned out of here!

EFFIE: Next time he makes a call, tell him not to come during business hours.

THEO: (*Stands, in a rage*) Why, you brazen slut! You whore of Babylon!

(*THEO slaps EFFIE on the face.*)

GERALD: Holy shit!

(*EFFIE rushes out while TINA drags THEO to the Veranda.*)

TINA: Uh, Mrs. Davidson, you mustn't let her upset you like this.

(*BLAKE enters with a fresh pot of tea and a clean cup.*)

MAUGHAM: Oh, boy, this milk is turning, take it away please, chop-chop.

(*BLAKE glares and mumbles.*)

BLAKE: 'Ai kae (*Eat shit*).

MAUGHAM: (*Chuckling*) He'll learn his place.

(*On the Veranda, TINA shakes THEO.*)

TINA: Are you alright?

THEO: What?

TINA: I think you gave Effie quite a scare.

THEO: (*Not that concerned*) I'm sorry. Just tell her I'm sorry.

TINA: You shouldn't have slapped her!

THEO: (*Shrugs*) I just got carried away with my character.

TINA: Darling, you can't keep all this guilt and anger bottled up. Why won't you . . . (*talk to me*)

(*THEO sees CROWLEY, who has just entered the Sitting Room. She rushes to him as TINA follows. REED has also entered.*)

THEO: Alfred, that woman came up here and insulted me.

CROWLEY: Her behavior is most unfortunate.

THEO: Don't you think we should have her turned out?

REED: But where would she go?

CROWLEY: I must speak with her one more time. She has an immortal soul, and I should do all I can to save it.

THEO: (*Staring blankly*) Nothing can save her. She's too far gone.

CROWLEY: (*Tenderly to THEO*) Too far gone for the mercy of God? Never! The sinner may be in the depths of hell itself, but the light and love of Jesus reach out.

(*CROWLEY exits while MAUGHAM and THEO follow him with their eyes. THEO and MAUGHAM then exit.*)

SCENE 17

(*TINA, CHARMIAN, and REED remain in the Sitting Room. EFFIE and BLAKE enter.*)

EFFIE: Wasn't Theo fabulous!

TINA: She was disturbed.

REED: (*Concerned*) What happened?

TINA: You needed to be here.

EFFIE: She wasn't disturbed. She was just really into it.

BLAKE: I'll tell you who's disturbed. That jerk who thinks he's Maugham.

CHARMIAN: But that's probably how Maugham really treated Polynesians.

BLAKE: If he calls me "boy" one more time (*he makes a fist with his right hand and smacks his left palm*), I'm going to speak to him in Sāmoan.

TINA: He's our guest, Blake. Behave.

BLAKE: I don't care.

EFFIE: I feel sorry for that Gerald person. It seems like something's really eating at him. Hey, what are their real names anyway?

TINA: You don't need to know that.

EFFIE: Why not?

TINA: Because then you won't make a slip.

EFFIE: Well, he's cute, no matter what his name is.

REED: He's cute and he's *gay*.

EFFIE: Maybe, maybe not.

TINA: He's our guest, Effie. Behave.

REED: They must have been practicing their parts for a long time. They don't miss a beat.

CHARMIAN: I'd just love to ask Mr. Maugham a few questions about his writing. The way he intends to portray natives and women, and see what he says.

TINA: He's our guest, Charmian. Behave.

CHARMIAN: I'll try, but it's too delicious.

EFFIE: Aren't you glad I found Peter? That he just appeared like magic?

CHARMIAN: He and Theo are a good match.

REED: I don't know about him.

CHARMIAN: Why do you say that?

REED: It just seems like he's hiding something.

EFFIE: Hah! We're all hiding something.

REED: Well, I just don't like him.

TINA: Reed—

REED: I know, and I *will* behave.

SCENE 18

(*MAUGHAM is writing and thinking in the Guest Room.*)

MAUGHAM: That Sefo—his attitude is inappropriate to his station, to say the least, and his presence makes me feel unsafe. I haven't met many of the native men here, but I suppose they're all the same—with that stealthy, quiet way of moving, pattering around in their bare feet. And those sinister, menacing looks. Why, he looks as if he'd like to stick a dagger in my back. (*Sitting down and writing*) I'm sure this is something that readers would like to know, since everyone talks about these people as being so blithe and childlike.

(*Enter GERALD.*)

GERALD: That Mrs. Davidson has quite a temper.

MAUGHAM: And a fixation on sexuality—typical of the repressed middle-aged woman.

GERALD: But she's not middle-aged. And do you really think she's repressed? After all, she *is* married.

MAUGHAM: I'm sure it's just a marriage of convenience.

GERALD: (*Sarcastic*) Like yours will be?

MAUGHAM: Gerald, I've explained everything to Syrie.

GERALD: Have you?

MAUGHAM: And I told *you* all about it from the first. She was pregnant before I met you. I have to marry her. I've never hidden anything from you.

GERALD: She's in love with you, isn't she?

MAUGHAM: We've agreed, for the child's sake. She knows how it is with me!

GERALD: I'm sure she thinks she can change you.

MAUGHAM: Don't be absurd.

GERALD: But what if she does love you? What if she believes you might really love her?

MAUGHAM: It's what she wants. She knows what she's getting into.

GERALD: Don't you care about who might get hurt in this web—her, you, me, the child?

MAUGHAM: I care about doing the right thing.

GERALD: Oh, is that what you're doing?

MAUGHAM: (*Irritated*) Of course it is! End of discussion! (*Pause, as he collects himself*) Now, let's get back to work.

(*GERALD shrugs, goes to his table, and rolls up a piece of paper in the typewriter.*)

GERALD: Do you really think Mr. and Mrs. Davidson don't "do it"? She's awfully young and cute.

MAUGHAM: She's a mincing little mouse that can roar.

GERALD: Maybe you're right. They probably think it's dirty. He's a real caricature, isn't he?

MAUGHAM: No, I'm sure there's a genuine religious feeling in the man.

GERALD: What?

MAUGHAM: A deep spirituality buried beneath his rhetoric.

GERALD: He's an ass.

MAUGHAM: A man with real concern for the welfare of others.

GERALD: (*Laughs at him*) This rain must be waterlogging your brain.

MAUGHAM: (*Exiting*) Just do the typing!

SCENE 19

(*MAUGHAM storms back into the Sitting Room, where CHARMIAN is reading.*)

MAUGHAM: Oh, I'm sorry, Mrs. McPhail. I don't mean to disturb you.

CHARMIAN: Not at all. Are you all right?

MAUGHAM: I'm fine. It's just this rain.

CHARMIAN: How is your writing coming along?

MAUGHAM: Splendid, splendid.

CHARMIAN: (*Fishing*) I imagine you find the Polynesians most interesting subjects.

MAUGHAM: Actually, I find them rather dull.

CHARMIAN: Dull? They seem to be a most lively and interesting people.

MAUGHAM: As a backdrop, I suppose, but my readers prefer stories about their own kind.

CHARMIAN: No Melville Fayaways for you, Mr. Maugham?

MAUGHAM: How delightful, Mrs. McPhail! You're a serious reader.

CHARMIAN: A doctor's wife must have things to occupy her time.

MAUGHAM: Quite frankly, the Polynesian female appears to me, if I may be candid without offending, a dangerous, perhaps fatal lure to a white man, but of no literary interest on her own.

CHARMIAN: A fatal lure?

MAUGHAM: Yes, and these half-caste women are even worse. Pretty on the outside, but coarse and scheming by nature. This climate, the women, the alcohol—a constant danger to the civilized man.

CHARMIAN: I suppose I had better keep a watch on my husband.

MAUGHAM: And yourself. I've studied medicine. It would be easy for a white woman to succumb to all kinds of illnesses here, even madness.

SCENE 20

(*On the Veranda, THEO sits directly across from CROWLEY.*)

CROWLEY: You *can* talk to me. You know I've been sent here to help you, don't you?

THEO: I do sense that there's something about you.

CROWLEY: As an artist, you see things, feel things more deeply.

THEO: I'm haunted by the woman I was, the things I did. I feel her like a weight on my back, a stain on my body (*looks at her hands and arms*), a bloodred, scarlet stain.

CROWLEY: You can fight that wickedness.

THEO: I do want to be rid of her.

CROWLEY: I can help you.

THEO: How?

CROWLEY: (*Moving close to her so their knees touch*) Just look up. Look at me. And trust. Trust that I can lead you the right way.

(*THEO stares into his eyes. He takes her hands.*)

CROWLEY: You must give yourself over to Mrs. Davidson. You want to, don't you?

THEO: Mrs. Davidson.

CROWLEY: Mrs. Davidson knows how to deal with women like that.

THEO: (*As if it's dawning on her*) Yes, Mrs. Davidson. I'm always safe there.

CROWLEY: Let Mrs. Davidson cast off the burden and wash the blood from your hands.

(*CROWLEY puts her hands together in a prayer position, kisses them, and then sings to her. THEO is completely mesmerized by him.*)

CROWLEY: (*Sings*)

There is a balm in Gilead
To make the wounded whole
There is a balm in Gilead
To heal the sin-sick soul.

(*Speaking*) Now, don't be afraid. You have me on your side.

THEO: Yes, Alfred, thank you. I don't feel so afraid now. (*Short pause*) About this evening.

CROWLEY: (*Smiling*) Yes, my dear?

THEO: We'll read a passage from the Bible, and discuss the commentaries. It's such a comfort to me.

CROWLEY: And it brings us closer together . . . in the sight of God.

THEO: That woman is downstairs now, isn't she?

CROWLEY: Yes, she's in her own room.

THEO: What if she tries to get at me again?

CROWLEY: We will fight together, my dear.

THEO: Have you spoken to her yet?

CROWLEY: I gave her every chance to repent. She's a very evil woman.

THEO: She should be punished for the things she's done.

SCENE 21

(In the Sitting Room, the table is set for tea. BLAKE, TINA, CHARMIAN, and REED are waiting to begin.)

CHARMIAN: No, Blake, I disagree. He's doing it as part of his Maugham role. I'm sure he's not really an asshole.

BLAKE: But why? Why do you think that?

CHARMIAN: Look, he's a gay guy from San Francisco, and he's smart, which is clear from his brilliant performance. He's got to be fully aware of the politics of oppression against gays, against women, against people of color. He couldn't articulate Maugham's position if he wasn't.

BLAKE: Then why isn't he aware of simple politeness?

TINA: Just ignore him if he does it again.

CHARMIAN: Good lord! It's as dark as night outside.

REED: This rain is perfect for your visitors' fantasy.

TINA: Uncanny is more like it.

BLAKE: Where are the divas? Everything is going to get cold.

TINA: I knocked on the door, and they said they'd be right along. Now, where's Theo?

BLAKE: She's waiting until they're here before she comes in.

CHARMIAN: Yeah, she's on the veranda, reading the Bible.

REED: Why is she doing that?

BLAKE: I guess she's getting in the mood.

REED: I think someone should—

(Sound of the chime.)

TINA: Quiet, here they come.

(*BLAKE begins pouring the tea and serving. Enter MAUGHAM and GERALD.*)

REED: (*To CHARMIAN*) The hospital was better than I'd expected in such a remote part of the world. I only hope it's as good in Apia as well. Oh, good afternoon, Mr. Maugham, Mr. Haxton.

MAUGHAM: Ah, another lovely tea. Who does the baking?

TINA: I do some, but Sefo does most of it.

MAUGHAM: I'm sure you have to supervise him.

(*BLAKE serves MAUGHAM with a big smile.*)

BLAKE: 'Ua pipilo kele 'oe (*You really stink*).

TINA: Oh, of course!

GERALD: The food here is so much better than the ship.

(*THEO enters.*)

TINA: Come in, Mrs. Davidson, and sit down. Will Reverend Davidson be joining us?

THEO: No, I believe he's gone back to see the governor.

TINA: Oh, I see.

MAUGHAM: And how was the reverend's talk with Miss Thompson?

THEO: She has refused to repent.

MAUGHAM: So, what will he do now?

THEO: He will take up the whips, as did the Lord Jesus when he drove the moneylenders out of the temple.

GERALD: (*Almost laughing*) Oh, boy, whips!

THEO: If she fled to the ends of the earth, he would follow her.

GERALD: We're *at* the ends of the earth already.

THEO: Do you mock me, sir?

GERALD: Why, no, I just—everyone is so serious here!

THEO: (*Irritated*) I think I'll take my tea on the veranda.

(*THEO exits.*)

GERALD: (*Shrugging*) I wasn't rude, was I?

MAUGHAM: Only marginally.

GERALD: Poor Sadie. Sounds like he's going to make trouble.

REED: Oh, he's a great busybody, that one.

CHARMIAN: Alec! (*Short pause*) Oh, won't this rain ever stop? It's getting on my nerves. The way it rattles on the tin roof is maddening.

MAUGHAM: Primitive nature is like a malignancy.

REED: It does make one feel powerless.

MAUGHAM: Yes, miserable and hopeless.

GERALD: Could we get any more gloomy?

(*Enter CROWLEY. He looks as if he's been out in the rain.*)

GERALD: (*Looking at CROWLEY*) I guess we could.

TINA: Good afternoon, Reverend. Would you care for some tea?

CROWLEY: Why, thank you, yes.

REED: Your wife tells us you've been to see the governor.

CROWLEY: It's terrible the way men of responsibility try to avoid doing their duty. The very existence of that woman is a scandal, and shifting her to another island will not solve the problem. In the end, I had to speak aggressively to the governor.

REED: You threatened him?

CROWLEY: Our mission board is not without influence in Washington. The governor came right around.

(*Enter EFFIE in a temper.*)

EFFIE: (*To CROWLEY*) You lowdown skunk, what did you tell the governor about me?

CROWLEY: Please sit down, Miss Thompson. I've been wanting to speak to you again.

EFFIE: You lowlife bastard.

CROWLEY: Your abuse is nothing to me, Miss Thompson, but there are ladies present.

GERALD: Sadie, what happened?

EFFIE: This feller just came and told me I had to beat it on the next boat out of here. Governor's orders.

CROWLEY: You couldn't expect him to let you stay here—

EFFIE: You! You did it! You did it!

CROWLEY: I won't deny that I urged the governor to do his duty.

EFFIE: Why couldn't you leave me alone? I wasn't doing you no harm!

CROWLEY: I wish you no harm either.

EFFIE: I hate you! Do you hear me? I hate you!

(*EFFIE storms out of the room. GERALD stands.*)

GERALD: (*To DAVIDSON*) You're a nasty, despicable person!

(*GERALD goes after EFFIE.*)

MAUGHAM: Gerald! (*GERALD ignores him*) Please excuse him. He's an impetuous soul.

CROWLEY: It's nothing to me.

REED: Why are you being so harsh with the poor girl?

CROWLEY: If a man had a gangrenous foot, would you have any patience with a doctor who refused to amputate it?

REED: Gangrene is a physical fact.

CROWLEY: So is evil, Dr. McPhail, so is evil. (*He turns and looks at MAUGHAM*) Just as true repentance through prayer brings forgiveness. Prayer heals all.

MAUGHAM: (*Rises, mesmerized*) Excuse me, there's something I have to do.

(*MAUGHAM rises and goes to the Guest Room. He kneels in prayer.*)

SCENE 22

(*TINA straightens up. REED and CHARMIAN help by clearing up the dishes and then exit. CROWLEY and TINA are left alone.*)

CROWLEY: I understand the principle of the charade. But why continue? They're not really your visitors.

TINA: Because the illusion keeps order. It's the only thing holding us together. Imagine what would happen if we told everyone the truth.

CROWLEY: (*Considering*) You're right, of course.

TINA: Now, you need to explain to me what you did.

CROWLEY: If I can remember.

TINA: What?

CROWLEY: I didn't really plan to do it. It was a spur-of-the-moment idea. An improvisation.

TINA: Just try to remember—anything, anything you can.

CROWLEY: I remember it was cold and gray and cloudy. Yes, it was in the afternoon, and it was raining. I was lying about on the divan, looking out the window. I was a bit drowsy. I was watching as the raindrops hit against the panes and then trickled down like tears. It was mesmerizing. There was a peculiar smell in the air, like sickly sweet flowers, and then all of a sudden, I was thinking about Maugham and that stupid book he wrote. I felt he needed to be taught a lesson. I got up, I went to the room, I took out the cauldron, and—

(*Noises of GERALD saying goodbye to EFFIE.*)

TINA: Oh shit, he's coming back. Out, out of the room.

(*CROWLEY exits as GERALD enters. GERALD looks dazed and has lipstick all over his face.*)

TINA: What in the world have you been up to, Gerald?

GERALD: Just talking to Sadie. She needs a friend.

TINA: (*Moves very close to wipe his face*) I would get this lipstick off before Mr. Maugham or Reverend Davidson or anyone else sees it. You'll only get the poor girl in more hot water.

GERALD: Oh, thanks, you're so kind.

(*MAUGHAM enters.*)

MAUGHAM: Mrs. Horn, I want to—Gerald, what are you doing?

(*GERALD jumps away from TINA.*)

GERALD: Nothing.

MAUGHAM: It certainly doesn't look that way.

TINA: You misunderstand, Mr. Maugham. Gerald had something in his eye, and he asked me to look at it.

MAUGHAM: Really? Well, what's that on his face?

TINA: (*Offended*) What kind of person do you think I am?

(*REED enters. He's surprised to see MAUGHAM and GERALD.*)

MAUGHAM: I wouldn't know.

TINA: What?!

GERALD: Oh, Dr. McPhail, I want to ask you—couldn't you do something for Sadie? Talk to the governor yourself?

REED: I suppose I could try.

MAUGHAM: Why do you insist on helping that creature?

GERALD: Because she doesn't want to leave on the next boat—it's the one that goes to San Francisco—her family lives there, and she can't face them.

REED: Poor lass. I will. I will try, but I can't promise anything.

GERALD: Thank you, doctor, thanks.

MAUGHAM: I don't think we—(*should be involved*)

TINA: Now what was it you wanted, Mr. Maugham?

MAUGHAM: Yes, oh yes. There were some wires outside our door. I didn't know what they were, and I pulled on one. I'm afraid I've broken it.

TINA: Oh no! The chime!

MAUGHAM: Of course, I'd be happy to pay if I've damaged something.

TINA: (*Exasperated*) It's—well, just never mind.

MAUGHAM: Now, Gerald, I need your help with some typing.

(*MAUGHAM and GERALD exit.*)

TINA: And what do you want, Reed? Don't tell me if it's anything bad.

REED: Me? No, I'm just going to the kitchen to get a beer.

(*REED exits and CHARMIAN enters.*)

CHARMIAN: Tina, I want to talk to you.

TINA: I have to sit down.

CHARMIAN: That guy who's pretending to be Maugham is just too good to be true.

TINA: Like the real thing.

CHARMIAN: Exactly. So, I'm wondering, could you ask him, I mean when his holiday is over, could you put him in contact with me?

TINA: What for?

CHARMIAN: What for? I was hoping he would come and do his little act for my Pacific Literature class. He has a great understanding of the racist and sexist nature of Maugham's personality, and he sees exactly how he fits into the postcolonial genre of Western writers in the Pacific. He demonstrates so clearly how preconceived ideas cloud insight. He goes straight to the core of things. It's like a living deconstruction of everything Maugham was. Is he an English professor or something?

TINA: I can't tell you that, Charmian.

CHARMIAN: Oh, I understand. I understand. But you will ask him, when it's all over, won't you?

TINA: Okay, sure, I'll ask him.

CHARMIAN: Too bad he's gay. Are you sure he's gay?

TINA: Do not even go there!

(*CHARMIAN exits, laughing. TINA watches her leave and shakes her head.*)

SCENE 23

(*MAUGHAM and GERALD in the Guest Room.*)

MAUGHAM: I can't believe you would embarrass me this way.

GERALD: What way?

MAUGHAM: First, finding you in that, that position with Mrs. Horn.

GERALD: I had something in my eye!

MAUGHAM: I'll bet.

GERALD: She's a very kind woman.

MAUGHAM: You need to be careful, Gerald.

GERALD: Of what?

MAUGHAM: Of your friendship with Mrs. Horn.

GERALD: Tina?

MAUGHAM: These native women are like healthy, erotic animals. She could devour you.

GERALD: (*Chuckles*) An erotic animal?

MAUGHAM: It's a well-known fact. And that Thompson hag that you insisted on befriending.

GERALD: She's hardly a hag.

MAUGHAM: How could you defend her like that in front of everyone?

GERALD: You mean in front of that minister with the broomstick up his butt?

MAUGHAM: Gerald!

GERALD: I've seen how you watch him.

MAUGHAM: I do not watch him.

GERALD: All gaga-eyed and full of admiration.

MAUGHAM: You're imagining things.

GERALD: So, are you going to get married *and* get religion?

MAUGHAM: Don't make fun of me.

GERALD: Don't be so—stupid.

MAUGHAM: And a spiritual life is something we should all seriously consider.

GERALD: What you need to seriously consider is the truth— about Syrie, about me, and about yourself. If

Davidson found out the truth about *us,* we'd be the ones leaving on the next boat.

MAUGHAM: No one would question me!

GERALD: No?

MAUGHAM: No! I'm a respectable gentleman, engaged to be married. A famous writer. No one would ever *dare* bring it up. And about "us."

GERALD: What?

MAUGHAM: I'm sorry to tell you, but there is no more "us." There may have been in the past, but from now on, you'll be my secretary and nothing more.

GERALD: What?!

MAUGHAM: I'm starting a new life now.

GERALD: I don't believe this!

MAUGHAM: (*Delighted*) I hardly believe it myself!

SCENE 24

(*THEO is reading the Bible on the Veranda. REED enters.*)

REED: Hey there.

THEO: Good afternoon.

REED: Theo, I—

THEO: My name is Mrs. Davidson, *Dr. McPhail.*

REED: Hey, come on. It's me, Reed. ʻO aʻu lau uō (*I'm your friend*).

THEO: Don't speak to me in that mumbo jumbo.

REED: You speak it too.

THEO: Only to the natives.

REED: We are the natives.

THEO: (*A little angry*) Don't be ridiculous. We're here to help them. If you insist on being rude, you'll have to leave.

REED: (*Now being careful*) Okay, I'm sorry. I'm very sorry. Let's start again. What are you doing, Mrs. Davidson?

THEO: Reading the Bible. I read to my husband every night. He suggested these verses from Proverbs: (*She reads*) "And behold, there met him a woman with the attire of a harlot. . . . And he goeth after her as an ox goeth to the slaughter. Her house is the way to hell, going down to the chambers of death."

REED: Your, ah, "husband" wanted you to read this?

THEO: Yes.

REED: And where is your "husband" now?

THEO: Doing the work of the Lord.

REED: And what would that be?

THEO: Taking care of that evil woman.

REED: (*Repeating*) That evil woman.

THEO: Yes. Soon, she'll get what she deserves. (*She sings*)
There is a balm in Gilead
To make the wounded whole
There is a balm in Gilead
To heal the sin-sick soul.

REED: (*To audience*) We'd known each other all our lives. One summer when we were back from school, we fell in love. She wasn't even twenty. We were wild and reckless, and Theo got pregnant. Of course, I asked her to marry me. Everyone expected it, but then she had a miscarriage. The last time we talked, I asked her if she thought we still had to go through with it, getting married. She just stared at me with no emotion, threw the ring in my face, and told me to leave. I felt so relieved. I felt like I'd escaped. (*Pause*) I did what every young man dreams of doing. I drifted around the world. I saw a thousand and one amazing sights. I slept with every woman I could. I found nothing.

SCENE 25

(*CROWLEY is in the Sitting Room. REED enters.*)

REED: What the hell do you think you're doing, Crow?

CROWLEY: Whatever do you mean?

REED: I'm talking about Theo. Did you tell her to read that trash?

CROWLEY: I was only humoring her. I don't see the harm.

REED: The harm is she's not herself. The harm is she's fragile, and encouraging her to dwell on sin and punishment is only making it worse.

CROWLEY: I can't help it if the poor child is disturbed. I'm not her keeper.

REED: Well, I am. So lay off.

CROWLEY: I wouldn't threaten me if I were you.

REED: Yeah? If you hurt Theo in any way, I'll kill you.

(*CROWLEY and REED stand facing each other. MAUGHAM enters. Because there is no chime, CROWLEY and REED are surprised out of their stare-down.*)

MAUGHAM: I beg your pardon. Am I interrupting something?

REED: No, I'm just on my way to bed. Remember what I've said, *Reverend*.

(*REED exits.*)

CROWLEY: The Lord will never abandon me when I'm about his business, *Doctor.*

MAUGHAM: (*As he pours a glass of port*) I was hoping to talk to you, Reverend Davidson.

CROWLEY: I'm always glad to be of help. Through your prayers, has the Lord lifted you?

MAUGHAM: Yes, I believe he's removing my . . . affliction. It's a miracle.

CROWLEY: His power is unlimited.

MAUGHAM: Do you really believe what you said today? That no sinner is ever too far gone for the mercy of God.

CROWLEY: Of course, I believe it. I couldn't call myself a Christian if I believed otherwise.

MAUGHAM: You see, I would like to believe it. I would like to believe that if I turned over a new leaf, if I threw off all my contemptible habits, if I started on a clean slate with my wife and our child, I could be, things could be—different. We could have a little estate, not too far from London of course, where I could retire to do my writing. We could mix with the very best. Our child could ride about on a pony, and at Christmas there would be a Yule log and a party with eggnog and caroling. We could sit together and watch the snow fall.

CROWLEY: Perhaps that secretary of yours is a bad influence.

MAUGHAM: Yes, I think you're right.

CROWLEY: He's consorting with Miss Thompson, and he seems to have no respect for religion.

MAUGHAM: Of course, he's just a young man. He's hardly—

CROWLEY: I fear he may be a moral degenerate. I think you must distance yourself from him.

MAUGHAM: I already have—in a manner of speaking.

CROWLEY: (*Takes MAUGHAM's hand*) You may place your trust in me, sir. Let me be the rock you lean on until you yourself can rise up on your own in God's light.

MAUGHAM: (*Mesmerized*) Yes, yes. I will.

CROWLEY: I am only too happy to bear the weight.

MAUGHAM: Yes, I do believe you understand me.

(*Enter TINA.*)

TINA: Oh, excuse me, gentlemen, am I interrupting?

MAUGHAM: (*Stepping back, flustered*) No, I mean, it was nothing, I—everyone here seems to creep around!

TINA: I do live here.

MAUGHAM: I thought this parlor was for the guests.

TINA: (*Irritated*) I do have to straighten up.

MAUGHAM: Yes, well, good night then, Reverend Davidson.

CROWLEY: Good night, Mr. Maugham, you are only beginning to feel his grace.

(*Exit MAUGHAM.*)

TINA: What are you up to with him?

CROWLEY: You asked me to play this part. Listen, Adonai—

TINA: Don't call me that!

CROWLEY: I'm not trying to upset you.

TINA: Upset me? Let's see. Gerald was doing I-don't-know-what with Effie. Charmian worships Maugham and thinks he's a brilliant actor and scholar. Theo is losing touch. Blake wants to kill Maugham. Reed is extremely suspicious of you. The chime's broken. I find Maugham gazing at you with puppy-dog eyes for God knows what reason. We're totally trapped here, and you can't remember how you got us all into this situation! How could I be more upset?!

CROWLEY: I'm simply trying to help, darling. Maybe you could spend some time with me, and help me to remember.

TINA: It doesn't look like I have much choice, do I?

CROWLEY: No, it doesn't.

(*Enter BLAKE. He and CROWLEY give each other a look.*)

CROWLEY: (*Exits*) Well, good night then.

(*A silence.*)

BLAKE: Who is that guy to you?

TINA: Peter Crow?

BLAKE: Yes, Peter Crow.

TINA: Why are you asking me this?

BLAKE: Because of the way he looks at you. Because of the way you look at him.

TINA: Do you love and believe in me, Blake?

BLAKE: I have so far.

TINA: And I could tell you anything about who I was, who I am.

BLAKE: Don't I know who you are?

TINA: No, darling. I'm afraid you don't know everything.

End ACT I

Act II

(*It is the next morning and still raining. TINA and BLAKE are on the Veranda drinking coffee.*)

BLAKE: I can't help being weirded out—magic spells, time warps—and I'm supposed to believe you're some kind of immortal being.

TINA: Everyone is an immortal being, darling.

BLAKE: And in your previous lifetime, or whatever you want to call it, you knew this Peter Crow character?

TINA: He was a famous alchemist. His real name is Aleister Crowley.

BLAKE: I *have* heard of Aleister Crowley. He was also a famous pervert!

TINA: He's caused all of this, and I'm doing my best to get him to undo it.

BLAKE: It's just too crazy to believe.

TINA: Go outside again and try to get out of here, if you don't believe me.

BLAKE: There must be some logical explanation.

TINA: Logic is relative to knowledge.

BLAKE: Are you saying I don't know anything?

TINA: Listen, Blake, there's no time for petty arguments. Aleister can be very dangerous. He's mastered an array of alchemical skills. He's extremely self-centered, and he has a real sweet tooth for power and promiscuity.

BLAKE: I guess that's why he always looks at you like you're the dessert.

TINA: Please, darling, I need you on my side.

BLAKE: (*Standing to leave*) It doesn't look like I have much choice, do I?

(*BLAKE exits as CROWLEY enters. BLAKE glares at him.*)

CROWLEY: Charming little life you have here.

TINA: I told you. It suits me.

CROWLEY: Although, I'm sure it's *dreadfully* provincial.

TINA: In these times, travel is quite easy.

CROWLEY: Time and travel, always an entertainment.

TINA: You know exactly how you got here, don't you?

CROWLEY: I could never hide anything from you for very long.

TINA: But you never gave up trying.

CROWLEY: This era seems most liberated—especially the women.

TINA: In some ways, you wouldn't like it at all.

CROWLEY: A time with some fascinating avenues to explore.

TINA: Look, as long as you and your two friends from 1916 are here, we're all stuck in this house and the very tiny area around it. Stuck in the rain. And you have to stop.

CROWLEY: Stop what?

TINA: Your desire— it's spreading out all over the house.

CROWLEY: I can't help it, Adonai.

TINA: Yes, you can. Your willpower is legendary.

CROWLEY: (*Sadly*) Except when it comes to you.

TINA: (*Quietly*) You have to go back, darling.

(*CROWLEY just looks at her.*)

TINA: You have to take them too.

CROWLEY: Why should I?

TINA: One, because this will get boring, and you know how you hate to be bored. Two, because if we wait much longer, it will become permanent, and three, if you don't want to completely lose my sympathy and compassion for all eternity, you'd better do it.

CROWLEY: For all eternity? What are you talking about?

TINA: I'm talking a complete karmic break, forever and ever.

(*Keep light on scene.*)

SCENE 2

(*CHARMIAN, REED, and EFFIE in the Sitting Room. THEO sits a little apart, reading the Bible.*)

EFFIE: I'm worried about this part. It just seems so over the top to me.

CHARMIAN: Just don't start laughing.

EFFIE: Oh, but I do. When I pretend to cry, I cover up my face and laugh. Watch.

(*EFFIE covers up her face and laughs, but it seems like crying. TINA and CROWLEY are on the Veranda.*)

CROWLEY: It doesn't look like I have much choice, do I?

TINA: No, it doesn't.

(*Lights fade on the Veranda as TINA moves to Sitting Room.*)

REED: Wow! That really looks like you're crying.

EFFIE: It's a trick I learned. Try it!

(*CHARMIAN, EFFIE, and REED all cover their faces and laugh/cry.*)

TINA: What is going on here?

CHARMIAN: We're rehearsing.

TINA: Can you keep it down?

EFFIE: Sorry. We're not allowed to laugh?

TINA: So, are all of you ready for the day?

EFFIE: I'm not quite sure how you want me to do this part here. In the story it says: "She gave a groan of horror and then burst into low hoarse shrieks which sounded hardly human, and she beat her head passionately on the ground."

TINA: Just do the best you can, but please *don't* beat your head on the ground, okay?

(*TINA exits.*)

EFFIE: I guess she's not interested.

REED: She does seem preoccupied.

CHARMIAN: I think you should just do the scene fast, collapse—

REED: Then I'll take you downstairs.

CHARMIAN: Where's Peter? He should be here.

EFFIE: You know, I just don't get it. Sadie's behavior seems so . . .

REED: So, what?

EFFIE: Well, she knows she's wanted by the police in San Francisco for prostitution. She barely escapes arrest in Honolulu for the same. Then she comes here and flaunts her profession, practically throws it in the faces of the authorities. Any dummy would be keeping a very low profile.

CHARMIAN: Gender politics aside, Maugham is often criticized for cliché, *and* for falsifying human behavior for the sake of his plots.

EFFIE: Reed's is the only decent character in the story.

REED: Davidson, he's a cliché if I ever saw one.

(*Enter CROWLEY.*)

CROWLEY: What was that?

REED: Nothing.

EFFIE: There you are, Peter.

CROWLEY: (*Kisses EFFIE's hand*) Good morning, darling. Still raining, I see. Good morning, Charmian.

CHARMIAN: We better hurry if we want to practice.

EFFIE: Let's go from my entrance.

CROWLEY: Give me just a moment.

(*GERALD and MAUGHAM enter unexpectedly.*)

EFFIE: Oh shit, it's them.

CHARMIAN: (*Shoves EFFIE toward the door*) The chime's broken, remember?

(*Lights out.*)

SCENE 3

(*Lights to GERALD, MAUGHAM, REED, CHARMIAN, THEO, and CROWLEY in Sitting Room having coffee. There is a knocking at the door.*)

THEO: Come in.

(*EFFIE sticks her head in.*)

THEO: (*Glaring*) What do you want?

EFFIE: May I speak to you, Mr. Davidson?

CROWLEY: Come right in, Miss Thompson. What can I do for you?

EFFIE: I'm sorry for what I said to you and for everything else.

CROWLEY: Have no fear, Miss Thompson. My back is broad enough to bear a few hard words.

EFFIE: (*Upset*) Look, you got me beat all right, but please, don't make me go back to Frisco.

CROWLEY: (*Stern*) Why don't you want to go back there, Miss Thompson?

EFFIE: My people live there. I don't want them to see me like this.

CROWLEY: Why don't you want to go back?

EFFIE: I'll go anywhere else. I swear!

CROWLEY: Why?

EFFIE: I told you!

CROWLEY: (*Gives a gasp*) The penitentiary!

EFFIE: Don't send me back! I swear to God I'll be good! I'll give all this up!

CROWLEY: That's it, isn't it?

EFFIE: If the bulls grab me, it's three years.

REED: You can't make her go back now. Give her a chance to turn over a new leaf.

CROWLEY: I'm going to give you the finest chance you've ever had. Repent and accept your punishment.

EFFIE: You'll let me go?

CROWLEY: No, you shall sail for San Francisco on Tuesday.

(*EFFIE shrieks, puts her hands over her face, and does her laugh/cry. She sinks to the floor. REED and BLAKE pull EFFIE up and they exit.*)

CROWLEY: I want you all to pray with me for the soul of our erring sister.

GERALD: (*Jumps up*) Go to hell!!

(*GERALD exits.*)

CROWLEY: (*Ignoring him*) And now, let us fall on our knees and pray for the soul of our dear sister Sadie Thompson.

SCENE 4

(*GERALD and MAUGHAM in the Guest Room. MAUGHAM is scribbling away.*)

GERALD: That was unbelievable!

MAUGHAM: Highly dramatic. I need to get every word.

GERALD: He's a monster.

MAUGHAM: His sense of right and wrong is unshakable.

GERALD: It's cruel.

MAUGHAM: Did you notice how he instinctively knew she was lying?

GERALD: He smelled it.

MAUGHAM: I've never seen such mastery over others.

GERALD: You mean tyranny.

MAUGHAM: He's God's shepherd.

GERALD: He's a wolf!

MAUGHAM: You just can't see the real him.

GERALD: I'll prove it to you.

MAUGHAM: Prove what?

GERALD: He's a predator.

MAUGHAM: Don't be silly, Gerald.

GERALD: It takes one to know one.

MAUGHAM: He's devoted his life to God.

GERALD: What is most appealing to a predator, Willy?

MAUGHAM: I'm not listening to anything else you have to say.

GERALD: (*To audience*) Prey, brothers and sisters, prey.

SCENE 5

(*CHARMIAN, TINA, and BLAKE in the Sitting Room.*)

CHARMIAN: That Gerald person is acting strange.

TINA: What do you mean?

CHARMIAN: He said, "Go to hell," and stormed out of here. What's up with that?

TINA: Gee, I don't know.

BLAKE: Maybe that's how he thinks Gerald Haxton might react.

CHARMIAN: Is there something you're not telling me?

TINA AND BLAKE:
Like what?

BLAKE: What we mean is—

(*TINA and BLAKE look at each other and back at her.*)

TINA AND BLAKE:
Like what?

CHARMIAN: You know, vacation relationship problems. Are the guests having a little spat?

(*TINA and BLAKE look at each other.*)

TINA: We might as well tell you, Charmian. They *are* having some problems.

BLAKE: Yeah, they've been in couples counseling for the last few months.

TINA: This trip is supposed to help them. You know, a break from their normal routine.

BLAKE: So that's why they seem a little—

TINA: Edgy sometimes!

CHARMIAN: I thought so. Is some of it sex confusion?

BLAKE: Sex confusion?

CHARMIAN: You know, like maybe that Maugham guy isn't sure about his—

TINA: (*Yells*) No! (*Quieter*) I mean, no. I mean, I don't know, but that's not the point. The point is we have to try to keep them happy.

BLAKE: We can't afford a bad review on the internet.

TINA: Or to have them ask for a refund.

BLAKE: It could ruin us.

TINA: Humor them.

CHARMIAN: I never realized what a difficult business this must be.

TINA: Believe me, it can push you to the limit.

CHARMIAN: Would it help if I told the others?

TINA: Yes, but be discreet.

CHARMIAN: Don't worry. Leave it to me.

(*CHARMIAN exits.*)

BLAKE: That was fast thinking.

TINA: Maybe it was for the best. We'll be able to explain any weird behavior for a while.

BLAKE: I don't like you dealing with Crow, Crowley, whatever his name is.

TINA:	I don't like it either.
BLAKE:	That's not how it looks to me.
TINA:	What?
BLAKE:	Are you sure there's nothing between you?
TINA:	(*After a pause*) Not now.
BLAKE:	Not now. Great. Just what I want to hear. "Not now."
TINA:	I've never pried into your past, Blake, so I don't think it's fair for you to pry into mine . . . even if it was much longer than yours.
BLAKE:	Is there anything else you're not telling me?
TINA:	Yes, there is, and it's very important. If you can't trust me, I can't stay with you.
BLAKE:	Can't or won't?

SCENE 6

(*CHARMIAN and EFFIE are on the Veranda.*)

EFFIE:	You asked him that?
CHARMIAN:	You think I shouldn't have?
EFFIE:	And he said we were only interesting as a backdrop?
CHARMIAN:	What else could he say?
EFFIE:	Did you ever feel that way?
CHARMIAN:	What way?
EFFIE:	Do you think that's bad? Being part of a backdrop?
CHARMIAN:	You mean always staying in the background?
EFFIE:	What do you think that means?
CHARMIAN:	Doesn't it mean nobody ever really gets to see you?

EFFIE: (*A beat*) Is your character getting to you?

CHARMIAN: Is yours?

EFFIE: Don't you think she must have felt sick inside?

CHARMIAN: Sadie?

EFFIE: Don't you think she was sick of all those men and her phony life?

CHARMIAN: Don't you see that's how he made her?

EFFIE: Doesn't she always do the stupidest things?

CHARMIAN: Don't you see she's not real?

EFFIE: Isn't she just a big fat loser?

CHARMIAN: Are you all right?

EFFIE: Do you think I'm a loser?

CHARMIAN: Why would you say that?

EFFIE: What have I done with my life?

CHARMIAN: (*Tries to be positive*) Well, you had your marriage, didn't you?

EFFIE: You think that's an accomplishment? Did you know most people thought it was a joke?

CHARMIAN: Because he was so . . . ?

EFFIE: Unfaithful? Do you know how hard it was to pretend I didn't care?

CHARMIAN: Oh, Effie, why didn't you leave?

EFFIE: What am I fit for?

CHARMIAN: Fit for?

EFFIE: A silly, shallow, superficial bimbo—do you think I don't know how everyone sees me?

CHARMIAN: That's not how you see yourself, is it?

EFFIE: Would I be wrong if I did?

SCENE 7

(GERALD enters the Sitting Room unexpectedly and surprises CROWLEY, who is drinking a glass of port. CROWLEY turns his back and gulps it down, but GERALD sees.)

GERALD: Well, if it isn't the man of God having a little nip.

CROWLEY: *(Chuckles)* Purely for medicinal purposes.

GERALD: You're missing out on a great dinner.

CROWLEY: I was—

GERALD: *(Starts to flirt)* Coq au vin.

CROWLEY: I was praying for the soul of that poor, unfortunate woman.

GERALD: Maybe you should pray for my soul.

CROWLEY: Why is that?

GERALD: Because I'm a genuine degenerate.

CROWLEY: Is that so?

GERALD: So very so.

CROWLEY: Where are the others, right now?

GERALD: Just about to come in for coffee.

CROWLEY: I see.

GERALD: How do you like your coffee, Reverend?

CROWLEY: With a little sugar.

GERALD: And cream? Do you like cream?

CROWLEY: Yes, as a matter of fact, sometimes I do.

(Enter TINA carrying a coffee tray. She immediately sees the way CROWLEY and GERALD are looking at each other.)

TINA: *(Clears her throat)* Coffee, gentlemen?

(Enter MAUGHAM, REED, THEO, and CHARMIAN.)

REED: Yes, two years at the front was quite enough for me. I'm looking forward to some quiet time in Apia.

MAUGHAM: Yes, it was terrible. I remember one hospital—a lovely white stone chateau on the outside, and inside hundreds of wounded men lying on straw . . . (*He becomes lost in the thought*)

REED: You met your secretary there?

MAUGHAM: Pardon?

GERALD: No, in Flanders. In the ambulance corps.

(*Silence. CROWLEY, REED, CHARMIAN, and TINA are all staring at the door off and on waiting for EFFIE to appear. BLAKE enters with a tray of cookies.*)

TINA: Sefo, fea Effie (*Sefo, where is Effie*)?

BLAKE: Ka'ilo (*Don't know*).

TINA: Fa'amolemole, vala'au 'o ia e sau (*Please, call her to come*).

BLAKE: 'Ia (*Okay*).

TINA: Fa'avave (*Hurry*).

CROWLEY: (*Trying to improvise*) War, so difficult on the soul. God says "Thou shalt not kill" but man fails to listen.

REED: Would you be a pacifist then, Reverend Davidson?

CROWLEY: As I've said, Doctor, I'm a soldier of the Lord.

(*EFFIE enters, looking a little disheveled.*)

REED: What are you doing here, Miss Thompson? I told you to rest.

EFFIE: I can't rest.

REED: You're exhausted.

EFFIE: I feel like I'll never rest again.

CHARMIAN: (*To THEO*) Poor creature looks near collapse.

THEO: She should expect to suffer for her sins.

EFFIE: I wanted to see you, Reverend Davidson.

CROWLEY: I knew you would come to me.

EFFIE: You got me beat.

CROWLEY: I knew the Lord would answer my prayers.

EFFIE: I've been a bad woman.

CROWLEY: Yes, child, don't be afraid.

EFFIE: (*Kneels*) I've been bad and—

CROWLEY: God is great in his mercy.

EFFIE: And I want to repent!

CROWLEY: Thank God! Thank God for this privilege to bring another lost soul to the arms of Jesus.

GERALD: (*Sarcastic*) Hallelujah.

EFFIE: (*Crying, clinging to CROWLEY*) Please, help me, help me. I want to be good.

REED: The lass needs to lie down!

CROWLEY: Yes, doctor, we'll take her downstairs.

EFFIE: (*To CROWLEY*) Don't leave me. Don't leave me. I'm afraid.

CROWLEY: Of course, I won't leave you. I'll pray with you day and night if you wish.

(*REED and CROWLEY take EFFIE out.*)

SCENE 8

(*MAUGHAM and GERALD head for the Guest Room.*)

MAUGHAM: It's a miracle.

GERALD: It's a bloody farce.

MAUGHAM: We've just witnessed a true conversion. How can you be so cynical?

GERALD: Sadie's not like that. It will never stick.

MAUGHAM: Can't you see that a person can change? That they can transform themselves?

GERALD: If you're talking about yourself, no, I don't see how a person can change the nature they were born with.

MAUGHAM: Born with?

GERALD: How have you described yourself to me over and over?

MAUGHAM: I don't know what you mean.

GERALD: For God's sake, stop being coy.

MAUGHAM: Alright, three quarters queer and one quarter straight. But maybe I've been wrong.

GERALD: Oh, please.

MAUGHAM: Maybe it's the reverse. Maybe the war—being thrown into those desperate situations with nothing but male companionship for comfort.

GERALD: Men don't become queer by going to war. That's ridiculous.

MAUGHAM: Maybe I'm just tired of feeling different. Tired of feeling like I'm not normal. Tired of people whispering and excluding—making fun of me behind my back.

GERALD: Well, I don't like it, but at least *that* I can understand.

MAUGHAM: I'll tell you how I wish I were born—with your confidence and your chutzpah. You revel in being different.

GERALD: Everyone's different, Willy. And none of those so-called normal people are any happier than you or me.

MAUGHAM: Reverend Davidson makes me believe that they are.

GERALD: You'd never be happy with a woman.

MAUGHAM: Reverend Davidson makes me believe I could.

GERALD: And I'm telling you, Reverend Davidson is just putting on an act.

SCENE 9

(TINA and CHARMIAN are straightening up the Sitting Room. EFFIE enters. She is angry.)

EFFIE: Where are they?

TINA: Who?

EFFIE: Your guests!

TINA: They're in their room. What's wrong?

EFFIE: I can't do this anymore.

TINA: Why?

EFFIE: It's making me crazy! *She's* making me crazy!

TINA: Calm down!

EFFIE: She's being bullied. He's bullying her with his stupid vision of the world. His religion.

CHARMIAN: Of course he is.

EFFIE: It's like he corners her, and then he rapes her.

CHARMIAN: That about sums it up.

EFFIE: He tortures her into redemption, and then he calls her angelic. It's bad enough what he writes about islanders. But he really hates women, doesn't he?

And I just can't stand to be in his fucking story anymore!

TINA: Effie, sit down. Come on now. Just sit down. Now, take a deep breath. Why is that, darling? What is the story about to you?

EFFIE: (*After a beat*) It's about a woman who runs around pleasing men. She makes her living pleasing men because that's all she knows how to do. And then one day, she becomes the victim of a powerful, twisted man, and in trying to please him, she gets betrayed in the worst possible way. He destroys her faith.

TINA: Does he?

EFFIE: Of course, he does.

TINA: Or does he just destroy her faith in him? Someone who didn't deserve her faith.

EFFIE: But she thinks he's speaking for God.

TINA: I guess that was her big mistake. And anyway, she could still change.

EFFIE: Maybe it's too late.

TINA: Nonsense. Without being bullied or victimized, she *could* change into something that suited her. We know the end of *his* story, but we don't know the end of *her* story.

EFFIE: (*Thoughtfully*) That's right.

TINA: And anything could happen.

CHARMIAN: It's not a nice role.

EFFIE: I'm already feeling bad about myself, and it's making it worse.

TINA: It's almost over, darling. You're so close.

CHARMIAN: Then you can toss it off.

TINA: Like a worn-out dress.

SCENE 10

(THEO is reading on the Veranda. CROWLEY enters.)

CROWLEY: Still awake?

THEO: Yes. I'm reading over a passage in the Bible. Were you with that woman?

CROWLEY: Praying with her.

THEO: She's the real scarlet woman, isn't she?

CROWLEY: What makes you say that? Scarlet woman, I mean.

THEO: It's a common expression, Alfred.

CROWLEY: But what does it mean to you, my darling?

THEO: A woman who sins, a woman who entices, a woman who could destroy a man.

CROWLEY: But, as I told you, a scarlet woman can be redeemed, my love.

THEO: Obedience, suffering, punishment.

CROWLEY: Yes, when her Lord calls her, she obeys. You do trust me, don't you?

THEO: Yes, you understand me.

CROWLEY: And you don't share our confidences with anyone, do you?

THEO: No one.

SCENE 11

(TINA and BLAKE are setting up coffee, tea, and pastries in the Sitting Room.)

BLAKE: It's been so dark all day.

TINA: Haven't you noticed? It's like it's always evening. The light never changes.

BLAKE: What does it mean?

TINA: I don't know.

BLAKE: I haven't seen you since breakfast.

TINA: Maugham wanted lunch in his room. I've been busy.

BLAKE: Busy meeting with *him*.

TINA: I have to meet with *him*. If this doesn't work, we're all lost.

BLAKE: What do you do when you meet with *him?*

TINA: Blake, I can't deal with jealousy right now.

BLAKE: I have a right to know. You shut yourself up with *him* for hours at a time.

TINA: Remember what I told you.

BLAKE: You were with *him* for years!

TINA: Yes, and now I'm with you.

BLAKE: How do I know what goes on in there?

TINA: By now, you should know me.

BLAKE: Maybe I should just kill him.

TINA: *That* would be a big mistake.

(*GERALD enters. Surprised, TINA jumps up, and BLAKE scuttles into the background.*)

TINA: Oh, good afternoon, Gerald.

GERALD: I'm sick of working.

TINA: Help yourself to some tea, dear.

(*MAUGHAM enters.*)

TINA: Good afternoon, Mr. Maugham.

MAUGHAM: It might be good, if it would stop raining.

TINA: If I could stop it for you, I would.

MAUGHAM: (*To BLAKE*) Boy, coffee if you please.

(*BLAKE pours a cup, hands it to MAUGHAM.*)

BLAKE: 'Ua 'ou fia mimilo lou ua (*I want to twist your neck*).

(*TINA gives BLAKE "the eye" as he exits.*)

MAUGHAM: What does that mean?

TINA: Oh, it means good day—only in *his* village, nowhere else.

(*Enter CHARMIAN, REED, and THEO.*)

THEO: (*To CHARMIAN*) He's exhausting himself with that woman.

CHARMIAN: He should mind his health.

THEO: I'm very worried about him.

REED: Yes, this has certainly been an ordeal for him, for all of us.

TINA: (*A little disconcerted*) Why, where is the Reverend Davidson?

THEO: He's ah—

(*CHARMIAN, REED, and THEO look around, wondering what to do because CROWLEY is missing from the scene.*)

CHARMIAN: I haven't seen him.

REED: I believe he—

THEO: Went for a walk. Yes, I believe he's out walking.

TINA: I hope he remembers to come to tea!

(*Enter EFFIE. She quickly looks around for CROWLEY.*)

EFFIE: Where is he? I mean, where is the Reverend Davidson? I need him.

GERALD: How are you, Sadie?

EFFIE: How am I?

GERALD: Yes, are you alright?

EFFIE: I—ah—I want the Reverend Davidson. I'm afraid when I'm by myself, but when he's with me I, somehow, I feel at peace with myself. I—ah—feel at peace with myself, and I feel my sins falling away. I—

THEO: (*Standing*) Hah! Don't kid yourself. Your sins won't just fall away. You're going to prison where you belong, you bitch.

TINA: Mrs. Davidson!

THEO: I hope you suffer there. I hope you're starved, tortured, humiliated. I hope you rot and die.

(*TINA and REED move to rush her out.*)

TINA: You're not yourself, Mrs. Davidson. Let's get some fresh air.

GERALD: (*To MAUGHAM*) See what religion can do to you?

CHARMIAN: She's just a little tired, that's all.

GERALD: She's off her rocker.

CHARMIAN: She's worrying about her husband.

GERALD: Maybe she's jealous.

EFFIE: Jealous?

GERALD: Yeah, with her husband spending all his time with you.

MAUGHAM: Leave her alone, Gerald.

GERALD: (*Aside to EFFIE*) Praying, or whatever else he likes to do.

EFFIE: (*Tries not to laugh*) Oh, Gerald!

(*CROWLEY rushes in. He looks like he just woke up.*)

CROWLEY: Miss Thompson, I heard you were looking for me.

EFFIE: Yes, I'm so afraid, but it's not so terrible when you're with me.

CROWLEY: I am always with you.

EFFIE: You're the only one who can help me now.

CROWLEY: You look so worn out, Miss Thompson.

EFFIE: I do feel very tired.

CROWLEY: Go downstairs to your room, and I'll join you presently.

(*EFFIE exits, and CROWLEY pours himself some coffee. He puts some sugar in it.*)

GERALD: (*Holding creamer, smiling*) Cream, Reverend?

CROWLEY: (*Sly smile*) Thank you.

MAUGHAM: I never would have thought it possible, Reverend Davidson!

CROWLEY: Last night I tore out the last vestiges of sin that lurked in her heart.

GERALD: (*Aside*) Holy shit.

CROWLEY: (*Ignoring him, looking at MAUGHAM*) Her soul, which was as black as night, is now pure and white like the new-fallen snow.

MAUGHAM: It's humbling to see the change.

CROWLEY: Her remorse for her sins is angelic. I am not worthy to touch the hem of her garment.

GERALD: But you have no problem sending her to prison.

CROWLEY: When she is in prison, I shall suffer as she suffers. Her suffering will be a sacrifice to God. I want her to accept it joyfully.

GERALD: Oh, bunk.

CROWLEY: You don't understand because you're blind to goodness. I love her as my wife—

GERALD: Your wife?!

CROWLEY: And my sister. Yes, my wife *and* my sister. I must go to her now.

(*CROWLEY makes a dramatic exit.*)

CHARMIAN: (*After a pause*) Mr. Maugham, do you mind if I ask you something?

MAUGHAM: What is it, dear?

CHARMIAN: Don't you find the Reverend Davidson's character a little overblown?

GERALD: (*Mimicking, melodramatic*) I tore the last vestiges of sin from her heart.

MAUGHAM: Men inspired by passion can appear that way to others.

CHARMIAN: And his metaphors, they seem a bit stale.

GERALD: Her soul was black, and now—it's white, like snow!

MAUGHAM: Stop it, Gerald. I find the metaphor totally appropriate in the context.

CHARMIAN: And what about his really obvious subtext of physical desire?

GERALD: I love her as my little wifey.

MAUGHAM: Good Heavens, Mrs. McPhail! This is real life. I don't know why you want to examine it like literature.

CHARMIAN: (*Laughing*) Hah! I *knew* you'd say that!

SCENE 12

(*On the Veranda, THEO paces, and REED watches her.*)

REED: Theo, would you just sit down, please?

(*THEO just stares at him.*)

REED: Okay, Mrs. Davidson, whatever, just sit down, okay?

(*THEO sits.*)

REED:	You didn't really mean that back there, did you?
THEO:	Mean what?
REED:	Hoping that someone gets humiliated, tortured. Wanting someone to suffer.
THEO:	Bad people deserve punishment.
REED:	Do they?
THEO:	Yes. That's the only way.
REED:	Look, we all know you feel guilty about—
THEO:	You know nothing!
REED:	Just listen, will you?
THEO:	Say whatever you want.
REED:	What if there's another way?
THEO:	There isn't.
REED:	There is, Theo. It's called forgiving.
THEO:	No, there's no forgiving.
REED:	If you can't forgive yourself, maybe you could start by trying to forgive someone else.
THEO:	Someone else?
REED:	Maybe someone you know. Some stupid person who took your love and trust and treated it like rubbish. Do you think you could ever forgive someone like that?

SCENE 13

(*It is evening. MAUGHAM, GERALD, and CHARMIAN are in the Sitting Room. CHARMIAN is knitting. REED enters during the opening conversation and pours himself a drink.*)

MAUGHAM: I've never been stage struck. I like the theater best when it's under dust sheets and the auditorium is dark.

CHARMIAN: Oh, but you must like something about it.

MAUGHAM: I'll never forget the thrill of hearing grown men and women repeat the lines of my first play.

REED: That must be an experience to remember.

MAUGHAM: And I have passed many happy hours at rehearsal.

GERALD: Don't believe a word he says. He loves all the fuss over him on an opening night.

(*CROWLEY enters looking haggard.*)

REED: Reverend, sit yourself down. You look all done in.

CROWLEY: Yes, I will sit, but only for a moment. I must get back to her.

GERALD: Perhaps you should have a snort.

MAUGHAM: Gerald!

GERALD: For medicinal purposes.

CROWLEY: Perhaps . . .

(*GERALD pours a brandy and hands it to CROWLEY.*)

REED: And how is Miss Thompson?

CROWLEY: We pray with all our might and main for the Lord to grant us his mercy.

GERALD: Us?

CROWLEY: I meant *her*. For the Lord to grant *her* his mercy.

REED: Have you gotten much sleep?

CROWLEY: Oh, a little, but whenever I fall asleep—it's the oddest thing—I have the same dream.

REED: What's that?

GERALD: Yes, let's hear it.

CROWLEY: I dream about the mountains of Nebraska. In the dream, I'm on a train. It starts out slowly, but then it goes faster and faster, and I realize I don't know where I'm going, and I've no way to stop the train. I look out of the window and see the plains—so wide and flat. And then the hills, two of them, rising from nowhere—huge, rounded, smooth, like giant mole hills. (*Pause*) Well, I must get back to her. She needs me.

(*CROWLEY gulps his brandy and rushes out.*)

REED: That's a very odd dream.

GERALD: We could have put money on it. Eh, Mrs. McPhail?

MAUGHAM: Let's just drop it.

REED: Whatever do you mean, lad?

GERALD: Talk about obvious metaphors. Our minister is dreaming about giant—(*GERALD lifts his two hands under his chest as if he's bouncing giant breasts*)

MAUGHAM: (*Standing*) I think we should retire now. I'd like to go over some of my manuscript with you, Gerald.

GERALD: If you say so.

MAUGHAM: Good night to you.

GERALD: (*Winking*) Sweet *dreams!*

(*MAUGHAM and GERALD exit. TINA enters.*)

TINA: That went well.

REED: That was his last scene, wasn't it?

TINA: His last.

REED: Good, then he can get the hell out of here.

SCENE 14

(*GERALD and MAUGHAM are in the Guest Room. MAUGHAM is making notes.*)

MAUGHAM: There, I think I've got everything down. He did say "Pray with all our might and main," didn't he?

GERALD: (*Yawns*) That's what he said, right before the tit dream.

MAUGHAM: Would you stop maligning him?

GERALD: Just because you're infatuated with him?

MAUGHAM: You have no idea how I feel about him.

GERALD: I'm telling you, he's a phony.

MAUGHAM: You're wrong. And he's right—you're blind.

GERALD: I'll prove it to you.

MAUGHAM: Don't be silly.

GERALD: I'll show you tonight—if you have the guts to watch.

(*GERALD goes to the Sitting Room and settles into a chair. MAUGHAM sits in the Guest Room, watching. Lights slightly dim as if hours pass and the two drift off. Lights bump up when CROWLEY enters the Sitting Room. He is going for a drink and doesn't see GERALD at first. MAUGHAM still watches.*)

GERALD: More medicinal fortification, Reverend?

CROWLEY: It's a very difficult business, saving souls.

GERALD: Willy, Mr. Maugham, seems to have gotten religion all of a sudden.

CROWLEY: (*Toasting*) Well, praise God.

GERALD: I don't hold it against you.

CROWLEY: I'm glad.

GERALD: You know, you really *do* resemble Aleister Crowley.

CROWLEY: So I'm told.

GERALD: I saw him once. I went to a talk he gave.

CROWLEY: Really?

GERALD: I wouldn't tell Willy, but I rather admire him.

CROWLEY: And why is that?

GERALD: Oh, I wouldn't want to offend your holiness.

CROWLEY: I won't be offended. I'm rather curious to know why you'd be attracted to such a—such a despicable person.

GERALD: He has an appealing attitude toward sex.

CROWLEY: Does he?

GERALD: With women *and* men.

CROWLEY: Sounds like debauchery.

GERALD: Or fun, Reverend. It could be fun.

CROWLEY: Humph!

GERALD: I've even memorized some of the things he said.

CROWLEY: Have you now?

GERALD: Like you memorize the prophets.

CROWLEY: And what did he say?

GERALD: Intolerance is evidence of impotence.

CROWLEY: Interesting.

GERALD: Do what thou wilt shall be the whole of the law.

CROWLEY: Do what thou wilt.

GERALD: I am above you and in you. My ecstasy is yours.

CROWLEY: True depravity.

GERALD: Ordinary morality is for ordinary people.

CROWLEY: You don't think I'm ordinary?

GERALD: Oh no! In fact, I've come up with my own little saying, just for you, Reverend.

CROWLEY: What's that?

GERALD: Women need a reason. Men just need a place.

CROWLEY: I believe there's an open storage closet just outside.

(*MAUGHAM watches shocked and hurt as CROWLEY and GERALD disappear.*)

MAUGHAM: Reverend Davidson! I'd like to slit his throat! All men are pigs!

SCENE 15

(*TINA and BLAKE are in the Sitting Room.*)

BLAKE: (*Agitated*) What do you mean, "If anything happens to you"?

TINA: I'm just saying—

BLAKE: I hear what you're saying.

TINA: I just have this bad feeling.

BLAKE: You've been setting me up like a patsy.

TINA: No, I just need you to be prepared for the worst.

BLAKE: You *want* to go back to him, don't you?

TINA: No, I do not want to go back!

BLAKE: The two of you've been planning this all along, haven't you?

TINA: No!

BLAKE: This whole crazy story about time warps and magic.

TINA: You think I would do that to you?

BLAKE: The only part I don't get is how you trapped us all in here.

TINA: I had so much faith in you.

BLAKE: So just go! I don't need you. Just go back with your asshole magician!

TINA: (*Distressed*) Oh, Blake, you don't know what you've just done!

SCENE 16

(*In the Guest Room, MAUGHAM is sitting in a chair. GERALD stands behind the other chair.*)

GERALD: Come on now, you have to get some rest. It's nearly dawn.

MAUGHAM: I can't believe I was so wrong.

GERALD: (*Sits*) He's an extremely persuasive fellow.

MAUGHAM: I don't know what came over me.

GERALD: You just fell for his line, that's all.

MAUGHAM: I had a serious think while you were . . . while you were . . .

GERALD: In the closet?

MAUGHAM: I'm not blaming you.

GERALD: You've been pretty beastly.

MAUGHAM: Yes, I realize that, and other things too.

GERALD: Have you reconsidered your queer percentage?

MAUGHAM: No, because it doesn't really matter anymore. I'll have to go back and marry Syrie because I've said I would, and because the child needs a name and a father. (*Pause, sincerely*) But believe me, Gerald, when I saw you walk out the door with that, that charlatan, something happened. There was this flash. It was like I woke up from a very bad dream. It was like I woke up, and . . . and I knew that, of all the people in the world, male or female, *you* are the one I want to spend the rest of my life with.

GERALD: Are you quite sure of that, Willy?

MAUGHAM: I've never been more certain.

GERALD: Then that's all we need to know. We'll find a way to work everything else out.

(*CHARMIAN rushes in and interrupts their conversation.*)

CHARMIAN: Please, you're wanted in the sitting room right away.

MAUGHAM: What is it?

CHARMIAN: Something ghastly has happened!

SCENE 17

(In the Sitting Room, REED, TINA, and BLAKE wait. THEO enters, and looks warily at everyone.)

REED:	*(Aside to TINA)* What's she doing here?
TINA:	I don't know. I told her she wasn't needed.

(MAUGHAM and GERALD rush in.)

REED:	Please, I think you'd all better sit down.
MAUGHAM:	What is going on?
THEO:	He didn't come back last night. I heard him leave Miss Thompson's room around two a.m., but he never returned.
REED:	I'm afraid there's been a terrible tragedy, Mrs. Davidson. I was called from my bed about an hour ago. It was Reverend Davidson.
GERALD:	What happened?
REED:	His body was found down by the water. He had cut his own throat from ear to ear. The razor was still in his right hand.
THEO:	*(Laughs, a little manic)* He's not really dead.
REED:	I'm afraid he is, Mrs. Davidson.
THEO:	*(To MAUGHAM, loud)* It's just a story. I'm telling you he's not dead!
TINA:	Poor thing, she's stunned.
MAUGHAM:	He killed himself?
THEO:	*(Yells)* He did not!
REED:	He most certainly did!
GERALD:	*(Mortified)* Oh my God! I didn't mean to drive him to—
MAUGHAM:	*(Shouts)* Shut *up*, Gerald! I mean, please be quiet, this is no time for your idle chitchat.

CHARMIAN: They've taken his body to the mortuary.

THEO: (*Loses it*) You're lying. You're all liars. Alfred would never—

TINA: (*Taking THEO's hand*) I think the strain is too much for her. Come, Mrs. Davidson, you've had a nasty shock.

(*TINA drags THEO to the Veranda and sits her down.*)

TINA: My God, Theo, do you even know who I am?

THEO: Of course I do, you're Mrs. Horn. Where is Alfred? I want Alfred.

TINA: (*Standing*) What the hell has he done to her?

(*THEO starts to softly sing the "Balm in Gilead" hymn. The Sitting Room scene continues.*)

MAUGHAM: I just can't believe he'd do something like that.

GERALD: Somehow, he just doesn't seem like the type.

CHARMIAN: I think we all could use some very strong coffee.

(*BLAKE begins to pour and serve coffee. The scratchy jazz music from EFFIE's room starts up.*)

REED: What the blazes is that?

(*Enter EFFIE. She is once again tarted up.*)

EFFIE: Say, Sefo, I'm all out of sugar.

REED: What the devil do you think you're doing? Stop that damned racket.

EFFIE: Hey, Doc, can that stuff with me. Who do you think you are?

REED: What the devil do you mean?

EFFIE: You men. You're nothing but pigs. You're all pigs!

CHARMIAN: Calm down, Miss Thompson. The Reverend Davidson has—

EFFIE: Hah! Some reverend! He pretended we were praying for my soul when all along he was praying for
something else. And when I wouldn't give it to
him, he just took it.

(*REED ushers her out.*)

EFFIE: (*Yelling as she exits*) Do you hear me? The hypocrite pig just took it.

MAUGHAM: (*Standing, grabbing GERALD, and dragging him
off*) Excuse us, please.

SCENE 18

(*TINA has been pacing on the Veranda and looking at THEO.*)

TINA: We'll just see who's got what it takes!

(*TINA closes her eyes and concentrates. She takes a few deep
breaths, opens her eyes, stamps her foot, and calls out like a
scolding mother.*)

TINA: Theodora Von Elsner! I know you can hear me!
I want you to get in here right now, young lady.

(*THEO stops singing and sits up straight.*)

TINA: Did you hear me? I said now!

THEO: (*Like a kid*) Yes, Tina.

TINA: Now do I have your full attention?

THEO: Yes, Tina.

(*TINA sits beside THEO and speaks sincerely but with conviction.*)

TINA: Now listen very carefully, darling, because I don't
have much time. You are *not* some sexy slut like Sadie
or some buttoned-up missionary like Mrs. Davidson.

Don't you dare fall for those images. They're very convenient for men like Reverend Davidson—like Peter Crow, or like Somerset Maugham, but they are *not* you. Do you understand? They are made up, false, phony, fun-house images. Have you heard everything I've said?

THEO: Yes, Tina.

TINA: (*Kisses her on the forehead*) Now rest.

(*THEO lies down, and TINA puts a blanket over her.*)

TINA: And if it's the last thing I do for you, when you wake, your world will be new.

SCENE 19

(*MAUGHAM and GERALD are in the Guest Room.*)

MAUGHAM: Start packing. We have to get out of here, even if it's by canoe.

GERALD: I don't think anyone actually *saw* us go into that closet.

MAUGHAM: We're not taking any chances.

GERALD: But *I* didn't kill him, not directly, I mean.

MAUGHAM: We want no further involvement.

GERALD: He must have gone straight from me to Sadie!

MAUGHAM: What an ending for a story! A minister who turns out to be a hypocritical pervert!

GERALD: Hasn't this whole stay here been a little strange?

MAUGHAM: Surreal, if you ask me.

GERALD: All of these people—they just don't seem quite right.

MAUGHAM: It's a bloody madhouse.

(*Enter TINA. She is surprised to see them packed up.*)

TINA: Oh! Excuse me, gentlemen. We got word the boat to Apia has been given the okay. They're leaving in just a few hours. Did you already know that?

MAUGHAM: Yes. Ah, yes, ah—Gerald stuck his head out the window and the quartermaster told him.

GERALD: Yes, the quartermaster. Isn't it great?

MAUGHAM: Please let me know what we owe you.

GERALD: Lovely stay we've had. Except for, well, you know.

TINA: I'll get your bill right away.

(*TINA exits.*)

MAUGHAM: What luck!

GERALD: We're saved!

MAUGHAM: The sooner we're in our cabin, the better.

GERALD: (*After a beat*) Say, you know, that Reverend—he really *did* have one final night on the town, didn't he?

MAUGHAM: Gerald, you are incorrigible!

GERALD: That's why you adore me, Willy.

SCENE 20

(*MAUGHAM and GERALD are DR in dim light, as they were in the beginning, with bags and an umbrella. DL, THEO is sleeping on the Veranda, also in dim light. CROWLEY stands in the Sitting Room in the center of a circle of light. TINA is helping him to set up a makeshift cauldron. CROWLEY wears the same robe he did in the beginning. Rain and wind are rising.*)

(*DR.*)

GERALD:	This rain is torrential. Maybe we should go back.
MAUGHAM:	I'd rather be blown to kingdom come.

(*Sitting Room.*)

TINA:	(*To CROWLEY*) Do you have everything you need?
CROWLEY:	Did you take care of the others?
TINA:	Maugham and Haxton are in position. I did a sleep spell on the others.
CROWLEY:	You need to leave me alone now.
TINA:	What?
CROWLEY:	Do you want me to do this or not?
TINA:	(*Mad, exits*) Have it your way.

(*DR, MAUGHAM and GERALD huddle together.*)

GERALD:	It's getting worse.
MAUGHAM:	I don't care. I want to get to the ship.
GERALD:	What is that out there in the bay?
MAUGHAM:	Where? I don't see anything.

(*CROWLEY begins to mutter his incantation. He throws something in the cauldron. There is distant lightning and thunder. DL, THEO bolts upright from her sleep in a trancelike state.*)

CROWLEY:	Mrs. Davidson, my dear, it's time now.
THEO:	I am not some buttoned-up missionary woman.
CROWLEY:	(*Singing*)
	There is a balm in Gilead
	to make the wounded whole.

(*THEO stands and faces CROWLEY. DR, GERALD is still looking out in the bay.*)

GERALD:	I tell you I see something out there.
MAUGHAM:	Where?

GERALD: Out there! See it? It's a huge column of water!

MAUGHAM: I see it! Yes, I see it. It's moving.

(*CROWLEY, still chanting, throws something in the cauldron again. Lightning and thunder are brighter and louder. The sound of wind and rain gets louder.*)

CROWLEY: You'll be rid of the evil woman once and for all.

THEO: I am not some sexy slut either.

CROWLEY: (*Singing*)
*There is a balm in Gilead
to heal the sin-sick soul.*

(*THEO tries to resist, but is pulled toward him. She walks to the Sitting Room and stands at the edge of the circle. GERALD and MAUGHAM are watching the water column.*)

GERALD: It looks like it's coming this way.

MAUGHAM: What shall we do? What shall we do?

GERALD: We have to go back!

MAUGHAM: No, we are not! We are not going back!

(*CROWLEY again throws something in the cauldron. There is bigger lightning and thunder as the sounds of the storm increase. MAUGHAM and GERALD hold on to each other. CROWLEY stretches his hand outside the circle to THEO.*)

CROWLEY: Now take my hand, Mrs. Davidson, my scarlet beauty.

THEO: No! That is a made-up, phony, fun-house image!

(*TINA enters the Sitting Room. CROWLEY sees her, reaches out, grabs THEO, and yanks her into the circle. THEO screams but, once in the circle, is docile.*)

TINA: Aleister, no, you can't take her!

CROWLEY: You come. She stays.

TINA: You bastard!

(*CROWLEY raises his hand for the final throw into the cauldron.*)

CROWLEY: Your choice, Adonai.

(*BLAKE enters to see TINA rushing into the circle. TINA pushes THEO out as CROWLEY throws the last something into the cauldron. THEO begins to walk in her trance back to the Veranda. TINA struggles to get away from CROWLEY. BLAKE tries to enter the circle but is thrust back by an invisible force. There is blinding lightning and deafening thunder.*)

(*MAUGHAM, GERALD, BLAKE, TINA, and CROWLEY all scream. Lights out.*)

SCENE 21

(*After a silence, lights slowly rise on the Sitting Room and the Veranda. The cauldron has vanished, and there is no storm. BLAKE wakes up on the Sitting Room floor.*)

BLAKE: (*Frantic*) Tina! Tina?

(*BLAKE looks on the Veranda. He looks in the Guest Room. He calls down both left and right, then exits from the Sitting Room.*)

BLAKE: What have I done? Tina? Tina?

(*BLAKE exits, calling for her. Lights rise in the Guest Room on CHARMIAN and EFFIE as they look around.*)

EFFIE: Hmmm. Should we help Tina by straightening things up?

CHARMIAN: It does look like they've gone, doesn't it?

EFFIE: I wonder why they didn't even say goodbye?

CHARMIAN: Do you think they were unhappy with the experience?

EFFIE: How could they be?

CHARMIAN: I wonder if Peter's gone too?

EFFIE: Did you like him?

CHARMIAN: Did you?

EFFIE: Well, he was perfect for the part, wasn't he?

CHARMIAN: But?

EFFIE: But didn't it seem like there were things going on with him, things you wouldn't want to know?

CHARMIAN: Like what?

EFFIE: I'm not making sense, am I?

CHARMIAN: Who says we always have to make sense?

EFFIE: Charmian, could I come and stay with you for a while?

CHARMIAN: Did you know I was going to invite you?

EFFIE: Do you think a place, a life, can close in on you?

CHARMIAN: Are you ready for a change?

EFFIE: We know the end of his story, but hers goes on— isn't that what Tina told me?

CHARMIAN: Doesn't she always know just what to say?

EFFIE: Do you think I could get into your university?

CHARMIAN: (*Laughs*) Effie, does it rain in Pago Pago?

SCENE 22

(*Lights fade on the Guest Room and rise on the Veranda. THEO is waking up, and REED enters.*)

REED: You're awake.

THEO: (*Disoriented*) How long have I been asleep?

REED: (*Sits on bed*) A long time.

THEO: I must have been dreaming.

(*Silence.*)

THEO: What scene are we in? Have I missed anything?

REED: Theo, everything's over.

THEO: No, I—

REED: You did the whole thing.

THEO: I couldn't have.

REED: What's the last thing you remember?

THEO: I remember that man, Peter Crow. He was singing me a song.

REED: I just hope we've seen the last of him.

THEO: Reed, I think something's not right.

SCENE 23

(*Lights rise on the Sitting Room. BLAKE enters, dejected. He sits. CHARMIAN and EFFIE enter with a cake and a tea tray.*)

CHARMIAN: Hey, Blake, I bet you and Tina are relieved it's all over.

EFFIE: Where *is* Tina?

(*BLAKE just stares at the floor. Enter THEO and REED. THEO sees BLAKE is distraught.*)

THEO: Blake, what's wrong?

BLAKE: She's gone.

CHARMIAN: Who's gone? Tina?

EFFIE: Where's she gone?

BLAKE: I've looked all over. I can't find her.

CHARMIAN: What do you mean you can't find her?

BLAKE: It was him.

THEO: Who? Peter Crow?

REED: Should we call the police?

BLAKE: No, no, it was my fault. She warned me. I didn't believe her.

REED: That bastard. The island is small. We could find them.

BLAKE: You'll never find them.

THEO: Tina wouldn't just leave you like that.

EFFIE: Never.

CHARMIAN: Unless he . . .

REED: Unless he what? He forced her? I wouldn't put it past him.

THEO: I think she's trapped somewhere.

CHARMIAN: Why do you say that?

THEO: I don't know.

(*THEO wanders over to the spot where the cauldron was and looks around, as if she is trying to remember something.*)

THEO: There was a man and something happened here. It's like I can almost remember. And there were two other men outside. One was older than the other. They were right out there. (*Pause as she looks out*) Blake! Blake! Look, there she is!

(*BLAKE jumps up and rushes out. REED follows him, and they return with TINA, who is completely bedraggled and a little dazed. Everyone clusters around TINA.*)

CHARMIAN: Tina, are you alright?

TINA: (*Regaining her composure*) Am I home?

EFFIE: What happened?

THEO: Was it Peter Crow?

BLAKE: (*Concerned*) Did he hurt you?

TINA: No, he didn't really hurt me.

BLAKE: I'm so sorry. I was wrong about everything.

TINA: *Almost* everything.

BLAKE: Those things I said. I didn't mean them.

TINA: If you really meant them, I wouldn't be here.

BLAKE: I *so* don't deserve you.

TINA: Too bad, because, as you can see, I'm pretty hard to get rid of.

EFFIE: Okay, enough with the coded messages.

CHARMIAN: Tell us what happened.

EFFIE: What did he do to you?

THEO: Yes, tell us.

TINA: (*Improvising*) He, uh—(*She looks at Blake*) He, uh—

BLAKE: (*Looks at TINA*) He uh—

TINA: He tried to kidnap me!

REED: I knew he was a criminal! You should press charges!

TINA: (*Yells*) No! (*Quieter*) I mean, no. No police. He's gone now. They can't touch him.

REED: How could he have gotten away?

TINA: Well, he had a, a—

BLAKE: A yacht!

TINA: Yes, a yacht!

REED: Of course, a drifting yachtie, up to no good in every port.

EFFIE: How did he do it? Did he drug you? Did he knock you unconscious?

TINA: He, uh, he used everything he could.

CHARMIAN: But how did you manage to get away?

TINA: (*Into her own fabrication*) Well, I'm sure you
              noticed, he's a very persuasive and powerful man.
              I resisted with all of my strength. We had a terri-
              ble fight, *on his yacht,* and I thought I would never
              be able to escape, but then—it came to me—Effie's
              all-purpose solution to unwanted male behavior!

EFFIE: You mean you—

TINA: Oh, yes. I took very good aim, and let him have it.

EFFIE: And it worked!

TINA: (*Smiles*) Like magic.

(*EFFIE and CHARMIAN start passing out cake and tea.*)

THEO: I'm glad you're here, Tina. I don't know what I'd do
              without you.

TINA: (*To THEO*) Are you back in the world, darling?

THEO: Yes, I've crossed over.

CHARMIAN: I baked this cake for our wrap-up celebration for
              "Rain" yesterday, but everyone fell asleep. So, let's
              celebrate now!

EFFIE: Hey, did you notice? It stopped raining.

CHARMIAN: (*To TINA*) You didn't happen to speak to the
              Maugham person before he left, did you?

TINA: I'm sorry, Charmian. He preferred to remain
              anonymous.

CHARMIAN: Oh, well, I guess I should feel lucky to have seen
              his brilliant performance.

TINA: Very lucky.

BLAKE: There was an email this morning from that other
              gay couple in San Francisco to reschedule—I mean
              schedule—the same "Rain" fantasy visit.

EFFIE: They're probably friends of our visitors!

REED: You two may have started something big.

CHARMIAN: Something cutting edge.

TINA: Do you think we could do this again?

BLAKE: Why not? It would be another adventure.

THEO: I'll help you.

REED: But this time you could be the doctor's wife.

EFFIE: (*Laughs*) Oh-oh, I think Reed wants to play doctor again.

THEO: Well, I don't want to be Mrs. Davidson again—ever.

TINA: Oh, Blake, look at you. You've gone and spilled cake all over your nice shirt.

BLAKE: Well, I guess I've just proved Sadie right.

TINA: What?

BLAKE: (*Laughs*) All men *are* pigs.

CURTAIN

SUGGESTED READINGS

There are many sources that reference the real people and their histories that I have fictionalized in these plays. These are some of the books I used as sources of information as well as inspiration.

AITU FAFINE

Suaalii-Sauni, Tamasailau M., Maualaivao Albert Wendt, Vitolia Mo'a, Naomi Fuamatu, Upolu Luma Va'ai, Reina Whaitiri, and Stephen L. Filipo, eds. *Whispers and Vanities: Samoan Indigenous Knowledge and Religion.* Wellington: Huia Publishers, 2014.

FANNY AND BELLE

Field, Isobel. *This Life I've Loved.* New York: Longmans, Green, 1951.

LaPierre, Alexandra. *Fanny Stevenson: A Romance of Destiny.* New York: Carroll and Graf, 1995.

Mackay, Margaret. *The Violent Friend: The Story of Mrs. Robert Louis Stevenson.* Garden City, NJ: Doubleday, 1968.

Sanchez, Nellie Van de Grift. *The Life of Mrs. Robert Louis Stevenson.* New York: Scribner's, 1922.

Stevenson, Fanny Van de Grift. *The Cruise of the "Janet Nicol" among the South Sea Islands: A Diary of Mrs. Robert Louis Stevenson.* London: Chatto and Windus, 1922.

Stevenson, Fanny Van de Grift. *Our Samoan Adventure, by Fanny and Robert Louis Stevenson.* New York: Harper, 1955.

THE HOLIDAY OF RAIN

Crowley, Aleister. *The Confessions of Aleister Crowley: Autoha-giography.* London: Routledge, Kegan Paul, 1979.

Maugham, Somerset. "Rain." In *The Trembling of a Leaf,* 241–301. Honolulu: Mutual Publishing, 1986.

Maugham, Somerset. *The Summing Up.* New York: Mentor, 1958.

ABOUT THE AUTHOR

Victoria Nalani Kneubuhl is a Hawai'i-based playwright and author of Hawaiian, Sāmoan, and Caucasian ancestry. She holds an MA in drama and theater from the University of Hawai'i at Mānoa. Her many plays have been performed in Hawai'i and the continental United States and have toured to Britain, Asia, and the Pacific. Her first anthology of plays, *Hawai'i Nei: Island Plays,* was published in 2002. She has also written numerous living-history performance programs for historic sites and community organizations, as well as the mystery novels *Murder Casts a Shadow, Murder Leaves Its Mark,* and *Murder Frames the Scene.* She is the writer and co-producer for the television series *Biography Hawai'i,* which has produced six documentaries that have aired on PBS Hawai'i. In 1994 she was the recipient of the prestigious Hawai'i Award for Literature and in 2006 she received the Elliot Cades Award for Literature. When not writing, Victoria can be found training or playing with her dogs.

Printed in the United States
by Baker & Taylor Publisher Services